FINAL DANCE: PART ONE

London Borough of Hackney	
91300001088215	
Askews & Holts	
AF ROM	£8.49
	6348565

Chapter One

Mateo hunched against the cold, his backpack feeling as if it were filled with rocks. He'd been walking around too long without enough food, and the dull ache that had started in his chest since he'd caught a cold was beginning to make breathing difficult. Every step was harder than the last. He must look like an old man — and a feeble, homeless one at that. Of course, that last part was true. Since bolting from the 'fresh start' the vice cop had given him, there was nowhere he could reliably bed down, no chance to stay out of the chill from the approaching winter weather to shake off the remnants of his illness. And meals were not a regular thing these days. Hunger magnified every crappy feeling he had.

He really needed to find that new place everyone was talking about. Word was they served plenty of hot food — and without the preaching part that even the nice Father Ted had laid on him as the price for help. He didn't need saving, but he did need a trick. Eating was only one of his needs. Money in his pocket would give him the other things that made life almost bearable, including a little weed to smooth out his nerves. The shit was legal now, although... Okay, so he wasn't quite over the age limit and the fucking vice cop had confiscated his fake ID. Still, he could pass for older, if only the licensed dispensaries weren't more uptight about carding a guy than most bars were.

The tickle in the back of his throat morphed into an undeniable cough. He nearly doubled over from the hacking and his chest hurt terribly. Something warm to drink would help that. Surely they'd have coffee — or maybe tea. *That's supposed to be good for lung problems, isn't it?* He just had to reach his destination. This part of town wasn't his usual hang, so it was hard to judge how much farther he had to go. Squinting past the wind, he looked at the street sign to make sure he'd taken the correct turn. It was supposed to be about a block away now.

He hitched his pack higher on his shoulder before picking up speed. His hope of reaching his destination soon overtook his lack of energy. The thin jacket he wore didn't do much to keep out the cold. Someone had said this new place had clothes as well as food. He hoped he could cadge a new coat, maybe a scarf. With a little bit of help, he'd shake this coughing problem and be better situated to survive the coming months. Winter in Boston was a major bitch.

Another turn had him catching sight of someone who nearly caused his heart to stop. He put on the brakes and struggled for breath. His sudden stress sent off another coughing fit, this time lasting longer and hurting a whole lot more. As he bent over, he kept his sight on the man down the street.

It can't be him! That fucker is gone. The cop said so...

The man who'd caught his attention didn't look his way. He merely leaned against the brick wall of a building, putting his big, booted foot flush against it while digging something out of his pocket. A few seconds later, he was puffing on a smoke. His stance was relaxed as he stared across the street. With his hair pulled back in a ponytail, his face was easy to see. That profile was what allowed Mateo's heart to start beating again as he fought to catch his breath.

Not him. Not the Creature. There was a superficial similarity in the height and breadth of the man, as well as the jet-black hair and pale skin. But this wasn't the asshole who'd fucked him over six ways to Sunday, forcing him to rent his body beyond endurance while keeping the profit. For a few awful months, he'd been a slave and living a life that had almost made him long for the abusive home he'd left years before. *Almost.* It had brought him as close to offing himself as anything ever had. And as scared as he'd been when the cop had pulled him in and made him snitch, it had been a relief, too.

It was too bad he'd also learned that the minimum wage, four-oh-fucking-one-k lifestyle was also not his jam. It was practically a different kind of slavery as far as he was concerned — or simply a way to stay alive without giving someone a chance to live a meaningful life. Sucking random dick might not be the best job in the world, but it was better, as far as he was concerned, than what he'd left. At least now he was working for himself, deciding who he did, when and how and keeping all of the money. And it paid better when he broke it down by hours versus effort. With the right technique, he could make a guy come in minutes. It was easy money. Mateo had become very skilled in certain areas. He considered it a vocation. Plus, when he was willing to also let a guy have at his ass, it could mean a nice place to sleep for the night. He liked sex with dudes, too. No 'gay for pay' in his case. He loved dick — the bigger the better.

This guy right here would almost certainly fit that category if he didn't bring back so many shitty memories. The similarities were too awful to ignore, even though this dude was totally hot. As he took a long drag off the ciggy, the man's profile exposed plenty to stare at. Mateo could admire the full lips and strong jaw. The nose couldn't have been any straighter and the cheekbones could cut glass. And yet, there was nothing effeminate about him. Every inch of him screamed alpha male, which was both scary and appealing. If not for his experience with *the Creature*, Mateo would have been on the guy at full-flirt speed. As it was, he had to swallow any trepidation, along with the phlegm clogging his throat, and take advantage of the opportunity to do a quick trick before finding the new soup kitchen.

Squaring his shoulders, he forced his feet to get moving and put a little swing into his hips. He was scrawny these days, but some guys were into that because it made him look younger than he was. Besides, his mouth worked fine so long as he could suppress his urge to cough, and that was all he was going to offer. A quick glance to his left told him there was a convenient alley to do business in. There wasn't much of anyone around anyway — a function of the location and the weather. He would pull out all the stops get the guy off quickly, too, so he wasn't going to have to spend much time on his knees on the cold ground.

He hadn't taken more than a few steps before the man swiveled his head in his direction. Mateo could have sworn his old Nikes made no sound while he walked down the cracked sidewalk, yet the man's reaction made him think he'd been beating a drum or something. Although there was too much distance between them to be sure, Mateo's heart skipped another beat with the certainty that the eyes boring into him were that same violet color as *the Creature's*. His steps faltered, even as he came within a few feet of the guy. And yup, he'd been right. That much was clear when the man's gaze didn't waver.

It's not him. It's not him. It's not him.

Mateo kept up the litany of reassurance, which was reinforced with his mark's full face now visible. The guy was gorgeous, although his expression was impossible to read. There was nothing particularly friendly in it. That was only because he hadn't yet heard the pitch. Any man could be seduced with the right effort. Mateo forced himself to smile and cocked a hip while he gave the man a slow once-over.

"Hi, Daddy... This is your lucky day." The words stuck in his throat just a tiny bit.

He cleared his throat with a quick cough as softly as he could before continuing, because, Jesus, this guy wasn't budging an inch—no response or answering smile, not even a leer. The man simply stood there, staring and puffing on his cigarette.

Mateo poured on the charm, his empty stomach and prickly chest urging him to make the sale and get going. "For today only, you can get the best blowy you've ever had for the low, low price of only fifty bucks." He fluttered his lashes, knowing that they were one of his best features — long and thick. Given that the guy who usually did his hair in exchange for this very service was currently in jail, he was otherwise looking like an alley cat. The green dye job had grown out and his hair hung in messy waves. But he needed to play to whatever strengths he had.

The man pushed off from the wall and turned to face him. The hard look on his beautiful face didn't change. He snuffed out his butt on the sole of one big boot before putting the stub into the front pocket of his jeans. Dressed in only a T-shirt covered by a chamois shirt, he looked remarkably unfazed by the cold.

Mateo twisted the strap of his backpack, trying to keep what he hoped was a coquettish smile on his face. He opened his mouth to pitch his offer again. The guy overrode him.

"Are you hungry?" The deep voice practically rumbled in Mateo's congested chest. Again, he flashed on *the Creature*, except this guy's accent was different. Harder. More clipped and without the almost sing-song quality he'd learned to loathe while spending only a few hours in hell.

He nipped at his lower lip before answering. "Enough to eat that big dick of yours." He could see the outline of the thing through the fly of the worn jeans that were slung low on narrow hips. "I'm sure your cum will more than satisfy me."

The man's eyes flashed before he said, "Don't be ridiculous. Follow me."

Without waiting for a response, the guy walked away, although not down the alley. Instead, he returned to the wide door he'd obviously come out of and, after opening it, held it for him in a silent invitation. He clearly expected Mateo to obey, and *sure, whatever...* At least it would get him out of the cold – although going inside was always riskier than being out, where escaping a bad situation was easier. A sudden gust of biting wind that threatened to send him into another coughing fit chased away his fears.

He approached cautiously, just in case something skeevy was waiting for him. A sign above the door caught his eye. Glancing up, he saw that – *Hey, what do you know?* – etched in silver letters against a black background was the name of the hang he'd been looking for. *Our Safe Place.* The realization helped him relax. If this guy was part of the new soup kitchen and meeting place for street rats, then he was probably at least not inclined to wring his neck. That didn't mean the blow job was off the menu, though. He'd been on his own long enough to understand that everyone had a price and no one gave anything away for free. There was always an agenda. Even Father Ted had wanted to save his soul in exchange for food. He'd only been kinder about the required *quid pro quo*.

So yeah, as he crossed the threshold, he knew he'd be on his knees eventually. At the moment, however, he could only stop and take in the warm, cheery surroundings. The big room was colorful and cozy, with throw rugs, beanbag chairs, tables and bookcases. At one end there was a large flat-screen TV where a couple of boys were playing a video game while others sat around and watched. There was a lot going on all over the place, but the smell of food caught his attention the most. His stomach growled.

"This way."

The sound of the man's voice so close behind startled him. He hadn't noticed that he'd come in on his heels and shut the door. The guy didn't seem to appreciate or care that he'd caught him off guard. He merely walked past him, heading toward an open doorway to the right of the screen area. Mateo hurried to keep up. Meal or no, he didn't want to lose track of the one person who was going to help with his current cash-flow problem.

The next room was a dining hall with a few dozen tables and lined with wooden chairs. Some kids were sitting scattered around, chatting, eating, drinking. At the far end, where his super sexy and jacked guide was walking, was an open serving area. Behind the counter was the kitchen and someone familiar stood there fussing with the hot trays that were lined up.

"Damien?" he called out before he could think better of it.

The guy lifted his face to look in his direction and, a second later, his face split into a smile. "Hey, Mateo."

Completely relaxed now that he'd spotted a kind of friend, he didn't hesitate to hurry over. "Dude, I should have expected you'd be here." He offered his fist for a bump. "A kid told me this was kind of a tribute to Father Ted, and you *are* a cook, right? I should have guessed you were involved."

Damien knocked knuckles over a warming tray that was filled with mashed potatoes. "Yeah, seriously, this was something I had to do. Losing Father Ted was a blow to lots of people and I'd like to think he'd appreciate this place. It's good to see you, man." His expression got somber. "I'd heard you were off the streets."

Shrugging, he gave the best answer he could. "The straight life's not my thing, you know?" He hitched his backpack, his gaze caught by the sudden appearance of the man from outside.

"He's hungry," the guy practically growled, and his expression read like he was mad, like needing food was a strike against Mateo.

Damien didn't seem the least bit disturbed by the colossus hovering behind him. He grinned. "Great, 'cause that's what we're here for. What would you like?" he added with a wave at the food laid out in front of them.

"All of it?" He grinned back, although he wasn't kidding. Everything looked and smelled wonderful and it had been a long time since he'd eaten. Even then, it had been a plain cheeseburger at Micky Ds because it was all he could afford. It had hardly been filling.

Damien's happy expression didn't waver. "No problem." Grabbing a plate, he began to load it with meatloaf, potatoes, cornbread and green beans. There were rolls, too, and pats of butter. When it was all piled high, he handed it over to Mateo, along with utensils wrapped in a paper napkin.

"Go have a seat and I'll join you. We can catch up. What would you like to drink? We have soda, but also hot chocolate, milk and various juices."

"Hot chocolate would be awesome." He felt a little silly asking, like he was a kid or something. But it had been ages since he'd had that sweet, warm drink and he was still cold from the long walk. Even in the heated room, a shiver ran through him.

"Coming right up."

"I'll get it." The man-with-no-name barked the words out, making them sound like an order rather than an offer.

Damien didn't seem to mind. "Thanks, Christos."

Christos. So that was the guy's name. It sounded European, although he wasn't quite sure what country he might be from. But Mateo was more convinced than ever that any similarity between him and *the Creature* was superficial. Someone who was willing to wait on a couple of street kids wasn't the kind of asshole who would beat someone senseless before fucking them until they bled.

He sat at an empty table, not intending to be more social than he had to be. While he didn't know Damien well, he'd always found him to be solid enough. If talking to him was the price of having all this food, it was okay with him. That didn't mean he waited for the guy to join him before attacking his meal, though. Table manners had never been his strong suit and, God, he was fucking starving. The first forkful had him lunging for more. He stuffed mounds into his mouth and chewed as fast as he could without choking. That proved hard when another cough shook him.

"Hey, take it easy. Eating that fast when you haven't eaten in a while will make you sick." The admonishment was given in a friendly tone as Damien sat down opposite him.

"Says the guy who isn't going hungry these days," he answered with his mouth full.

"Yeah, I hear you. I haven't forgotten what it's like, though."

Mateo took a second to look his companion in the eyes. He saw a kind of sadness that reminded him that Damien wasn't very far past a life on the streets. "Our kind of life sticks with you...like herpes," he added with a grin to show he was trying to keep it light. Being morbid and feeling sorry for oneself was a sucker's game.

"Things can change."

"Sure," he agreed with a wave of his fork, "if you don't mind being paid shit wages while people in suits yell at you about how you got too much foam in their fucking lattes." He shook his head as he took a big bite out of his piece of cornbread. "Give me an honest blow job any day. At least I know in advance what kind of screwing I'm getting."

Damien frowned. "Was it that bad?"

Mateo nodded. "Seriously. And the shithole I could afford on what I was getting paid was no better than living on the streets. It was worse, honestly. At least out there I *expect* rats to run over me."

Damien ran his finger along a groove in the wooden table. "I'm sorry. I forget how lucky I was to find the job I did." He looked around. "We're working on establishing dorm rooms upstairs so that we can offer safe, warm places before the winter hits for real. We've started a list for the beds. I'll put you on it."

Mateo simply shrugged and kept eating. He couldn't think farther ahead than a couple of hours or so. There were fewer disappointments that way. "I bet it's hard to get the do-gooders to hand over the money, huh?"

"It's not a money thing. It's paperwork, red tape with the city." Damien cleared his throat. "The funds for this place are actually all coming from my man."

Mateo swallowed hard and grabbed his roll to butter it. "Dude, you've got a full-time rich daddy?"

Damien's cheeks pinked. "It's not like that. We're in love."

"Oh, sure. That's awesome for you," he replied, because if that was the fantasy his friend wanted to weave, who was he to ruin it?

Damien leaned in. "It can happen. There are good guys out there who want more than your body, Mateo. You have to believe in yourself." That pearl of wisdom was delivered right before the mugs of hot chocolate.

Damien's giant elf put the drinks on the table between them with surprising gentleness, given his size. He glared at Mateo with his violet eyes for a few seconds before he left again without saying a word.

Mateo put his fork down long enough to grab the mug and scald his tongue with a big slug of his drink, but it was worth it. He closed his eyes and hummed in appreciation before another coughing fit took hold. Damn, it felt as if his lungs were trying to escape his body or something.

Damien frowned. "Are you all right?"

Mateo used more of his drink to settle himself. "It's nothing, just the leftovers from a cold. I'm fine." Although his reassurance was punctuated by another shiver, and weird, but he felt kind of hot now. He took off his jacket and tossed it on the floor beside his pack.

"Are you sure? That doesn't sound good — and you're kind of sweaty."

"It's hot in here." He shrugged away the concern and tackled his food once more. "So what's up with that guy?" *Christos.*

"You mean Christos? He's a relative of my man. He's come to Boston to help out…with stuff." He blew on his drink before taking a sip. "He's been really nice about volunteering here."

"What's his jam?" He tucked back into his plate, although with the worst of his hunger satisfied, he slowed down. Man, Damien was right. He was sweating, as if the sudden amount of food in his stomach was overheating his whole system.

"As in?" Damien put his hand up. "Please don't mean what I think you do."

With a shrug, he said, "Why not? Don't tell me you have a 'no fucking' rule here."

Damien gave him a pained look. "Not exactly. But this is a safe space, so no drugs or drinking and no turning tricks."

Mateo drank more of the chocolate and nearly came in his pants because it was so good. "No problem. I'll blow him in the alley."

"Mateo," Damien said sternly, "Christos isn't like that."

"Dude, every man is like that, thank God. And I need the cash."

"I can give you a few odd jobs around here."

"What, like sweeping or doing the dishes? No offense, but I'd rather suck dick. Didn't we just have this conversation?" He popped his eyes at the guy before adding. "Besides, I can tell that behind those jeans, there's *some* dick to suck."

"That's not the point, Mateo."

"Cock size is always the point — that and the amount of cash it takes to buy weed." On some level, he knew he sounded like the trashy boy his family had always accused him of being. He couldn't help it. When it was on his terms, sex made him feel good. It chased away the demons clogging his head for a little while. It was the same with being high. It mellowed his anxiety and allowed him to forget for a little while how totally fucked his life was.

Something made him uneasy. Shifting his gaze beyond Damien, he saw the subject of their conversation staring at him from the kitchen. Those freaky eyes bored holes into him, yet without leaving him with the dread he'd first experienced out on the street. There really was no comparison to the depth of emotion in those eyes compared to the utterly dead ones of *the Creature*. He wasn't sure how the attention made him feel, so he went with the most pressing and obvious answer.

"Don't look now, but I think the guy is way into me. It seems like he doesn't share your view."

Christos leaned against the divide between the kitchen and the serving table, not caring that he was being rude by human standards. He'd long past given up worrying how the strange inhabitants of this planet viewed him. His quiet life in the mountains, tending to his goats and his vineyard mostly on his own, didn't require him to be social. In fact, one of the things he appreciated about his Greek neighbors was that they let him be. He'd gotten out of practice at hiding the fact that he was an alien, not that he'd ever been good at it. He didn't have Alex's smooth social graces or Val's 'fuck off' ones. He'd always let slip something about his true nature whenever he got comfortable with a human. His living alone made more sense all around and the solitude suited him, except when it didn't. Loneliness was just one more thing he had to accept as a consequence of the crash. He found it disorienting to suddenly be thrust into a sea of humans. Coming to Boston was proving to be difficult on many levels.

Except for this one indulgence... No one around him seemed to mind his open appreciation for young males. Certainly it was the norm in Alex's club. Such a clever man, his captain. He'd found the perfect cover for their natures and had cocooned himself and his most loyal followers in a friendly environment. Their actions were easily hidden from the general public while they were also living the most authentic lives they could since crashing on this ball of fractious and primitive beings. If he couldn't have the peace of his mountain home, this would do well enough until they put the whole Dracul nonsense to rest once and for all.

Perhaps he was supposed to be more circumspect here in this place that Will and his boy worked hard to make into a safe space for some of those that humans loved to discard like garbage. And he had been, so far, careful to maintain his distance and use his muscles in mindless work that nevertheless kept him occupied while they waited for...God knew what. Dracul was planning something and, as always, the fucker had no consideration for others. Although it was hard, Christos had ignored all the possible temptations flooding him here.

This new seeker of succor, however, was different. The boy that Damien knew well enough to sit with had been the one to make that charming offer of a most intimate service. Christos could hardly be blamed for being intrigued. While his imagination wasn't as vast as say...Val's, when it came to sex, he had no trouble picturing those pretty lips wrapped around his cock. He'd been painfully hard since the moment the coquette had opened his mouth.

A barking sound raked his ears, making him frown. There wasn't anything appealing about that cough, however. This human wasn't all that well, apparently. Out in the cold, it hadn't seemed particularly alarming. Inside the almost-stifling heat of the old building, the underlying illness was more obvious. Not that Christos' dick minded. It wasn't as finicky or empathetic as he was. It wanted to empty his balls, and a little thing like consumption of the lungs wasn't going to put it off.

"What are you doing?"

Christos didn't bother to look at Will when he answered. "Isn't it obvious?"

His shipmate leaned into his space. "You said you understood that the mission of this place is to provide safety for kids. They have enough people preying on them. The way you're ogling that boy, you're like a cartoon wolf with eyes bugging way out. He appears to be a friend of Damien's, besides."

"He calls him Mateo."

"Oh shit, really?"

Now Christos did bother to look at Will, although briefly. "Why? Does that mean something to you?"

"Yes. That's someone who helped Alex and the others to bring down Cadoc. He was one of the boys who had been exploited. I thought they'd gotten him off the streets," he added with a frown in his tone.

"Apparently not, given that he offered to suck my dick for fifty dollars. Is that a good price?" he added, his gaze still locked on the boy, who stood while another coughing fit overtook him.

"How the fuck would I know, and why would you even—?"

The rest of the words were lost on him. The boy had stumbled past the chair he'd been sitting on, his body shaking as he fell. Christos vaulted over the serving counter, not caring who saw. When he landed, he whirled to place his hands on the table and used his momentum to cartwheel over it. He ended right where he needed to be to catch the boy before he hit the floor.

The kid was hot as a cock, in a bad way—too much so, even for a human. Christos wasted no time scooping him into his arms. The kid weighed practically nothing, likely a testament to how hard he'd been living for a while. One big, hot meal wasn't going to solve his problems. He needed a lot more than that to fatten him, plus what he really needed was a doctor. One look at the beautiful face with its flushed cheeks told him as much. A crowd had gathered already — the kids who'd been eating, Will and his boy, plus the woman who was a friend of Emil's and an ally of them all.

Christos focused on Will. "He needs medical care."

"Damn," Damien said with a shake of his head. "I knew that cough sounded bad. There's a hospital a few blocks away."

Christos considered what that meant. Humans no longer left their sick to fend for themselves, mostly. Taking him to a big institution with overworked doctors who wouldn't treat this boy until they'd worked through the even-more-urgent cases didn't seem the best idea, however. His grip tightened as he considered whether that was the right move. His charge moaned and shuddered, his pretty lips puffing out hot breath while his eyes remained closed.

Christos made his decision an instant later. "No. I'm taking him to Harry for help."

The woman — Logan, she was called — snorted before clapping her hands. "Okay, kids, the show's over. Go back to what you were doing." She eyed Christos. "Good luck with that." Then, as she walked away, she muttered, "What is it with these guys and pretty boys? Grabs them by the short hairs every goddamn time."

He ignored the snide remark, mostly because he couldn't exactly argue with her observation. He was overreacting to someone and something that shouldn't concern him in the least. And yet, the idea of simply handing this boy over to the emergency department at a hospital was not viable. He intended to see to his care himself, and it had nothing to do with promised blow jobs.

It *mostly* had nothing to do with that.

"Bring your SUV around to the front, Will."

The man shook his head slowly. "Seriously, Alex isn't going to like the decision to bypass the hospital. This kid is not *in the know*, and bringing him to the family home is risky, especially with Mackie's condition being obvious at this point."

"So, I'll bed him in one of the rooms at the club." His cock twitched because, on some level, his wording was not an accident. "I mean, I'll settle him into one of those rooms. That should handle any security concerns."

Will's expression telegraphed that he wasn't convinced, but Damien put his hand on his man's arm. "I'm with Christos on this. Mateo suffered a lot at the hands of a certain someone, and he risked his life to help. I didn't understand it at the time, but Demi has filled me in on the whole thing. We kind of owe Mateo, don't you think?"

Whether Will agreed with that assessment or not, the look in his eyes when he stared at his boy was clear. The guy wasn't about to deny his lover anything. With a nod, he gave Damien a quick kiss and headed for the kitchen. It had a back door leading to the alley where the vehicle was parked.

"I'll come with you. Logan's got this place covered and I don't want Mateo to freak out when he wakes up with strangers."

"As you wish." Christos hefted Mateo closer and frowned. "His clothing is not suited to the weather. Can you get a blanket to wrap him in?"

"Sure... That's a great idea. I'll meet you by the front door." Damien didn't wait for a reply. He simply strode away.

Christos complied with the plan because it made sense, although he wasn't yet used to how these human boys had gained prominence in their inner circle. But Alex was obviously comfortable with it, so it was Christos' problem to adapt. For most of their time on this planet, they'd treated humans like the inferior creatures they were, albeit benevolently. He'd never developed the close ties that some of his comrades had with men regardless. It seemed pointless to become emotionally attached to beings with such short lives. Forming romantic entanglements was something he'd particularly avoided. Feeding blood to transform the humans to lengthen their lives had also never appealed. He'd seen how badly it could end. *Why bother?* It would never compare to living in a hive.

Of course, now that they had Annika, their Queen, things were different. And he wasn't sure how he felt about that. It had taken nearly a thousand years to accept his new reality. It was hard to change his mindset once again.

Not that any of that was relevant at the moment. He ignored the stares and blocked out the whispers of the young around him. They were irritating at the best of times, loud and messy. His volunteering to help was not done by any altruistic disposition of his. It simply gave him something to do, and staying at the family house was frankly much of the same. The hybrid boys orbited the Queen like newborn planets jockeying for position around the sun. The amount of noise they generated with their television shows, video games and endless music was an assault on his ears and sanity. His quiet solitude for so many years had rendered him overly sensitive to the chaos he now found himself in.

His wait for Damien by the door was brief. The human had started taking Will's blood and had developed a hair more speed than the average human. He raced over with a blanket in hand and draped it over Mateo's still-unconscious body.

"That should do it until we get in the SUV," Damien said, tucking in the edges as best he could.

When Damien opened the door, their ride was already there. They hustled to get in, Christos taking the entire back seat with his bundle. Mateo stirred as Will was pulling away from the curb. Those thick, dark lashes fluttered for a few seconds before he opened his eyes to watery slits.

"What's...?" He started to squirm.

Christos tightened his hold. "Hush. You fainted. We're taking you to see a doctor."

The boy tried to lift his head. "No, I can't. I don't have money and the free clinic is too crowded." His protest was cut short by a cough that shook his whole body. Christos lifted him to more of a sitting position in an effort to help.

Looking over his shoulder, Damien said, "It's fine, Mateo. We're taking you to a private place. Will and Christos have an uncle who is a doctor. He'll fix you up."

Mateo moaned and dropped his head on Christos' chest. "I guess I'll owe you more blow jobs, then."

"Don't be foolish," Christos bit out. "There is no payment expected."

The boy grunted in what could be termed a laugh. "That's not what your dick is saying."

Ah yes. That stupid thing was pressed hard behind his fly and right up against the boy's small ass. It couldn't be helped. That would naturally happen when someone pretty sat on his lap, even though the pretty something was coughing up his lungs and hot with an obvious fever.

He stared out of the window. "Perhaps if you stop offering sexual favors, my ignorant cock will stop getting the wrong idea."

"I'll see what I can do, but no promises." Once again, he shook as his lungs tried to expel the sickness within them. These humans were easily laid low by illness. *Such delicate creatures.*

"God, I feel terrible."

"You will get better soon." If that promise sounded more like a command, so be it. Christos wasn't sure he was in complete control of the situation.

One thing was for sure, though. For the first time since coming to Boston, he wasn't bored.

Chapter Two

Mateo was surrounded by creatures — or so it seemed. There were lots of big men with dark hair and pale skin. Scowls were the main expression, although the doctor treating him was kindly, smiling and reassuring. His son, too — someone Mateo had already met, he realized — flitted around and played Nurse Nancy. Between the two of them, Mateo was propped up in a huge bed with what must be thousand-thread-count sheets and a thick, warm comforter. He'd been stripped of his grungy clothing and, after a quick sponge bath, had been dressed in soft, fleecy pajamas. He felt like the heroine in *A Little Princess* — before her father had died. The pampering wouldn't last forever. He fully expected to end up in the attic at some point, shivering in the cold and working his debt off. In the meantime, he was going to milk this for all it was worth.

It was too bad he also felt like death. It was hard to enjoy the comfort when his head ached and his chest hurt as if one of those massive men in his room was sitting on top of it.

Christos, who'd apparently caught him mid-swoon — or so Damien had relayed — was standing in the corner like a really pissed-off sentinel. He hadn't retreated from his spot since carrying Mateo in and depositing him on the bed. A few others of his family had come in and out since then. One had a Mohawk and really reminded him of *the Creature*. The other wore his hair even longer than Christos did and had 'boss' written all over him. The rest of the men showed the guy deference, that was for sure. He wasn't unkind when he looked Mateo over, but he clearly wasn't happy for him to be there, either.

No one was, other than Christos and Damien, and even they were likely acting out of kindness and nothing more. Although everyone had spoken in low tones while the doctor had treated him, there had been a word here or there that came shooting across the room. And the F-bomb in all of its various iterations had been the most prominent. 'Crazy' had been batted about, as had 'moronic' and a few other less-than-complimentary adjectives. All of them had been lobbed in Christos' direction and he'd let them bounce off him without a lot of response. He was the immovable object to the others' irresistible forces. Mateo wanted to feel guilty for causing such trouble. His shitty health made that impossible. How had he gotten so sick?

"Here." Demi's smiling face came into view. "This is your first dose of antibiotic." He held out a pill and a glass of water.

Mateo wrinkled his nose. "Do I really need that? It's just a cold and a cough." Even as he said it, he knew that wasn't true. But after a childhood in which prayer had been used in place of medicine, he had an ingrained distrust of pills.

"You have bronchitis and a fever, which means it may be bacterial. You need this and, afterward, I've got a dose of cough medicine with acetaminophen. Be a good boy and take it all without a fuss and Damien will bring you a bowl of chicken soup."

Mateo rolled his eyes and did as he'd been told. He really just wanted to feel better, maybe get some sleep. And if the price of all of this was offering the big guy in the corner a little 'something, something', that was okay. He'd done more for less in the past. Besides, the guy was a gay boy's wet dream. He was even more impressive now that Mateo could stare at him openly, and the way he'd held him in his massive arms had been embarrassingly comforting. He hadn't felt that cherished in…well, never, actually. The memory of it made him shiver.

"Oh, you poor thing," Demi cooed. "Drink this and hopefully you'll feel better once your fever comes down."

Okay, if the dude wanted to assume his reaction was sickness and not lust — or some softer emotion that he didn't want to think about — that was fine. The syrup poured into him tasted almost not bad. He chased the remnants away with more water and relaxed against the pillows behind him. God, this really was the best bed he'd ever been in, and some of his tricks had been well-off. A guy could get used to this luxury if he were stupid — which he wasn't. This was a temporary fairyland event, and while he'd relish the time for as long as he could, he wasn't going to start weaving fantasies. Unlike Damien, he had his feet firmly on the ground.

And speaking of which… The cook came into the room like he owned it, carrying a tray and unfazed by the large, dangerous-looking men he weaved through. He replaced Demi by the side of the bed and settled the tray over Mateo's lap before removing the metal cover. A delicious smell wafted straight into Mateo's nose. Despite the meal he'd eaten not long ago, he was still hungry.

"This is my homemade chicken noodle soup. I make it in big batches and freeze it so that I can warm bowlfuls whenever I want. Do you think you can eat now?"

Pushing himself to more of a sitting position using arms that were way too weak, Mateo nodded. "Absolutely." A cough racked him for a few seconds, causing Damien to hold the tray steady. But it wasn't as bad as before, so the medicine was already working. "Thanks."

He grabbed the spoon beside the steaming bowl and dipped into the soup. The burst of flavor that hit his tongue had him moaning. It was that good. His gaze happened to home in on Christos and the intensity of the man's stare made his hand shake. There was no denying the desire in his eyes. If Mateo played this right, he'd have a safe, warm place for a few days. That wasn't a bad deal and he did want to get a look at what was tucked into the dude's pants.

"Let me help you," Damien said, his face coming into view. He took the spoon from Mateo's hand. "You're obviously weak. I'm sorry I didn't realize how sick you were back at *Our Safe Place*." He scooped more broth and held it to Mateo's lips.

There didn't seem any point in arguing about the pampering, and he was grateful for the help. "Dude, seriously," he said between mouthfuls, "I didn't get how fucked I was. There's no way you should feel guilty about it."

There was a lull in the conversation, both theirs and others', the room falling silent. Beyond Damien's shoulder, Christos' stare never wavered. The scrutiny was intense. Mateo vaguely wondered if the guy was going to stay there for the rest of the day and into the night. *Is he going to watch me sleep?* It was a creepy yet oddly thrilling idea.

The guy with the Mohawk threw up his hands. "Well, I fucking give up. We may as well get towels monogrammed with his initials, given how this is going."

"Indeed," the bossman said. He raised his eyebrows at Christos. "This is your project, regardless of what Willem and Harry say. You will keep it under control."

"Yes, sir," came the answer, Christos barely glancing in the other man's direction.

The behemoth brigade left the room with surprisingly graceful and quiet steps, leaving only Damien and Christos. Other than the scraping of the spoon against the bowl and an occasional coughing fit, silence reigned over the room. It was both soothing and disquieting. Mateo was used to the noise of the city, even when inside. Here, it was as if they were secluded somewhere far away from Boston. He realized with a jolt that he wasn't entirely certain where they'd brought him to. The last time that had happened, things had taken a horrible turn.

"Where are we, exactly?" he asked between bites.

"Somewhere safe," came the reply from the man in the corner, and his tone implied that no further information was required.

Damien rolled his eyes, and his obvious lack of fear helped ease Mateo's nerves. "You're in one of the bedrooms of the club I work in."

"Oh." Mateo dutifully ate his next mouthful before daring to ask, "What club is that?" He didn't know Damien well, and although he knew that he was a cook in some private place, that was the extent of his knowledge.

"Club Lux. It's a members-only club for wealthy gay men. They come for the entertainment and the chance to relax among others who understand them, mostly. The food is also excellent," he added with a grin. "Some of them like to play, so there are rooms for that, too."

It took him a moment to appreciate what the guy meant by 'play'. He swept the room with his eyes but saw nothing in the way of spanking benches or whips.

"The family used to live in the upper floors. They moved to the building next door a little while ago. Now, bedrooms like this one are for those club members who want to spend the night in a more conventional way."

Mateo peered over Damien's shoulder to look at Christos. "So, this isn't your room, Daddy?" It was a bold question, one that he needed answered because he liked to know exactly where he stood.

The man shifted his stance, if not his expression. "No—and do not call me that."

He widened his eyes as he sipped more soup, swallowing before he replied. "Sorry, *Sir*."

"Not that, either."

"Master?" Some guys did get off on that sort of thing, even if they didn't use the rooms the club offered. He didn't really care, so long as he was treated well.

"Absolutely not."

Okay, tough nut to crack. "What should I call you?"

A few seconds ticked by. "I am Christos."

He wasn't used to being given real first names and never last names, so that was nothing new. "That's unusual. I hope you're not like the original one," he couldn't resist saying. "You know, pure in thought and deed." Damien tipped the bowl for him to drink the rest of the broth. When he'd drained the last drop, he lay back and sighed. "That was wonderful. Thank you."

"My pleasure." Damien picked up the tray. "Why don't you try to get some sleep? That button on the wall there," he said, jutting his chin to a spot behind the bed, "goes straight to the kitchen. Push it if you need anything."

"Really? That's pretty cool."

"Well, the members pay a lot for the best service."

Mateo snuggled into his covers, feeling sated and sleepy. The ache in his chest had lessoned and he hadn't coughed in quite a few minutes. "I won't bother you."

"It's no trouble, really. I'm sure it's strange being here."

He worried a spot in the edge of his comforter. "It's great, actually. I only need a few hours' sleep and I'll get out of everyone's hair." He hoped that wouldn't be the case, but he wasn't going to make assumptions.

"No." That from his beautiful gargoyle in the corner.

With obvious exasperation, Damien looked over his shoulder. "No offense, Christos, but you're kind of freaking him out." He turned back to Mateo. "What he means is that you are welcome to stay as long as you need to recover. It's totally your call, of course, but Harry wants to keep you here until your fever has completely broken and your cough is under control. It's no imposition."

Mateo shifted his gaze from Damien to Christos and back again. "What does *he* want?"

Once again, Damien rolled his eyes. "I think that's pretty obvious, but that is also totally your call. There is no payment required or implied for our help. The family who owns this club is generous with its time and money. Helping you is not going down on some ledger. Isn't that right, Christos?" he added without taking his eyes off Mateo.

"*Naí*"

"That means yes in Greek," Damien clarified, and that was a good thing, too, because it sounded like a negative.

Disconcertingly, he wasn't sure how he felt about that. Relief? Yes, although that had more to do with how awful he felt physically. There wasn't much he thought he could do at the moment. There was also disappointment, which was plain dumb. He didn't need to be pressured to be willing to hop into this man's bed. He could make that decision on his own. His muddled thinking and feelings must be due to the fever. A little rest and he'd be able to figure things out better. He'd been on his own for years, now, and except for that one time, he'd done well making his way.

"Okay, that's good know." He licked his lower lip and dropped his voice. "Is he going to, you know, stand there for the rest of the day or something?"

Damien shook his head. "No." Moving toward the door, he said, "Come on, Christos. Let's give Mateo peace and privacy."

For a moment, the man didn't move and his stare didn't waver from drilling a hole right through Mateo's forehead. Then he abruptly looked away and followed

Damien. "I'll be in the hall," he said gruffly. "Say my name, and I'll come in."

"Can I call you *Chris*?" Mateo asked the man's back.

"No." The door shut quietly behind him.

"Christos?"

The door opened again before he'd gotten the entire name out. "What?"

Mateo couldn't hold back a smile. "Nothing. Just checking."

Still smiling, he closed his eyes and waited for the latch to snick before rolling onto his side and willing himself to sleep.

* * * *

"This is boring." Merlin regretted his words the moment they'd come out of his mouth.

Annika's stern gaze locked on his. "Idris needs help with his hand-eye coordination. Tossing the ball is excellent training."

He resisted the urge to squirm. In his relatively short life, only males had affected him so, though not the pitiful humans like his father, of course. The ones who'd crashed on this planet and had fought to conquer it or protect it, depending on their whim, were capable of turning his insides to jelly. He'd learned early to hide his reaction behind bravado and cruelty — and it had worked. At least his sire, before his death, had praised him for it.

Living under the thumb of this female was new territory. There hadn't been any women at the castle and he'd been inclined to treat those that he'd met after his capture with the same contempt as any human. Annika was different. She was like him, a hybrid, although he dismissed his human half as something akin to a genetic affliction to be overcome. He thought of himself as wholly like his sire and the other males. Annika seemed to be similarly inclined. Whatever part of her was human seemed buried deep inside, if one discounted her eyes and hair. Her beautiful blonde hair was almost white. It flowed down her back either free or in a braid, like now.

Looking at her did funny things to him. Part of him calmed in her presence while another part became agitated. It was confusing and irritating and he loved it all the same. He woke with the desire of seeing her every day and went to sleep to dream of her. Regardless of how he thought about her orders, he followed them as if his entire body was tethered to her commands. His brain couldn't make it do anything different. He'd tried — once — to disobey her and it had physically *hurt*. Compliance had brought sweet relief, and when she smiled at him and praised him for his actions, his chest swelled with pride and a feeling he was beginning to think of as happiness.

So, here he sat in a small circle with Annika, Idris and the two other hybrids who'd come to stay. They were tossing a large, soft ball to the toddler, who gleefully tossed it to someone else, using both of his small hands. The kid was relentlessly cheerful, something that Merlin wasn't used to. No one in his early childhood had dared to giggle unless it was at someone else's expense. Idris appeared delighted with simply being alive. Annika's silly dog Babette pranced around the circle as if trying to catch the ball with her tiny mouth. Those antics also entertained Idris, while Merlin wanted to smack the thing out of his way.

Much of each day was devoted to hanging with the little boy. Annika insisted. They were exercising his mind and his muscles as if he were training for something — although for what, if anything, was a mystery. The Queen didn't go in for a lot of explanation. Merlin found spending time with such a young kid mind-numbing. At least he wasn't alone. Yaro and Matti shared the load without complaint and were decent enough company when they weren't at Annika's beck and call. And he had to admit that this building they all lived in was loaded with awesomely fun stuff, probably because the men were paired up with humans not much older than he was — biologically speaking, of course. He'd been born long before any of them.

Annika clapped her hands as Idris tossed the ball way over her head. "That's very good, Idris. You are getting strong." The dog scampered after it and sank its teeth into the cloth.

The kid giggled, with drool running out of the corner of his mouth, and clapped his hands in response. "Strong!"

"That's right. Matti. Get the ball away from Babette before she tears it. Be firm with her now." Annika folded her hands in her lap. Her legs were tucked to one side, stretching the soft green fabric of her long skirt. She was always dressed like one of those princess characters in the movies she adored. The look suited her. Sometimes her beauty made it hard for Merlin to breathe.

Matti popped to his feet and hurried to do her bidding. *Of course he did.* He and Yaro seemed as devoted to her as Merlin was. It should have made him mad, he thought, that her attention was taken from him to shine upon others. It didn't. Somehow, it felt right that there were a few of them orbiting her every day. Besides, when she snuck into the basement to see Petru, she always brought him and neither of the others. It made him proud that she trusted him with the secret that she was keeping, even from her father.

Matti hurried back with the ball — which, Merlin had to admit, Idris had managed to fling pretty far. Before they resumed their game, however, a soft knocking on the door interrupted them.

"Enter," Annika called out.

The door opened to reveal the pathetically weak human who'd brought Merlin into this world. It was hard not to sneer at the stupid thing that shuffled in with his eyes cast downward and hair obscuring his face. Alun carried a tray filled with cups and a plate piled with cookies. The scent of chocolate and sugar preceded him and made Merlin's mouth water. He might be worthless in all other ways, but this human was good in the kitchen.

Annika smiled brightly. "Oh, how thoughtful, Mr. Alun. I'm sure we could all do with some hot cocoa and sweets. You are very kind."

"It is my pleasure."

The soft, timid voice made Merlin grit his teeth. How was he supposed to respect someone such as that? His sire had always showed his human slut contempt, and Merlin saw no reason to question that. Except...

"We are all very grateful," Annika said as the guy set his tray on a side table.

Matti and Yaro immediately voiced their appreciation. After a moment's hesitation, Merlin joined in. "Yes, thank you...Father," he added without having to be prompted by the Queen. She'd been quite firm on that point already. He must treat this human with respect, even if he couldn't find any love in his heart for the man.

Love. That wasn't an emotion he was sure he could feel. There had been none back in Dracul's castle. The males had treated their human slaves and sons as useful tools of different sorts. There had been no tenderness, nor could he remember wanting any. Maybe he had once as a baby. If so, the memory was lost to him, beaten out of him. No show of kindness or weakness had been tolerated. Merlin still wasn't sure he faulted his sire for that upbringing, although everyone here, even the badass Val, was open about their softer emotions. But they were scary-strong at the same time. Maybe it was okay to feel love, and if so, he thought perhaps he loved Annika. He knew no other word to describe the terrible, yet wonderful, effect she had on him.

Merlin and the older boys waited until Annika had risen, taking Idris by the hand, before doing the same. Alun served her the first steaming cup, along with a sugar cookie coated in icing and a napkin. She let go of Idris to take the offering with a gracious smile and went to sit on the nearby couch. Idris toddled after and climbed up beside her. She broke off half the cookie and handed it to him.

Merlin let the others go next, hanging back to be the last, because interacting with his father made him uncomfortable. He didn't want to experience his reaction in front of anyone. It was impossible to look the man in the eye, not that Alun's gaze was anywhere other than downcast. Centuries of being slapped for doing differently wasn't going to be changed in only a few months. It served Merlin's interest well. He took his mug and two cookies and hurried over to a vacant chair.

To his dismay, Alun didn't leave. Instead, he removed the last mug from the tray and joined Annika and Idris on the couch. He sat on the other side of the toddler and, using one arm, moved him over to his lap with surprising ease. Then he helped Idris drink his cocoa by holding the mug to his small lips. Idris grabbed it with both hands, yet Alun's grip never wavered. As he watched the scene, Merlin found himself wondering if that had ever been him. Had he sat on his father's lap while being given food or drink? As he chewed on one cookie, he cast his mind back and found no memory of such.

All he could remember were communal meals in which the men were served at tables while the hybrids fought over platters of lesser quality food in a corner. He'd never seen his father and the other humans eat, although he supposed they must have. The customs were different here, with everyone sitting together and eating the same thing. He wasn't sure which he preferred, given how he expected to join the warriors at some point, gaining his own power. What future did he have now? He didn't know. Worse, he wasn't sure what he wanted.

Annika smiled at him over the rim of her mug. The look cast a warmth in his chest that the hot drink couldn't match. It reminded him that he didn't have to worry about that. His Queen would show him the way.

* * * *

"This is moronic."

From where he sat on the hallway floor, Christos flicked his gaze to Willem. "How so?"

"Seriously?" The man shifted the tray he held to one hand before gesturing around them with the other. "You're hanging out in this wasteland of tasteful décor as if some ravening horde is going the breach the room unless you're here to stop it."

"Given the type of men who belong to this club, that's not an unrealistic concern."

Will shook his head. "As if Alex would allow that. Val has already hung signs that this floor is off limits to club members for the foreseeable future. Your boy is safe from unwanted attention."

"He's not *my* boy."

Will snorted. "You are fooling no one."

Christos let his head fall against the wall. He really missed the quiet and comfort of his mountain home. "I simply state the truth. He is not mine. That is not to say I don't want him to be," he added before his shipmate could jump in, "at least for a little while." The release of sex with someone other than his own hand would be welcomed. He wasn't looking for a greater entanglement, and he was glad that the boy sleeping in the room behind him wasn't interested in that, either.

"You don't have to play nursemaid to a human to find that kind of pleasure. There's more than a few downstairs who'd be very willing." He paused before adding, "Why did you bring him here?"

That question had already been asked with the kind of fury wrapped in idle curiosity that only Alex could deliver with his clipped words and mild stare. Christos gave the same answer as before. "I have no idea. At the time, it seemed the right thing to do."

That was a lie of sorts. It had been imperative that Christos bring the boy somewhere within his control, where he'd have access to the fetching human with the outrageous mouth. The things he said made Christos want to laugh, which was a terrifying effect. He didn't do humor—not since the crash. Nothing about his situation in the last thousand years had been remotely amusing. It was disconcerting, to say the least, to fight to keep his normally passive demeanor. This boy was dangerous. He should have left him somewhere far away. Instead, only one relatively thin wall stood between them.

Willem snorted. "I'm hardly one to cast stones. I knew the moment I laid eyes on Damien that I wanted him. No amount of rational thinking dissuaded me." He shrugged. "It has turned out great for us. You might have the same good fortune."

The observation disturbed him, so he chose to ignore it. Surging to his feet, he held out his hands. "Give me that. I assume it's for the boy."

Will did as he'd been asked. "Yes, Damien is busy with feeding the members and asked me to bring it. Plus, the kid's next dose of both medicines is here. Harry says it doesn't matter whether he has a full stomach or takes the pill and the cough syrup then eats."

Christos frowned at what the tray contained. "This isn't much food."

"It is for a human who weighs less than one of my legs."

Christos merely grunted, not convinced. Ah well, if the boy was still hungry after consuming this, he could get more. He immediately did a mental facepalm. This really was rather ridiculous, and yet there was no helping it. It was his decisions that had put the entire family in this position, therefore it was his responsibility to handle the details.

"Thank you for bringing it. Next time, text me and I will come to the kitchen. There is no reason for you to put yourself out."

Willem shrugged. "It wasn't a bother, and I did it to help Damien, in any event. It's not like there's something more pressing to do, either. With all of us wandering around waiting for...you know what, I'm getting a little stir-crazy."

"As am I. Something must happen soon—or perhaps driving us insane from boredom has been the plan all along."

"It's certainly torturous. Good luck in there," Will added before leaving.

Christos stood in front of the bedroom door for a few seconds, debating whether he should knock. On one hand, he didn't want to wake the boy if he was still sleeping. On the other hand, he didn't want to scare the shit out of him by walking in unannounced. In the end, he took the chance of the latter by entering without knocking and making as little noise as he could.

He needn't have bothered. Through the darkened room, he could see the human turning in his direction. "You're awake." A stupid observation, but stupidity was apparently his new watchword.

"Mm-m." Whatever the boy might have said was drowned by a fit of coughing.

Christos hit the dimmer switch to bring the overhead light on to a soft glow. "I have your medicine."

It took effort to slow his movements when all he wanted to do was race to the boy's side and pour relief down his throat. As it was, he made the tray's contents rattle with his speed. He put everything on the nightstand and found himself holding the human's shoulders as the deep, hacking cough shook his whole body. When it was finally over, he helped him sit against a mound of pillows. A heat unnaturally high, even for this species, radiated through his clothing.

"Here." He held the cough syrup already measured out in a cup to the boy's lips and helped him drink it. Then he did the same with the glass of water.

"Thanks." The boy slumped against the pillows. "I was feeling better when I fell asleep earlier. Now, I'm crappy again."

"Your kind sicken easily and recover slowly."

The boy gave him the side-eye. "My *kind*?"

Christos nearly kicked himself. His loose lips, as usual, required clean-up. Plus, living either alone or among those with full knowledge of his nature had made him sloppier and more complacent than he'd ever been. He mustn't forget that this human was ignorant of his origins. "I meant no offense. It is merely that you live on the streets. That is hardly conducive to good health and a speedy recovery."

The boy grimaced. "Tell me about it. Is that my dinner?"

Christos was happy to have a change of topic. "Yes." He removed the metal lid to a bowl of creamy tomato soup and a grilled cheese sandwich. "That seems inadequate for the evening meal."

"Are you kidding? That's like one of my favorite things." The boy made an abortive move to grab the bowl, but his arm shook badly enough that he had to drop it. "Fuck, I'm so weak."

"No matter… I will feed you."

The idea struck him as absurd. He had no skill at serving anything to anyone unless delivering double pops to the head of an enemy counted as such. Somehow, he doubted it. Nevertheless, this was his mess to manage, as Alex had made clear. And truly he didn't mind, so long as he didn't dump the hot soup in the sick boy's lap.

Taking the bowl and spoon in hand, he considered how to achieve his mission. There really was no hope for it. The only way was to sit on the side of the bed. The human helped by scooting closer to the middle, and still, their hips and thighs collided when Christos parked his ass on the narrow strip of mattress afforded him. The boy didn't seem to mind. He batted his eyelashes while quietly waiting for the feeding to begin.

And wasn't that the worst word to think? His gaze homed in on the quick pulse at the base of the human's neck. This close, Christos could hear the rushing of the blood through the artery. He could smell it, too, which was just as well, given that the sickness invading this small body gave it a slightly bitter odor. It reminded him that regular human food was the only thing on the menu.

He started to dip the spoon into the soup then remembered the napkin. Grabbing it from the tray, he flicked it open and laid it onto the boy's chest. The first effort was the hardest, with a bit of a colliding and some spillage. But they found a rhythm and soon it got easier, if no less awkward. At least, that was how he felt. It was hard to say what the human thought of all this. He was hungry. That much was clear. He eagerly slurped every mouthful that was offered. Once about half the bowl was gone, Christos switched over to the sandwich. That took less effort and arguably the boy could do this part himself. Regardless, Christos didn't make the suggestion and neither did his patient.

There were no words spoken while he carefully fed the boy, alternating between soup and sandwich, with the occasional sip of water whenever coughing started. The whole effort was practically clinical, and yet Christos was aware of every breath the boy took, the twitches of his fingers, the fluttering of his lashes. Where their bodies touched, it was as if fire pressed through the bedding to lick at him. His cock had long become painfully hard and his fangs itched to descend.

This is bad. Very, very bad. You imbecile.

The boy saved them both by slumping against the pillows with a sigh. "Thanks. I think I've had enough."

"You haven't finished." Like it was any of his business.

The boy smiled in a way that didn't reach is eyes. "Thanks, but I'm not feeling great and don't think I can handle any more."

"Of course." This was his opportunity to escape the sweet torture of being next to what he wanted but couldn't have. Instead, he stayed sitting on the bed as if his ass had been glued there and he grabbed the antibiotic. He held it out, along with a glass of water. "Can you take this on your own?"

"Sure." Their fingers touched with the transfer of the pill. There was more fire with a spark chaser. Christos pulled his hand away at the same time as he passed over the glass of water for a repeat performance.

Thankfully, the boy put the glass back on the nightstand himself when he was finished. Of course, that meant he had to lean over and he rubbed against Christos' thigh. That additional contact gave his dick the false signal that things were getting more interesting. Naturally, they weren't, and a smarter person would have stood to take the tray out of the room. And again, he proved he was a barking moron, as Malcolm would say, by staying right where he was.

"Thank you...for everything," his guest said in a low tone.

"Gratitude is unnecessary," he replied with more gruffness than he'd intended. He looked anywhere other than the boy. That way led to madness.

"If you say so. There must be something you want, though, right?" The boy slid his hand over to Christos' thigh. The touch was like a brand.

"No!" He grabbed that hand with a firm grip and placed it back on the bed. The offer had the positive effect of getting him off that damn thing. He rocketed to his feet, struggling to get his breath under control. For some reason, he was puffing like a locomotive.

"I'm, ah, sorry if I upset you." The boy's voice sounded small. Christos couldn't help looking at him. Wide eyes stared back. "You want me. I can see that."

Ah yes. His dumb cock was on full display now. "It is of no importance. I am hardly going to impose myself on someone as ill as you are."

The boy lifted one shoulder. "I won't be sick forever."

Christos ran the fingers of one hand through his hair, dislodging the tail he'd forgotten he wore. "Were you not listening to Damien this afternoon?"

"He's sweet and kind of naïve, despite having lived on the streets himself. I know how the real world works."

"That may be, but you don't know how *I* work. Now, although there is nothing I want from you, is there anything else you need from me?"

The human lowered his gaze, twisting his bedding in his hands. "I guess not, except…is there a remote for the TV?"

Christos nearly leaped at the chance to do something that didn't tempt him more than he already was. "Of course." He retrieved it and practically tossed it onto the boy's lap.

"Thanks." The human didn't turn on the television right away, however. He kept staring downward. "There's one more thing, if you don't mind."

"Certainly." He crossed his arms and waited.

"Could you maybe stay with me? I'm sort of…I don't know, scared I guess, to be alone. This is a strange place and it's really quiet. I'm not used to…" That was when he raised his eyes to Christos. The look of vulnerability shining through was his undoing.

"If that is what you wish." He couldn't believe he was saying it. He should take the tray and go back to his post in the hall. It was as if someone else had control of his tongue and the rest of his body. Instead of doing any of that, he moved to go sit on a chair in the corner.

"No, come here, where you can watch too." The boy patted the other side of the bed.

Christos hesitated only a moment before complying. He sat before toeing off his boots, then gingerly lay against the headboard with one pillow to cushion his back. He remained stiff and awkward. The heat of his companion did nothing to ease his discomfort, either. Every nerve-ending jangled and his dick was screaming to come out. His balls were likewise begging for relief. He couldn't do this and turned his head to say as much.

But the boy, the human, *Mateo* beamed back at him.

That was when he knew for sure that he was in deep trouble.

Chapter Three

"*This* is my new army?" Dracul gripped the arms of his chair with enough power to nearly crush the wood to pulp. The line of humans standing before him were the very dregs of what this pitiful world had to offer.

His slut sidled closer. "Yes, Master. They aren't much to look at, but I've vetted them all and they are formidable."

"For the right price, naturally," he sneered, although he had to admit that having fighters who could be trusted to serve the human god of money would make for a nice change. These pieces of living trash appeared to be wholly amoral. He could work with that.

"I have proven to them how generous you will be for faithful and successful service. They like how shiny your Krugerrands are."

"Hmm." Humans were pathetically predictable. For his next question, he switched from English to Welsh for privacy purposes. Humans were idiots when it came to their many languages. "Do they also understand the price of betrayal?"

"I thought it best to leave that demonstration to you, Master," the boy answered in the same tongue. "There is a perfect candidate, if I may be so bold?"

Dracul's mouth pooled with saliva and his fangs itched with anticipation. It had been too long since he'd tasted new blood. He didn't even care that his slut had overstepped himself, as was his want. There would be time enough later to beat the smugness off his face. "Who?"

The boy cocked his hip, licked a finger and pointed it in the direction of a human standing in the front center of the group. The man was big, as they all were, yet younger perhaps, and he looked like he hadn't seen as much fighting as the rest of them. His skin was smooth yet bulging with muscles. His carotid popped out of his thick neck, while light blue eyes held the kind of dead quality that he admired in some of the species. He was probably someone totally devoid of empathy. As he was pointed at, the others moved away from him, sensing something bad was about to happen, even though they likely hadn't understood what was being said and they didn't want to be close to the action. *Wise.* The man himself remained cool, unafraid. *Not so wise.*

He leaned forward with anticipation, his cock hard. "Why?"

The slut pulled his accusing finger back to clasp his own throat. "He grabbed my ass and made an improper proposal. That was *after* I clarified that I am your property."

"Ah."

A pity. This one seemed a gem among the dreck, but some things were unforgiveable. The boy might not be much, but he still was *his.* This would be the perfect lesson in case any of these fuckers thought he was an easy mark to kill and rob instead of follow. They were his best option to finally bring Alex down and reclaim his remaining son. And he salivated anew at the thought of the vengeance he would wreak against the sluts who had dared defy him. It would be sweet in particular to drain Dafydd of his blood, then maybe he'd force-feed chunks of the husk to that cunt who'd dared to run from the pleasure of his attention.

First things first, however.

He rose slowly, letting his silk robe slip off his shoulders and slide to the floor. Being unencumbered was always the best way to feed. Ignoring the raised eyebrows of the humans at the sight of his scarred body, he kept his focus on his quarry. The man's expression was of boredom. One could almost feel sorry for his lack of understanding. On the other hand, it had been ages since he'd done a big reveal for unwary monkeys without tails.

"You touched what is mine," he said, switching back to English.

The moron actually shrugged. "He is piece of ass. I think maybe you share." His broken speech revealed his lack of education and his accent indicated something Balkan, perhaps. Too bad, indeed, that this was the sacrificial lamb, as humans from that region tended to make excellent fighters.

It was critical, however, to establish his power and decimate any ideas that these pieces of shit might have about overtaking him and stealing his wealth in return for no service. He knew what they saw — a broken man, alone with one small twink and a whole lot of valuable stuff. It was critical that he demonstrate how truly fucked they all were if they crossed him.

"You thought wrong! What is mine, is mine alone. You worthless scum have to earn whatever I decide to give you. Disobey me, turn on me and you will know my wrath."

The fucker dared to grin. "You big guy but not so tough, I think." He looked around at his coterie before adding, "I think we are a lot and can do as we want."

"And now you are wrong once again."

He let his fangs descend and waited a few more seconds to draw out the suspense before opening his mouth and hissing. There was a moment of perfect looks of horror on these hardened soldiers' faces before he pounced. The men scattered in comical fashion, although he kept his attention on his feast. He tackled the man, even as he struck at that beckoning vein and sank his fangs in deep. He latched on with an unbearable thirst.

His victim thrashed beneath him, rubbing delightfully at his ruined cock. He came from the friction alone. It took nothing to hold on to his meal. The warm salty blood flowed down his throat as he sucked and sucked with wild abandon. How long had it been since he'd fed to full satiation? Well, before he'd lost his home and his army of loyal crewmembers… The reminder of what had been taken from him spurred him to tug ever harder.

The wild movement within his embrace slowed then stopped. He paid it no mind, savoring his long drink and coming time and again until the flesh he'd torn into dried and the clothing he was holding became drenched in cum. When there was nothing left to suck out of the human husk, he ripped his fangs free and lifted his heavy head. He would sleep well this night once he had his new army secure. There was silence, the humans around him standing unmoving, saying nothing, barely breathing. Dracul delighted in their shocked looks.

He licked the blood from his lips as he swept the room with his gaze. "Any questions?"

* * * *

Mateo reached across the bed before his eyes opened and he came up empty. He cracked his lids to confirm that Christos wasn't with him anymore, not even in the room. Rolling onto his back, he tried not to be bothered by it. There was no reason for him to expect that the man would have stayed the whole night, except he did remember being woken at one point to take another pill. Christos must have been there for some while after they'd turned off the TV.

He stretched and yawned before sliding out of bed to use the bathroom. For a few seconds the room spun and his legs felt like jelly. Christos had helped him during the evening to make the short journey. The attached facilities seemed farther now that he was walking on his own, mostly because the bedroom was like some fancy hotel one, big and with a plush carpet where his feet sank a few inches. The bathroom was much the same. He'd been in a few nice places with tricks, so he wasn't completely floored by the shiny fixtures and the polished stone. Awed, yes, but not dumbstruck.

Weak as a kitten, he still had to sit to pee, which made the fact that he was alone all the better. It had been embarrassing as fuck when Christos had helped him into position the previous night. Funny how easy it was to get naked and nasty when it was all about sex for money. Somehow, when it was just a guy helping him, being kind, it had made him want to slink away with shame. He was used to being self-reliant. This bizarre turn of events left him confused and uneasy.

Christos had said there was no payment expected, and his sincerity had rung true. And that was the problem. Kindness wasn't anything Mateo was used to. He didn't know what to do with it.

He gave himself a few seconds to gather the strength to stand again. Eyeing the huge multi-headed shower, he longed to get clean. He'd sweated through the nice pajamas Damien had given him. That was maybe a good thing, like his fever had broken. There was no way he could manage to stay upright that long, however. So he settled for being able to wash his hands and stagger back to bed without falling flat on his face.

A soft knock was followed by Demi entering the room with a bag over his shoulder and carrying a tray. "What are you doing up by yourself?" he scolded. "You should have pushed the buzzer."

Mateo didn't get back into bed so much as fell into it. "I thought that was for when I needed food, not someone to hold my dick while I pee." He couldn't help moaning as he pulled the covers over his shaking body. "Dude, this sucks. Shouldn't I be well by now?"

Demi *tsked* like an old man as he set the tray on the nightstand. "What part of *'You have bronchitis'* don't you understand? It's not simply a little cold that makes you miserable for a few days. This is serious. It could lead to pneumonia if you're not careful."

"Yeah, I know. I'm not good being helpless." He was whining but couldn't quite help it.

Demi pulled out an ear thermometer from his bag. "No one is. Let's see if you have a fever still." He stuck the thing in Mateo's ear then frowned at it after it beeped. "A hundred and one. Better."

Mateo frowned. "I think I was sweating during the night. Doesn't that mean it broke?"

"Yes, that was the acetaminophen at work, except that isn't the end of it. Your temperature can rise and fall until the antibiotic really does its thing." The guy put Mateo through a medical check-up, taking his blood pressure and listening to his lungs and heart.

"What are you, Doogie Howser or something?" he asked when it was done.

"Huh? Oh right, I get the reference. I liked that show, actually."

"You caught it in re-runs too? It was one of the few things I was allowed to watch on TV."

"Um, right, re-runs. Anyway, I'm studying to be a doctor. Harry is my father, you know." Demi replaced his equipment neatly back in his bag.

Mateo furrowed his brow. "But, when I met you with Damien, you seemed like another street kid."

Demi paused in the middle of revealing the food on the tray. "No, that was me just messing around. I was kind of trying to piss off my lover, Sergeant Trey Duncan."

"Except you were chasing Umi that night and he ended up dead." His chest tightened at the memory, and it had nothing to do with his illness. "You all look like *the Creature*," he added in a low voice, fear welling up once more. Now that he wasn't quite as sick, his thinking was clearing and he remembered his initial reaction to Christos.

Demi gnawed at his bottom lip. "What? Who?"

Mateo sat straighter. "You know. He hurt me then I ratted on him. If you fuck that cop, Duncan, you must know the whole story."

"Um-m."

"Demi!" They both turned to find Christos entering the room. "I will handle this."

"Excellent." The boy practically ran from the room. "Medicine's on the tray," he called out from the doorway.

The sight of Christos, his long hair in a tight braid that shone with wetness, was a balm to Mateo. Even though this man looked more like his tormentor than Demi, somehow he chased most of Mateo's fear away. It didn't make sense, yet it was true nonetheless. That didn't mean he wasn't going to press for answers though.

He folded his arms. "I have questions."

"I am aware. You will start your breakfast first. I will tell you what I can."

Mateo accepted the tray over his lap and was momentarily distracted by the delicious smells of scrambled eggs and toast. "I'm not sure I understand what that means." There was a glass of orange juice and, being thirsty, he started there.

Christos sat on the side of the bed, his heavy body depressing the mattress. Better, though, was the way his solid leg brushed against Mateo's. "Ask your questions and I will answer as best as I am allowed."

"Do you know about how that asshole forced me to accept him as my pimp?"

Christos' eyes turned flinty and, for a brief moment, there was a look that raised goosebumps on Mateo's arms. "I have been told of it, yes. He can't hurt you ever again."

"I know. Sergeant Jefferson told me that he disappeared after a raid and fled Boston. Jefferson claimed that it would be more trouble than it was worth if the fucker tried to return here."

"I have not met that particular member of the police force, but Sergeant Duncan is Demi's man and he speaks highly of his colleague. I'm sure he gave you his honest assessment of the situation."

"Yeah, I met Duncan, too. They both seemed trustworthy... for cops, that is." He tucked into his eggs, because he was as hungry as he was curious. Speaking with his mouth full, he said, "So you understand why the sight of everyone around here freaks me out? Or maybe not. You all remind me of him — big and scary and whatever."

"Yes, I understand there is a resemblance and we are...different."

"You've got that right." He bit off a big hunk of toast that was lightly buttered. "You look like he did, but you sound different. Does that mean he's a relative who was raised in a different country?"

Christos turned his violet eyes on him and almost grinned. "You are smart to think of that and you are exactly right. The man who hurt you was a distant member of the family, but he was also a vicious predator raised by one who has no conscience. He was someone that I, and everyone else that I now live with, despised."

Mateo froze mid-bite. "You keep talking about the guy in the past tense. Is he...dead?"

For a brief moment, it seemed as if Christos' eyes went from violet to red. "Oh, yes. He most assuredly was. We clean up our own messes. And that is why you have nothing to fear from him ever again."

Mateo swallowed hard. "How come, then, Jefferson doesn't know that?"

"Because the authorities would frown on our housekeeping methods."

"But you're telling me."

The man inclined his head. "You deserve to know, and I'm trusting that you will keep the information to yourself."

Mateo grimaced. "Plus, no one's going to believe me anyway if I say something."

"There is that."

"Thanks for being honest about my lack of power, at least."

"You would not benefit from my sugar-coating your situation, nor is it in my nature to lie. I detest it, as well as keeping secrets, although it isn't my place to control my life in that regard."

"I don't understand what that means."

"I'm not my own man." He looked away. "It is hard to explain, especially to one who was born in a place of democracy."

Mateo snorted. "Like that's gotten me anywhere. Anyway, if you're talking about family obligations, I get it. When I was a kid, the rule in my parents' house was that my father was the head of the family. What he said was law. Everyone toed the line, including my mother, no matter what. It's like that, huh?"

Christos gave him a thoughtful look. "Yes, it is something like that, although for us, there isn't a father."

"But there's Alex, right? He's the boss?"

For a second, it seemed as if the man would disagree, then he nodded. "Yes, Alex makes the rules."

"Will he be mad that you told me the truth about...you know who?"

"Possibly. If he finds out."

Mateo made a locking key motion across his lips. "I won't tell. It would be a pretty shitty thing to do after all you've done for me."

"You owe me nothing. We've had this discussion before." The censure was mild.

Mateo let the topic go because it was obviously important for Christos to believe that there wasn't going to be a settling of a bill before they parted company. Instead, he ate what he could of his breakfast and dutifully took his medicine. Then he collapsed into his pillow, feeling foolish over how weak he still was.

He tugged at a stringy strand of hair that flopped across his cheek. "God, I'm so gross. I'd give anything for a shower."

"Has Harry or Demi advised against it?"

"No," he sighed. "I haven't even bothered to ask, but I'm so weak that I doubt I could stand long enough to wash my body, let alone my hair."

Christos pulled his phone out of his pocket. "That is no barrier. I can help you, so long as it's not detrimental to your health."

Mateo's brain did all kinds of gymnastics at the image created by those words. Did that mean what he thought it meant, that Christos would come into the shower with him? Naked? Together in that big space he'd spied in the bathroom? Soapy and slippery and…nope, that wasn't possible. If he lacked the strength to clean himself, he was in no shape to do any of the fun things two men could normally do together.

Christos appeared oblivious to all those implications. He kept his focus on his phone as he texted, waited, then texted again. "It's fine so long as I help you and we make sure to dry you and your hair thoroughly before you get back into bed."

He walked over to the door and fiddled with something on the wall. "There… I've jacked the heat to make the room as warm as possible for when you come back in." He returned, and putting his phone on the nightstand, held out his hand. "Do you feel up to it now?"

Mateo's heartbeat stuttered as he contemplated the offer. The chance to get the grime of the streets and his sickness off him warred with the trepidation of getting naked in front of a man who both intrigued him and made him wary in equal measure. Of course, he could be completely out of line. Nothing said that helping meant stripping and getting into the shower with him. Perhaps Christos would merely hang around the bathroom, ready to leap in if he started to pass out.

Practicality won over trepidation. Throwing back the covers, he reached for that helping hand. "Thanks," he said as he tottered to his feet.

Christos threw a strong arm around his shoulders and steadied him. Mateo couldn't help leaning into the support and even dared to grab hold of the man's waist. Every bit of the big man was lean and hard and weirdly cool. He was like *the Creature*, except Mateo immediately banished those thoughts because his rational mind could tell the difference between the family members. So far, everyone here had treated him with surprising kindness, as different from his experience with their thankfully dead relative as could be.

The trip to the bathroom was short yet tiring. He didn't object when Christos steered him toward the toilet and sat him down after lowering the cover. "Wow, that's pathetic. I can't believe how wobbly I am."

"You put too much pressure on yourself. Illness does that to hu — people."

He looked up at him from under his lashes. "I bet it doesn't happen to you."

"No, it does not," the man allowed after a second's thought. "Let me help you disrobe. Lift your arms."

Mateo chuckled. "Sometimes you talk like you're from some long-ago time." He stopped abruptly at Christos' touch.

As the man grabbed the hem of his pajama top, his fingers brushed against Mateo's sides. The coolness was both a relief from the hotness of his own fevered flesh but also electrifying, causing a heat of a different kind. He could swear his dick was trying to rally past the sickness.

Christos swore under his breath, apparently affected by the contact as well. "I should have thought to start the water before doing this." He pressed the top against Mateo's chest before walking over to the shower.

Or not affected at all, merely planning the best way to nurse me through my bath time. Jeez.

He watched Christos fiddle with the temperature of the various shower heads, then turn some gizmo by the towel racks. Immediately, the floor beneath his bare feet started to feel warm.

"Is that heating the tiles?"

"Yes — and the towels."

"Wow, being rich is really awesome, huh?" He tried not to resent how shitty his life was in comparison and appreciate that he could benefit from this luxury for the next few days.

Christos returned. "The economic inequality of people on this planet is a major point against it."

"Like it's better on other planets?" he teased.

"Possibly." The man acted as if the question was perfectly legitimate, while wasting no time stripping off his own clothing.

Mateo sat, clutching his shirt to his chest, curling his toes along the heated tiles while every inch of Christos' magnificent body became exposed. The expanse of pale skin stretched over tight muscles had the effect of looking like marble. The lack of obvious hair heightened the effect, not that any of the details took his attention for long, not when that big cock came swinging into view. And swing it did, because the guy went commando, and removing his pants meant that the weapon he'd been containing took full advantage of its sudden freedom. Hard and sticking up in a nearly entirely vertical position, it loomed into Mateo's line of sight. Here, finally, was a hint of color, a pink tinge blooming over the shaft all the way up to a wide head. Big balls clung tightly to the base.

He must have made some kind of noise, a gasp or a squeak even. Christos paused in his efforts to fold his clothing. "Please do not be concerned with that. I am unable to control it, but it is meaningless."

Mateo blew out a breath. "Seriously, dude, that means a fuck load of *something*."

"I am sexually attracted to you and am especially aroused at the idea that I am going to be seeing you naked and touching you." Tossing his clothing on the sink counter, he gave Matteo a hard stare. "I will not act on my desire nor will I take advantage of your vulnerability. You have my word that you are safe with me and, other than possible inadvertent contact, I will not impose my unruly dick on you. I am here to help. That is all." His words and tone made it all sound like a vow, and the serious expression on his face made Mateo want to reassure *him*.

"I trust you, and I'm not afraid of you or your dick."

"That is good. Can you stand? Here... Use my arm for leverage."

Mateo took hold of what felt like an iron rod and rose on legs that were just as jelly-like as they had been moments before. Of course, now there was another reason for his weakness besides sickness. If Christos could be adult about this, he could as well. There was no sense in rewarding the man's kindness by being provocative. He resolved to ignore the obvious attraction and just be grateful his own body was too ill to react similarly, because that would be embarrassing as hell.

He kept his gaze on the spray of water while Christos pulled his pajama bottoms down to his ankles, then he dutifully lifted first one foot, then the other, like a toddler, until he stood equally naked. There was almost a muscle memory of what it meant to be in such a position, making him shudder in anticipation of something that he knew wasn't coming.

Christos misinterpreted the reaction, thank God. "Come. Let me get you under the water to warm you." He elicited another startled sound from Mateo when he lifted him into his arms. It didn't help that the tip of that cock brushed against his ass briefly in the process.

Mateo clung to the man much like a baby rhesus monkey, too overwhelmed with the bizarre situation to be embarrassed. Christos wasted no time stepping into the giant shower. Once he did, he lowered Matteo gently onto his feet, keeping a firm grip on his shoulders while positioning him under the hot, powerful spray. The moment it hit him, Mateo groaned from the exquisite sensation of being bombarded with the soothing water. It was better than sex.

Christos willed himself to become a statue, like an ancient piece of marble carved in the image of the Egyptian God Bes, with his phallus on full display yet intending to be a protector, not a predator. Damn his unruly dick anyway. One would have thought rubbing out a few orgasms in his own shower would have tamed the beast and made him acceptable company for this poor, sick boy. *Apparently not.* Of course, he hadn't anticipated this particular form of temptation. It was more like torture, really. How could he expect to remain passive while holding the body of a beautiful boy, shiny with water sluicing down his golden skin?

By reminding himself how ill and defenseless this human was, that was how. Mateo was there because he was in dire straits and had been felled by a sickness that had the power to kill him, if not for the care he was receiving. He needed kindness, something Christos suspected the poor child had received little of in his short life. And reminding himself of how young this human was helped. Yes, technically he was an adult, but that meant nothing. Emotional maturity came later in this species. There was no chance anything between them could be counted as consensual and equal. Mateo believed he owed payment for this help. For that reason alone, Christos was determined to keep himself in check. He would prove to this boy that there were decent men on this planet who wanted nothing from him, even if those men were actually aliens.

His head a little clearer on the matter, he turned to the mundane task of helping Mateo wash. Bottles of various kinds stood lined up in caddies attached to the wall. Holding the boy steady with one hand, he pumped shampoo into the other before lathering it through his hair. He'd intended to make it quick and clinical. The way the boy reacted to his touch, however—pretty little moans and leaning his head back to offer better access—had him changing his mind. Humans liked being scratched and petted, like many animals he'd encountered. It was satisfying to press the pads of his fingers into the scalp and massage.

He was rewarded by breathy groans and the occasional shiver. Given the warmth of the water beating down on them both, he couldn't pretend it was anything other than pleasure.

They both got so lost in the activity that it was startling when Mateo leaned a little too close and brushed against Christos' hard dick. Each of them jerked away and he had to let go of the boy's head in order to keep him from taking a tumble into the wall.

"Sorry," the boy mumbled.

"My fault entirely," he replied and returned to finish the job of washing then rinsing Mateo's hair.

After making short work of the conditioner, he filled his palm with liquid soap and contemplated how he was going to manage this little nightmare task without embarrassing himself and alarming the boy, because naturally he'd forgotten to bring in a washcloth and would have to do all the cleaning by hand. He considered offering the soap to Mateo to do on his own, then decided that would be cowardly. Instead, he went about the job as if he were rubbing down a horse. He started with the safe bits—the shoulders and back and on to the arms. That enticingly small and high ass was more of the same. Wipe down and around, and not— *sweet Jesus*—inside the crack. The flow of suds and water would do the trick just fine.

Turning Mateo around to rinse away his efforts and start on the front, he averted his eyes. The chest was exactly like the back, only with nipples, and they didn't require any attention at all. The flat stomach was simply a reminder of how underfed the boy was— something to pity, not covet. There was nothing of interest south of there. That was what he told himself over and over, and yet he couldn't help but peek at the slender cock that was on display, because there was hardly a shred of hair surrounding it. What nature gave humans, they constantly sought to alter and remove. And yet, he couldn't complain at the lovely sight. It all but killed him to pass that oh-so-desirable piece of flesh through his fingers without lingering. A quick flirtation with cleaning small, soft balls and he continued on to the legs. That was the most cursory effort of all. Otherwise, he'd have to bend over, putting his eyeballs right in front of that which he was dying to suck into his mouth.

He turned Mateo around again, treating him like a doll, to rinse his front clean. Mateo remained compliant and quiet, but his body was beginning to shake with fatigue. Christos hurried to turn off the water and scooped him once more into his arms. The human's light weight continued to disturb him. They might not have many days together, yet he was determined to fatten the boy up as much as possible. The towels were warmed through and he hastily wrapped two around his charge, one for his body and one for his hair. Then he sat on the toilet with Mateo in his lap, because he just couldn't imagine letting him go. *Not yet.*

Thank God for thick towels. His dick was valiantly trying to break through the barrier, but it remained firmly trapped instead of poking at Mateo. At least the boy seemed to be comfortable and not fearing he was under assault, because the moment they were seated, he leaned against Christos' chest with a humbling amount of trust.

"Thank you. I can't believe how tired and wobbly I am after doing so little."

"It was a lot, showering like that. Your, um...hair needed a good cleaning."

"Hm-m. It's been a few days and I was sweating last night because of the fever. It felt wonderful the way you washed it."

The boy's soft, sleepy tone gave Christos all kinds of bad ideas. "I'm glad to have been of help," he said gruffly before beginning to rub the boy's wet hair with the towel.

"I should do that." Mateo moved to pull away.

Christos held him firmly in place. "No, you are too weak. I will do it. It is no bother. There's likely a hair dryer in here and I'll use that once I get most of the water wicked away. I don't want you to get a chill. Harry will take a dim view of me if I set his patient's recovery back through lack of care."

Mateo snuggled closer into his towel. "You could call for Demi to do this if you think I can't."

"No."

"Because I'm your responsibility?"

"That—and because I want to be the one to do it." He regretted the confession the moment the words left his mouth. In the next instant, he decided that he didn't. What difference did it make if the boy knew how he felt? He'd vowed not to touch him or make any kind of demands. Keeping his promise was all that mattered.

Mateo tipped his head back and looked at him. "You want me."

He stilled his movements and stared at him. "I have said as much."

"Except you don't want to"—he frowned—"or you resent the fact that you do."

Christos restarted his efforts, keeping his movements slow, almost a caress, much like the way he'd washed it to begin with. He didn't miss how Mateo's eyes dropped closed with obvious delight.

"How I react to you or how I feel about it has nothing to do with you."

"You think? It seems like it has everything to do with me."

Christos huffed. "Well, naturally it does. I mean that it's nothing for you to be bothered about. It has to do with my failings, my weaknesses. You aren't responsible, nor should you give it a moment's thought. Your only concern is to get well."

"Hm-m." Mateo cuddled against him once more. "What if I want to think about it? What if I want to encourage it?"

Christos' breath hitched, as did his movements, before he regained his composure. "No. You must do neither of those things. You aren't in a position to make any kind of decisions and I refuse to allow you to do so."

"You're no fun."

"I have never claimed to be. Now, no more of this. I will dry your hair and the rest of you, then dress you in fresh clothing."

Another thing he'd forgotten. Fortunately, once he had eliminated every drop of water from the boy's skin, wrapped him in another warm, dry towel and returned to the bedroom, he found that someone had removed the breakfast tray and laid out clean clothing on the bed. It took little time or effort to see his charge fully dressed and tucked in tightly once again.

"There," he said, straightening by the nightstand and realizing belatedly that he was still naked. And…yeah, still totally erect. His cock hadn't gotten with the program at all. "Excuse me a moment."

He nearly used his natural speed in his haste to return to the bathroom, slowing abruptly enough that he stumbled like a drunk—one whose cock preceded him by about a foot. There was a burst of a giggle from the bed. Ignoring it and his own sense of shame, he entered the bathroom and practically slammed the door shut. He snatched his clothing from the counter then realized he could never get his pants on in his present condition. There was nothing for it but to rectify the situation.

Hating himself, knowing that the boy was out there almost certainly picturing what he was doing, Christos nevertheless took his cock in hand. He made his grip as punishing as he could, both to give vent to his anger and also to make short work of the affair. He had to bite back a groan and brace one hand against the wall as he jerked his shaft. Coming didn't require any kind of imagery, given how primed he was. He still conjured up the memory of Mateo, slick and sleek like a seal under that spray, with his firm ass facing Christos in an unintended invitation. He allowed himself to fantasize it was just that and imagined accepting it — to clasp those slim hips and draw that ass toward him, to slide his dick between the wet cleft, to find that hole awaiting him, circling it with his cockhead dripping with pre-cum and to press forward, past the puckered ring and up the tight channel to drive balls-deep inside the willing boy.

This time, the groan made its escape. He let it out long and low as he milked the climax. His arm shook with the effort to keep himself upright, making him think of the boy waiting for him in the next room. When the next wave of orgasm claimed him with even more intensity, he went to his knees, relishing the pain caused by bone hitting tile. When his vision cleared, he used one of the wet towels to wipe the cum from his hands and everywhere else it had managed to splatter.

Then he used it to rub his cock clean with vicious vigor until he hissed from the burn.

Staggering back to his feet, he proceeded to dress, although his fucking dick wasn't quite as limp as it should be. It remained a struggle to wrangle it back into his pants. He managed, though, and gathered the dirty linen to take down to the laundry. No way was he leaving this mess for someone else to deal with. And he'd handle the washing machine himself. He didn't need the ribbing that would come from others scenting his lack of control.

Christos was quiet when he reentered the bedroom, not sure if Mateo had fallen asleep. No worries there. The boy was lying where he'd put him minutes ago, his gaze fixed firmly on him.

"Honestly, did you find that more satisfying than anything you might have done with me?" There was an accusation in his tone, which was adorable as well as aggravating.

Christos didn't bother denying anything and went for the truth, as always. "Certainly not. I would have much preferred drilling you into the mattress." Ah, that sudden widening of the human's eyes was most gratifying.

He headed for the door. "As that is not an option and will never be an option, for reasons that I have already stated on multiple occasions, it was all that was or ever will be available to me." He stopped with his hand on the knob. "Now, is there anything else you need or want before I leave?"

Mateo slunk into the covers. "No. Thank you."

"Very well. Get some sleep. That shower took a lot out of you."

"No, it didn't. I'm fine." A large yawn laid waste to that claim.

Christos hid a smile. The boy really was adorable beyond measure. It was going to be agony keeping his hands off of him. "I will return shortly to check on you."

With that promise, he put distance between them, even knowing that nothing was ever going to be enough of a barrier to curb his mounting desire.

Chapter Four

Merlin suppressed his eagerness and dutifully went through the warm-up exercises that the warriors insisted on before they got to the good stuff. Aside from the pleasure of being in Annika's presence, this training was the one good thing about being forced to live in Boston with his father's enemies. Alex and his men had decided that, with the existential threat of Dracul, it was important for all of the young males to be trained in combat. This hand-to-hand shit was second only to the awesome fun of trying out various badass weapons in the basement shooting range.

Not that he looked forward to fighting his former master and any of his men who might have survived the attack. In fact, he'd intended to be a traitor in the midst of these suckers who hadn't known a powerful leader when they'd been given the chance. He'd had visions of turning the tables on them at the right moment, which had been his only solace while trapped in Malcolm's highland castle. Then Annika had entered his orbit and, like a bolt of lightning illuminating the world around him, he'd realized that both Dracul and Alex had been wrong. They were pale shadows of whom they all truly should bow down to. Her plans trumped them both and Merlin no longer imagined how he would participate in this fight. He understood that his mission was different, and learning these skills had taken on new meaning for him. He would use them for her benefit, and fuck anyone who got in his way.

He was careful not to let any of his thoughts show, however, and he listened carefully to everything he was being taught. Val and Malcolm were the main teachers for both personal combat and weaponry and he appreciated their skill. They got occasional help from the other hybrids' fathers, Tony and Claude, who were pretty fierce, although they were nothing compared to those first two dudes. Merlin soaked up everything each of them had to pass along, slowly gaining in strength and skill.

There were also first-aid classes taught by Harry, but those were a bore. It hadn't occurred to him that someone would ever stop fighting to help a downed comrade, either. He couldn't imagine playing medic to any of these guys. Harry had insisted, though, and Alex had gone along with it. Val had announced that it was mandatory, using a look that promised serious trouble if anyone argued. Merlin had no intention of crossing the guy unless absolutely necessary. Besides, he might need the medical training to help his Queen. That alone made the lessons tolerable, though he still hated them.

"Get more of a stretch in your hamstring, Merlin," Val barked out.

"Okay, Val." In his mind he rolled his eyes, but of course, he didn't dare show that kind of disrespect in the open.

The familiarity was acceptable, however. Everyone was okay with first names being used, which was strange and a little hard to get used to. Back at the castle, it had been 'sir', or 'master' in the case of Dracul, and forgetting that show of deference could earn someone a sore jaw or cracked ribs. That was one thing he didn't miss. And he didn't make the mistake of thinking that informality meant weakness. Alex and his men could break him in half without working up a sweat. He didn't push his luck with them or question their judgment. They were the ones who'd kicked ass back in Wales, after all.

"Grab your ropes, everyone, and start skipping." This from Malcolm, who trained in only a kilt. The man didn't even flinch when someone's kick got to close to his balls. That was some badass shit right there.

Merlin thought this girly stuff was stupid, but again, he did as he'd been told. The humans found it great fun. But they were weird about a lot of things, in his estimation, always dancing and playing games. Their frivolity made them children in his mind, although they were sharing beds with very grown-up warriors and didn't hesitate to get in their faces if they were mad about something. In that way, they obviously had guts to spare. He still thought training them was a waste of time, and hated sparring with them because he didn't want to muck up any of their pretty faces and get into trouble. But again, Alex had insisted. He didn't want his boy or any of the others to be at a disadvantage, and they were all drinking blood now, so they were getting stronger and faster than any regular humans. Only the knocked-up one, Mackie, was exempt from the hand-to-hand lessons. He'd witnessed the guy fighting with his husband about that. Of course Val had won the argument. And Mackie got to shoot as a consolation. He was better at it than any of them, which rankled Merlin.

Malcolm clapped his hands once. "All right, that's enough. Put the ropes away and pair off by species the same as last time."

Merlin turned to face Yaro, who was his sparring partner. Matti was coupled with Demi. The humans always started with their own too—Quinn with Jase, Brenin with Damien—except when Val chose to mix them with the hybrids to increase the octane of the training. Merlin had to admit that the humans didn't hold back when he fought them. They got right into it and took their licks without any tears or complaining. He hadn't expected them to be so fierce. Alun, however, had been the biggest surprise of them all. Alex's decree about training had included him, and Merlin wouldn't have thought the pitiful human had it in him to be any good at fighting even Idris. Yet the guy sparred with Dracul's former bitch, Dafydd, and surprisingly held his own. He could almost respect him, then remembered how this was the human who'd cowered in the corner whenever Merlin's sire had disciplined him. He wasn't someone to count on if there was trouble.

Putting aside any further stray thoughts, he squared off against Yaro as they circled each other, looking for an opening. Yaro was a sneaky little fucker, always feinting in one direction before attacking from another. He was slightly older than Merlin as well and, while lean, he was all ropey muscle and slippery as an eel. Merlin had a slight advantage in height, though, and was meaner. Yaro had been raised in some posh, gentle home. He not only didn't know how to fight dirty, but he was also constantly surprised when Merlin did. *Sucker.* Yaro was too nice for combat. But Val had said that when in battle one should use any means to win. There were no Marquess of Fucking Queensbury Rules in this war.

He'd just found a weak spot when the door opened and the scent hit him like a slap. Freezing, he turned only his head to watch the visitor come floating in. Everyone was doing the same. Such was the effect of the Queen. Even Val and Malcolm had stopped in their tracks, their focus on the young woman coming toward them. Annika's beautiful hair was pulled back in a swinging ponytail and she was dressed much as most of the humans were, with leggings that fit her like a second skin and a sleeveless top with a hem that didn't quite meet the waistband hugging her hips. As she approached, a flash of taut, creamy-smooth skin caught his eye. The air got sucked out of the room and Merlin found it hard to take in a breath.

Val sketched a bow. "My Queen, how can we help you? Have you come to watch?"

Annika smiled brightly at the man. "No, Mr. Val, I have come to participate. I am rather disappointed that I haven't been asked to join." Her tone was sweet and brittle as ice at the same time.

Val seemed lost for words. He stood blinking at her for a few seconds before turning to Malcolm. "Where's Will?"

It was Annika who answered. "Papa is with Alex, looking after the club—not that this is any of his concern." She folded her arms.

"Och, I think it is indeed very much his concern, lassie, given that he's your father," Malcolm intervened. "This is no place for you."

"And why not?"

Now it was the Scotsman's turn to look confused. It was amusing how these big warriors turned into puddles around the Queen. Merlin relaxed his stance, entertained and intrigued about what she was going to do next.

Damien stepped into the breach, hustling over. "Hey, Annika, you're freaking these guys out, you know?"

"I don't understand why, Father Damien. Are we not all in danger from Dracul? Hasn't Alex decided that everyone in the household needs to be able to fight instead of putting the entire burden on the warriors? We don't know what kind of complement Dracul has put together since the raid on his castle. We all need to be prepared to fight, do we not?" She included everyone in that last question, her gaze flitting around the room.

Val opened his arms wide. "My Queen, we are here to protect you. Each of us will die in that service if need be."

Fucking right, we will. Merlin was only slightly surprised at his own vehemence.

"Very prettily said, Mr. Val, but I do not intend to cower behind any of you while you fight for me." Dropping her arms, she added, "Do you think I can't look out for myself? You see me as weak?"

"Never that. But you are..."

"What?"

"Small—and perhaps not quite as strong as you'd like to be." Val's tone was not unkind.

"I am not much smaller than these humans you are training and I have my papa's blood as well as my human father's. I think you underestimate me." When Val shook his head, she added, "Try me."

"I beg your pardon?" Val's normally impassive face had taken on a look one could almost describe as terror.

Annika shook her arms and legs and stood in a loose stance before him. "Try to hit me."

"Um-m, that's a hard no. *Ma'am*."

"Annika," Damien said, "that's not a fair thing to ask of him." For a cook, the guy had giant balls to keep inserting himself in the stand-off like that. Or, more likely, he didn't feel the same awe for her as the warriors and hybrids did. *More fool him*. Her power was obvious to Merlin. It shone around her like an aura.

Annika looked down her nose at the human, for all that she was about five inches shorter. "Why not?"

Val answered. "Because I don't want to break your face—or any other part of you, for that matter." Now Val was clearly getting agitated.

Merlin almost volunteered to do it himself. His trust in the Queen was absolute. If she believed she could protect herself, he was sure she was right. What was wrong with these men? How could they question her obvious wisdom in anything?

Annika's lips quirked in a brief smile. "I promise you won't lay a hand on me. Now, must we continue with this silly argument or are you going to do as I ask?"

Val made eye contact with Malcolm again, who merely shrugged. "Okay, you're the Queen. Damien, I'm counting on you to keep Will from killing me when this little experiment goes south."

Stepping aside, Damien replied, "Don't worry. I'm a witness to your efforts to prevent this. All's good."

Val snorted. "Not even remotely, but okay." The warrior put himself in an offensive stance, with his left foot forward, body angled to the side and his right arm pulled back. When he made his swing, even Idris could have avoided the fist. It was that slow.

All Annika had to do was step back for him to miss. Instead, she moved only her upper torso, bending back at the waist so that Val's fist punched through empty air. As his swing followed through, she twisted up again into a straight position. He tried the same thing using his left hand, this time, and with a faster velocity. Once again, he found nothing to connect with where her upper body had been a split second before. Her feet remained planted right where they'd been from the beginning.

Annika grinned. "Is that all you have, Mr. Val? Don't hold back on my account."

Val grinned as he bounced on the balls of his feet. "Yes, ma'am. Give us some space, boys."

There was a moment of hesitation before everyone moved back to create a large buffer around the two of them. Excitement permeated the room. Val wasted no time renewing his assault and he obeyed his Queen without hesitation now. He jabbed with one hand then the other in quick succession. Annika twisted her torso again, this time from side to side, greeting his efforts with more air. When he switched unexpectedly to a roundhouse kick, Merlin held his breath with sudden fear. He needn't have worried. Annika avoided that deadly foot with the same graceful ease.

After that, Val's attacks became a blur of punches and kicks and Annika's body twisted and turned like a soft rubber band. She bent herself at unimaginable angles and yet never lost her balance. She lifted a foot and pirouetted when he came in low and immediately flowed into a bow with her ponytail brushing the floor to avoid him as he went high again. The faster and harder Val came at her, the more she practically danced around the room with an economy of movement that made it seem as if she were merely doing warm-up exercises instead of engaging in an epic battle.

Merlin lost track of how long it went on. Quite a while, that was for sure. It ended abruptly without any kind of signal being made that he could detect. Annika stood nearly dead center of the room, her arms stretched high and one leg sticking out at a ninety-degree angle. Val was in front of her, breathing hard enough to hear. His arms hung loosely to his sides in a clear sign that he was done fighting. Annika slowly lowered her arms and leg. They stared at each other for a few seconds before he bowed low.

"Apologies, my Queen. You are more than capable of defending yourself and are welcome to join our classes, although I'm not sure there is anything that we can teach you," he added with a grin.

"I'm good at defense, obviously," she replied, then blew out a breath. "It's the offense I need help with."

"It will be my honor to train you," Val said with another bow.

"And I'll show you how to shoot," Malcolm chimed in.

"Oh, thank you. That would be most wonderful." Annika practically clapped with glee.

"I'm glad we got all of that settled. Obviously no one cares what I think." Willem stood by the open door with Alex and Damien by his side. The human must have gone to fetch his man while the rest of them had been enthralled by the demonstration.

"Oh, Papa!" Annika pranced over to him and threw her arms around his neck. "Of course I care what you think." She kissed his cheek before resting hers against his chest. "Did you see how well I did?"

Will hugged her. "Yes, I caught the tail end of it — with my heart lodged in my throat."

Val slid his hand over his killer Mohawk. "I didn't lay a finger on her, Will. I swear, I didn't. And man, I tried. I really did. I had no idea queens could move like that."

"I don't think any of us did," Alex interjected. "It's never come up before. There was no need for it to on the home world — or maybe the women deliberately kept this knowledge from us."

Annika stood back from her father and beamed at the man. "I honestly have no idea, Mr. Alex. I only know that I can and I want to be a part of this war, not hidden away in a tower like a helpless princess."

Alex gave her a stern look. "You are our Queen. Protecting you is as natural to us as breathing. However," he added when it looked as if she would argue the point, "I cannot dispute that we live on this world now and to a large degree must abide by their customs. Young women have always fought on this planet to protect what is their own. We can hardly expect you to do less."

Will turned to eye the man. "Can't we? 'Cause I sure as hell want to."

"Alas, no. Your daughter shall not allow it, no matter how we feel, in any event. Val, continue with your lessons as you see fit. Come, Will. We best leave them to it."

"I suppose." He pressed a kiss on his daughter's forehead and Merlin knew a moment of stupid jealousy. He wanted his lips to be able to do that—and more. "Take it easy on the boys," Will warned with a grin.

Annika took it seriously. "I will, Papa. I promise. But we must all train very hard. Dracul is coming soon." Her tone of voice sent a shiver up Merlin's spine.

Alex froze in mid-stride and turned. "How do you know that?"

She shook her head. "I can't say—but I'm sure it's true."

Alex nodded once. "Then continue with all speed. We must be ready. I will lose no one else in this pointless war."

When he was gone, Annika turned to the rest of the room. "Who would like to be my partner?"

Yaro and Matti stepped forward with a 'me', at the same time Merlin did. He didn't hesitate to shove them both aside hard enough for them to land on their asses. "It will be my honor." He gave her a courtly bow and was pleased that he did so with as much power and grace as Val had.

"In your dreams, boy," Val growled. "Get back to your usual pairings, all of you." He merely arched one eyebrow when Merlin glared at him. "Malcolm, take over the training while I show Annika some moves."

"All right then, laddies... You heard the mun."

Merlin wanted to argue. He glared at Val's back for only a few seconds, though, because he was both afraid of the man and he knew that Val's plan was sound. Annika needed to be run through the basic moves before sparring with anyone.

Plus, as he went to return to his place, Annika caught his eye. She smiled and winked at him before following Val. That small affirmation sent his blood soaring and his heart racing. He felt ten times stronger and a million times more motivated to do well. Poor Yaro had no idea what was coming his way.

And neither did Dracul.

* * * *

Andri's vision dimmed, a sure sign that the Master was taking too much of his blood. He didn't become overly concerned. There was no point, given that he wasn't in control, plus the Master needed him and would soon stop tugging at his vein. In the meantime, the feeding made the alien stronger and come harder — and Andri so wanted to do both for his Master, the most powerful creature on the planet. It didn't matter that he'd been impaled on the guy's massive cock for hours. He would happily remain in place for the rest of his life. Nothing gave him greater pleasure than being fucked by that monster dick.

Besides, he was part of an object lesson — another one. Having sucked one new recruit until he was nothing more than a dried-out husk, Dracul had cemented his power over the dozens of humans that had heeded the siren call of mere money. They now appreciated how much they were embroiled in an epic change for their planet. They were already petrified of the Master, even if they didn't admit it, but also fully committed to their new future as servants of he who would soon rule the entire world. Riches and power were within their grasp and the scent of greed that clung to them was detectible to even Andri's rather dull senses. Seeing the Master watch them work out while continuingly fucking his slut demonstrated anew how much stronger and more virile he was than them. And if they envied his access to such a fine piece of ass, so much the better. Andri reveled in being part of the play.

Moments later, cum blasted into his channel. He'd lost track of how often it had been filled. He practically swam in the stuff, and the amount that leaked past his hole had already permeated the air. It had its undoubtedly desired effect, because many of the men were hard, their cocks tenting their loose track pants, sweats and shorts. Their gazes occasionally flicked in his direction, and although he had nothing to compare it to, he would swear they were putting in extra effort, lifting extra-large weights and striking the punching bags as if to literally knock the stuffing out of them. He fancied that he was their muse, something to spur them on to greater training in order to conquer the world to have their own pick of sex toys.

It also gave him something to look at, with their bare chests and arms slick from their exertion. Not that he would ever want any of them over his Master... Physical beauty was nothing compared to the attractiveness of organic power. And he had access to that simply by sitting sprawled against the cool chest of an alien vampire. The fangs that had been sunk into his neck retracted. A few cursory licks of the Master's tongue meant Andri wouldn't bleed out. He hardly cared at the moment because his own orgasm made him gasp and close his eyes. But for his Master's cock anchoring him, he would have fallen onto the floor. The rim of a glass bumped against his lips and he greedily drank the sweet juice the Master offered. It restored his energy enough for him to crack open his eyes.

His gaze immediately homed in on two men wrestling at the far end of the large room. The way in which they grappled with each other made him think this wasn't a sparring session. There were too many vicious punches thrown and one of the men kneed the other when he had the chance. It made Andri wince, although his cock tried to rally once more. He was too spent for it to go anywhere, but he could appreciate the show nevertheless, especially when the one whose balls had been crunched retaliated by biting the other man's earlobe off. A howl and a spray of blood momentarily caught everyone else's attention. After a few seconds of curious looking, they returned to what they'd been doing.

Dracul's dick swelled inside him and he began to lazily hump once more. Andri moaned in part pleasure, part pain. His insides were being rubbed raw, but that hardly mattered, so long as the Master was happy... He hesitated to think that perhaps part of the Master's unrelenting fucking was based on worry that, despite the skill and determination of this new human army, they would not be up to the task of defeating the other aliens. Sheer numbers would only work if they were overwhelming. The few dozen recruits he'd obtained hardly seemed enough, but the Master had been very clear how many to get. If he had wanted more, Andri would have moved heaven and earth to please him, which wouldn't have been necessary anyway. There was no end to the availability of human psychos looking to wage war for the right price.

He dared to voice his concerns in Welsh, as they always did now for privacy. It made him feel even more special in the Master's eyes, part of the inner sanctum. "Master, may I ask a question?" He braced for a blow that never came. It was a bit of a disappointment, actually. Dracul slid a palm lazily across his chest and pinched a nipple hard enough to make him whimper. *Oh, even better!*

"What is that?" The pressure on his nipple increased.

It was hard to speak through the fog of pain, but that was the whole point. "Will this be a sufficient number of soldiers for your plan?"

The pressure ramped up briefly, making him yelp. Once again, the men in the room paused, this time to look at him. Through the tears swimming across his eyes, he saw them smiling. Some adjusted their crotches. Even the men in a heated wrestling match gave him their attention. Well, one of them did. The other's eyes were fixed on the ceiling. *Is he dead?* Dracul growled and everyone went back to what they'd been doing, as if goosed by an electric prod. And, yeah, the victorious wrestler simply swiped blood from his lips, pushed to a stand then went over to the speed bag.

"We might require one more." The Master's breath tickled the top of his head. "Two, given my meal yesterday." Then, "No, it doesn't matter. These cretins are all I need."

"They are certainly strong and brave in the way of the utterly stupid, Master, but surely your enemies can handle such a small group."

The Master drew him in tightly to his broad chest and rolled his hips to embed his dick as far as it would go. His lips brushed Andri's ear. "Of course they can," he said in a whisper. "Most of these idiots are already dead. They just don't know it yet. And they won't until it is too late. Do you understand?"

Andri shivered at the menacing tone. "Yes, Master. They are red herrings for your plan." It made sense now, although he still couldn't see the bigger picture of what was being put into place.

"Exactly."

He dared to go further in his thinking. "All this training is giving you a chance to pick which of them are the best. Those you'll reserve for the more important roles while the others become cannon fodder?"

"That is also correct." Dracul scraped his teeth down Andri's lobe, making him think of the man still lying in the corner. "There is more to you than a tight hole, which is a good thing, given how tired I am of fucking just it."

Alarm shot through him. He instinctively clamped down on the cock inside him to increase his Master's pleasure. "Please… I will do anything to make you happy, Master. Fuck me until I bleed. Or I'll gladly suck you. I love being choked by your amazing cock."

Dracul chuckled. "Oh, you'd say or do anything to keep your place, wouldn't you, slut?"

"Yes, Master."

"I can destroy your body and drain it of blood and you'd still want me, isn't that right?"

His fear ratcheted, as did his arousal. "Anything you desire, Master. I belong to you and only you." His heart hammered and his breathing sped up.

Dracul chuckled again. "Not to worry, slut. You have your uses and I will soon have others to amuse me. Stay loyal, do as I say and I will reward you."

"Yes, Master. You can count on me. You are all that I've ever wanted, the one I was always destined to serve."

The man's grip tightened around Andri's chest, making it harder to breathe. "Even when you were taking Petru's cock?"

"Especially then," he gasped. "He was nothing compared to you. He was never worthy of your patronage."

The hold eased. "You always know the right thing to say. You are clever, indeed. And if he comes crawling back and I tell you to kill him for me?"

Andri didn't hesitate to answer. "I will cut out his heart and feed it to you." It didn't matter if he meant the words or not. Petru would never dare ask for forgiveness. He knew Dracul better than anyone. Mercy and second chances were not an option. He wouldn't see his old master again.

"Again, the right answer, and so prettily said that I almost believe you."

"It's the truth, Master. I swear."

"I never trust words, slut, only reward actions." With that, he bent Andri almost in two and took hold of his hips with a punishing grip. Andri clasped the end of the chair to brace against the assault.

"You at the speed bag, come here!" the Master barked in English. It was the one common language of all the mercenaries.

The man made one more strong punch before heeding the Master's call. His gaze flicked to Andri for only a second as he approached. "Sir?" He stood with legs braced and his weight on the balls of his feet. No fool, he was expecting an attack. Flecks of dried blood still dotted his lower face.

"You fight dirty."

The guy grinned. "Yeah, 'cause winning's the point."

"Well said."

"And I don't like it when some asshole gets into my space."

"I'm sure he had it coming," the Master agreed in an oily tone that nevertheless held menace in it.

"I'll clean up the mess."

"No, the slut will."

The soldier glanced at Andri again with indifferent eyes. "He doesn't look strong enough."

The Master pumped harder into him. "You'd be surprised at what he can do, how much he can take." There was a pause. "Try him." The Master grabbed a hunk of Andri's hair and used it to pull his head back.

Knowing what was coming, Andri's skin tingled with anticipation. His spent cock found new life. Here was a unique kind of experience. Petru had never shared him with anyone and, as amazing as his Master was, even he couldn't fuck him and choke him at the same time. He licked his lips to prepare to take what he could see would be a big dick.

But the soldier didn't get any closer. Instead, he said, "I've seen what happens when someone tries to use your toy."

"Without permission, of course. I'm issuing an invitation, so there is no need for concern."

The room was quiet, everyone else unmoving, except for a few who were rubbing their bulges, if not sticking their hands down their pants. The man still hesitated.

"I don't know. I'm not into dudes."

Dracul tugged at Andri's head some more, making his face jiggle. "But he's so pretty, as much as any *girl*. And a mouth's a mouth, for all that. Close your eyes if you must. I insist." Now it was clear—if hadn't been before—that this generous offer wasn't a suggestion.

"Yes, sir." The man slid his track pants down to mid-thigh as he got closer. He might not have been into boys, but his dick was certainly hard. And it was mouth-wateringly big.

Closing his eyes, Andri opened wide and relaxed his throat. A moment later, something big and blunt slid all the way down in one brutal thrust. He'd been prepared for this, delighted in it, and already had a taken a lungful of breath. The salty, bitter taste of sweat coated his tongue.

It was exquisite, being impaled at both ends. It didn't matter that the men using him didn't coordinate their movements or that the human was hopelessly awkward at skull-fucking. He let his body go loose, not fighting the push-me-pull-you of the experience. He didn't remain entirely passive, however, working the dick with his throat muscles while squeezing his hole rhythmically.

The cocks impaling him swelled at the same time, so he braced himself for the flood of cum that shot into him at both ends. He gagged and whimpered and came harder than he'd ever done before. This had been the right choice, throwing his lot in with Dracul. His life was just as he wanted it and would only get better. Once Dracul took over the world, Andri would be sitting right beside him at the top.

Chapter Five

"How'd you get stuck with this babysitting duty again?"

Christos eyed Logan, who slouched in the passenger seat. "I'm merely making myself useful, given that I am superfluous in the training. Val and the others have that covered. My presence adds nothing to the effort. And as Damien needs to participate and worries that *Our Safe Place* is properly staffed, and Will worries when Damien does…" He shrugged. "Just helping the hive."

His carefully crafted nonchalance hid the fact that he was practically jumping out of his skin with the need to return to Mateo's side, which was ridiculous. The boy was fine, well-fed and monitored by Harry, and he was on the mend sufficiently to be exhibiting signs of boredom. For that, he had a television with the bajillion channels that satellite offered. He would easily survive without Christos hovering over him. And it wasn't as if Christos had the right to do so anyway. The boy was not his, was never going to be, and the earlier he started accepting that, the better.

Not that his dick agreed. It was hard again, still hard really, having never completely subsided, no matter how many times he'd jerked off that day alone. Being at the charitable center to feed homeless youth would be a good reminder of how vulnerable Mateo was, damaged in a way that would benefit from a good job and some psychotherapy, not a one-sided relationship in which his body was the glue that held them together.

Logan chuckled. "It's funny how everyone used to refer to you all as the family. Now, it's this weird concept that I associate with bugs."

"It's always been hard to describe our relationship in human terms. We used to refer to each other as shipmates. Then we settled on family as humans became more sophisticated, even though those of us from above are not truly relatives. With Annika, we have finally become a hive once more. I understand," he continued, "that hive is not quite right, but it's as close as we can get to defining our social structure."

"Yeah, I get it. She's a pistol too, that one. It's hard to accept how she's effectively growing right in front of my eyes."

"I can imagine how disconcerting that is." He couldn't, actually, but he'd been on this planet a long time and knew which words eased human minds.

Logan twisted around to talk directly to the timid man in back seat. "I guess that is nothing new to you, huh?"

"Not really," came the quiet reply.

The poor man was practically a ghost, wandering around the home they all shared and having little to do, scared of his own shadow. And who could blame him, given what he'd experienced living the hell that had been Dracul's castle? The shipmate that had claimed and brutalized him was dead. Their hybrid son, however, was not. His contempt for his father was obvious, although Annika did wonders to keep his vicious habits and learned behavior in check. There was hope for Merlin, but less so for Alun. His participation in the training was earnest, according to Malcolm, but not very effective. And his stamina was limited for that sort of thing. His willingness to help out with the homeless kids was a good thing all around. It got him out of the new prison he was inadvertently stuck in and eased Christos' and Logan's burden of playing nice with the needy boys and girls. Christos didn't do well with heartfelt aid and neither, by her own admission, did the woman warrior.

"They mature quickly and slowly at the same time," Alun offered. "It is…confusing." It was the most Christos had ever heard the man say in one sitting.

Logan snorted and turned to face the windshield. "You've got that right. At least she keeps that brat of yours in line. Man, has he got a mouth on him, and he takes 'sullen teenager' to new heights."

Christos raised his eyebrows at the harsh assessment of the poor human's child. To his surprise, Alun neither rose to his son's defense in the knee-jerk fashion of parents everywhere, nor did he join in the criticism.

"It was hard for him growing up in Dracul's castle. There were many expectations and no mercy. And I failed my child all the time. I couldn't protect him from the one who sired him. He was lucky in being strong and able to survive things that others couldn't. I am fortunate at least to have him still and not have to weep over the loss of someone I carried into the world."

Okay, now they'd had a record-shattering amount of communication from the man. His ability to feel guilt over his child's upbringing and pity for him as well informed his nature and spoke of his inherent strength. To come through that hideous fate and not be irretrievably broken, as only humans could be, was remarkable. Christos' estimation of him increased in that short ride to *Our Safe Place*.

As he pulled into one of the parking spaces in their alley, Emil came out with a load of trash for the dumpster. He nodded at them, then waited as they all climbed out.

The chef raised his hand. "Hey, good to see you, and right on time. I need to get back to the club and check on how dinner is coming along." He didn't try to touch any of them. Hugging and shaking hands was a purely human thing and Logan didn't like to be touched unless absolutely necessary, Christos had come to learn. Alun hung back, as was his want, trying to look invisible. His earlier loquaciousness was now a distant memory.

"I trust everything here is already prepared," Christos said. Cooking was not his forte, even by the relatively easy standards of what was served in this place.

Emil grinned. "Don't worry. All you have to do is serve and do the dishes. It's nothing you can't handle, and if you run into any trouble, Logan and Alun are here to pick up the slack."

Logan shook her head. "Yeah, like domesticity is my thing, either. Alun's the one I'm counting on at this point."

The man in question ducked his head, running his fingers through his ponytail. "I'm happy to help in any way I can." He really was very pretty, especially now that he'd gained some weight. Emil had said the poor guy had looked like a scarecrow when he'd first been rescued. While still slender, he appeared healthy, with his pale skin and high cheekbones. His black hair was glossy. Really, if Christos was going to pursue a broken sex slave, he may as well set his sights on Alun. It made far more sense than this ridiculous interest in Mateo.

"Okay, then," Emil said, "I'll get Shawn. He's been helping out this afternoon but is working at the club tonight."

They trooped into the building's kitchen together. Emil hustled the go-go boy with the brown skin and bright green eyes out to his SUV, leaving Christos and the others to take charge. There was a seemingly never-ending line of kids coming in to take a tray and fill it with plates of food and tall glasses of soda, milk or water. Some elected to get coffee or tea but the hot chocolate was the overall favorite.

Christos went on auto-pilot, because it was easy to keep the warming trays full, while Alun served and Logan juggled prepared foods in the kitchen behind them. The lack of anything substantial to occupy his time meant that his mind was able to wander in the wrong direction. He kept wondering what Mateo was doing. Had he eaten his dinner already? Was his fever down? Had he sweated through his clothing and needed a sponge bath?

Okay, now that was a very bad thought, because it led to him to imagining him doing that chore, which in turn reminded him of how he'd spent part of his morning naked and in the steamy shower with a slippery boy who was offering himself on a platter for Christos' use. Thinking of all that silky skin he'd found under the grime made his palms itch and his dick throb. He forced himself to look at the kids getting food — to really study them, to see how desperate they were with so few options about how to better their lives.

This is Mateo, every one of them. He doesn't want me, not really. It's survival sex he's offering, moron, nothing more than that. I want him because he's available and it's been too long since I've taken a lover, even for a single night.

The talking helped. Except when he tried to picture wanting any of the other humans before him, he couldn't. No boy or girl interested him. Over each face, he saw only one — Mateo's, his pretty light-brown eyes, his lovely high cheek bones framing a cute nose. Disgusted with himself, he turned to ask Logan to change places so that he could at least stare at something that didn't remind him of the boy. A strange ripple of unease rushed through the room, taking his attention.

He braced for trouble, even though there was nothing to indicate that it was coming. Instead, a man walked in, large for a human and carrying himself with the kind of confidence that Christos associated with a soldier. Plus, he definitely had a gun holstered under his arm. The telltale bulge was there, at least to his eyes. An untrained human might miss it. The kids in the room quieted and every one of them was staring at the visitor. Whoever he was, they knew him — or knew *of* him in some fashion.

"Cheese it, boys. It's the cops," Logan said from behind him then barked out a laugh.

He gave her the side-eye, unwilling to lose track of their visitor. "Do you know him?" She didn't seem particularly concerned.

"Yeah, he's a friend of Duncan's. Your little boy-toy was under his protection at one point while we took care of a *family problem* before you blew into town."

Ignoring the dig about his relationship with Mateo, he simply said, "Ah." He relaxed a fraction as well, knowing now that this wasn't a source of danger, at least not for him. The kids, however, were another matter. "What is his name?"

"Jefferson. Sergeant, I believe."

He went with that. "Sergeant Jefferson, is it? How may we help you?" Although he plastered a smile on his face, he kept his tone firm. There would be no trouble on his watch.

The cop approached with an equally cheery expression, even as his eyes darted around. "Hi, I'm sorry. Have we met?" He stopped in the now-empty space in front of the warming trays. Everyone was giving him a wide berth.

"No. I'm a friend of Duncan's, though, and your reputation precedes you." That was mostly true. He didn't have to be told that this man was in the dark about how and what they were, so he gave the kind of answer that a human would expect.

"I see. It has been a while since I spoke with Trey." The man gave him an assessing look. There was a flash of appreciation before he settled back to business. "How's he doing?"

"Well." He supposed. The truth was that he hadn't seen the cop in a while either. "What do you want here?"

"That's blunt," the man replied cheerily.

"My previous effort at being more polite didn't prove fruitful. As you can see," he added with a wave of his hand, "you're making our guests uneasy."

Jefferson look around the room again. "You've done remarkable work in such a short time. Father Ted would be pleased that so much is being accomplished in his name." He returned his gaze to Christos. "To answer your question, I'm looking for a particular boy."

"There's a joke in there somewhere," Logan chimed in. "Like, aren't we all?"

Jefferson gave her an indulgent smile. "Yes well, his name's Mateo—" He bit off his sentence and glared at Christos. "I'm sorry... Did you just growl at me?"

Oops. Christos pounded his chest with the side of his fist. "A bit of indigestion. What do you want with Mateo?"

"So you have seen him. Is he here now?"

"What. Do. You. Want. With. *Him?*" Christos had to work to keep his eyes from changing red and stay the impulse to leap over the counter and rip the man's throat out.

"Hoo boy." Logan slid away from him and over to Alun.

Jefferson didn't back down. If anything, he leaned onto the balls of his feet. "I only want to make sure he's okay. I was responsible for him a short while ago, found him a job and an apartment. Then he went off the grid again. I'm worried, that's all. I figured this was a place he'd likely go. Has he been here?"

Christos managed to talk himself down. This cop was obviously alert but didn't show any signs of lying. He stared straight into Christos' eyes, and while his pulse had quickened, it appeared only related to his own aggression.

"He was," he admitted. "And he's in a safe place, although not in *Our Safe Place.* There's no point in your staying here. It's only making the others nervous and I can assure you that Mateo will not be returning here any time soon."

Jefferson relaxed a hair. "What makes you so sure?"

"Because he's with me, in my home." Alex's home, really, but why quibble? And he did a brief and mental facepalm at the admission then chose to not regret it. It was the truth, and if this man decided to read more into the situation than there was, tough shit.

Jefferson's eyes narrowed. "Really? So what? You're one of those predator fucks who volunteers to help kids like these out because it's good hunting grounds?"

Christos grimaced and fisted his hands. Behind Jefferson, there were about a million wide eyes staring at them and hanging on to every word. Damien and Emil would be really pissed if he caused those kids to become leery of the place.

"I will forgive the insult because many men would do exactly that. I am here as a favor to my family, whom I'm visiting and who are behind this endeavor. Mateo took ill and is actually a guest of the family while he recovers. I misspoke when I referred to it as my home. In reality, we are both temporary residents and he is under a doctor's care."

The cop's demeanor changed again, relaxing more, his expression going from hostile to more friendly. "I know about them. They're the people who own the club, right?"

"Lux, yes." Christos also relaxed, trying to make it seem like a normal conversation, when it felt anything but.

"Yeah, that's Duncan's fiancé's family. There's lots of money there. I've looked into that club, too, figuring their go-go boys might be exploited. I bet there are transactions going on in those rooms that I wouldn't like."

"I really couldn't say." His distrust rose again. This was turning into a fucking nightmare. He longed for the boredom of slinging food. "No one is being exploited, however. Of that, I can assure you — not that my word means anything to you."

"You've got that right." The cop sighed. "Duncan says the same, and while I wouldn't trust him with my heart, he's too good a cop to turn a blind eye to anything." The man stood quietly, staring at him, for a few seconds before saying, "Mateo's going to be all right, huh?"

"Yes. It's bronchitis that my uncle, the doctor, has under control."

Jefferson nodded. "Good. That's good." He rubbed at the back of his neck and suddenly his fatigue and worry were obvious. "I didn't like finding out he'd taken off. It's winter and, you know… I really thought I'd gotten through to him, that he was off the streets for good."

And now Christos felt sorry for the guy. "He'll be fine. I'm sure we can find him a job at the club." He held out his hand when the man frowned. "I know what you're thinking, but he'll be off the streets and making a good wage, no matter what he chooses to do. My cousin Alex owns the place, even offers dental insurance." He didn't know why or how he could make such assurances, and yet as he said the words, he was determined to make them true.

"Okay." The cop sighed. "So what's for dinner?"

As Christos was trying to figure out a polite way of saying 'fuck off', Alun surprisingly intervened. He spoke in his usual soft voice from where he stood hovering over one of the trays.

"We have macaroni and cheese, fish fillets and hamburgers for the main course and honey-glazed carrots and corn for sides. Plus, there are white and whole-wheat rolls." The man said all of this while staring downward, except at the very end, when he lifted his head and looked over the steaming food right at Jefferson.

The cop's face lit up. "That sounds delicious. I know this is for homeless teens, but I don't suppose I could finagle some of that mac and cheese? I promise to make a generous donation, but that stuff's like my kryptonite."

Alun dropped his gaze again while he went for a plate. "Of course, sir. All are welcome."

That wasn't entirely true. Cops weren't among those for whom this place was intended. Christos didn't want to make an issue of it, not given how Alun had solved the problem of at least moving Jefferson off the topic of Mateo. And the poor man had again broken his own personal record for being bolder than Christos would have imagined. The cop had 'scary' written all over him. Maybe that wasn't a problem for Alun, who had surely learned to navigate in such dangerous waters while living under Dracul's roof.

Jefferson moved to where Alun stood. "Great. I appreciate it. And my name's Craig, by the way. 'Sir' is for my father and my superiors on the force."

"Oh my God," Christos muttered. "Seriously?"

Logan sidled over to him. "Oh, you boys... Always looking for a place to stick your dicks."

He would have bristled at the comment if it weren't so true, for humans and aliens alike. "That drive has the benefit of keeping your planet populated."

"Yeaaah," Logan drawled. "And speaking of which, isn't there a potential problem here?" She tossed her head in Alun's direction. "I mean, he's not like Lucien or Dafydd, is he? He hasn't been, um, *fixed*."

"Oh, right." He understood what she meant now. Harry had ensured that both his husband and Dafydd wouldn't be able to get pregnant again by performing a hysterectomy. Alun, as far as he knew, still had his womb. And wouldn't that be an interesting turn of events in Sergeant Jefferson's life? They already knew a human was capable of siring a hybrid. Annika was proof of that. If Alun and Jefferson produced a baby, what would that be? A full human created through an alien process. Was that permutation possible?

Fuck, now I'm being ridiculous. There was never going to be anything between these two men, although thinking about it had managed to dispel thoughts of Mateo for about two seconds.

"This isn't going anywhere," he declared.

"You sure about that?" Logan shook her head and moved back into the kitchen.

"Is this enough, sir? Craig." Alun smiled shyly at the man as he held out a plate piled high with food.

The cop gave him a megawatt smile as he accepted the offering. "Perfect, thank you." He scooped some of the mac and cheese and moaned through the bite. "Wonderful. Did you cook this?"

Alun hung his head and made himself busy stirring the corn around its tray. "No, I'm just helping, like." His accent sounded a bit thicker.

Jefferson seemed disinclined to go sit at one of the tables, which was probably a good thing. The wary kids had finally decided that he wasn't a threat to them and had gone back to eating and talking, albeit in lower tones than before.

"What's your name?"

"Alun."

"Alan?"

"No, Al-*un*."

Jefferson nodded his head as he ate. "I get it. It's nice. Different. And your accent, is that English?"

Alun whipped up his head and, for a second, he looked affronted before his typical deference returned. "No, Welsh."

"I thought it wasn't quite what I'm used to hearing on *Downton Abbey*. I like it. It's...prettier."

Alun's face pinked and Christos found himself hoping that more kids would come in for food. He scanned the doorway and nope, nothing.

"It's like a bad porn movie." Logan had snuck up on him again, obviously at loose ends like he was. "All that's missing is the *bow chikka wow wow* background music."

"I'm blissfully ignorant of what you mean." Except her words evoked images of Mateo lounging in bed, looking at him through sleepy eyes. Glancing at the clock, he saw that he had another miserable four hours before he could return to the club. "This is torture."

"Aw, I think it's kind of sweet," Logan replied, misunderstanding what was bothering him. "I think Alun can handle himself pretty well, surprisingly, but I'll leave it to you to keep an eye on this and intervene if necessary."

"Of course."

His attention was mercifully taken by the entrance of a few kids. They sort of clung to each other, with their gazes ping-ponging around the room. Obviously new to the place and distrustful of the situation, they didn't race to the serving area. When they spotted the cop, they stopped as one.

"It's all right," Christos called out to them. "Sergeant Jefferson is only here to eat. Come get some food. It's all free and you can have as much as you want." That seemed to do the trick. They came eagerly now, and he happily started filling their plates.

Alun broke away from his little confab with the cop. "Oh, I'm sorry. Let me do that."

"It's fine. I've got it."

The Welshman helped anyway and very soon, all the new kids walked away to find seats with plenty of food on the trays in their hands. The process hadn't taken more than a few minutes. The clock hands had moved too little to Christos' way of thinking. He resigned himself to a boring night punctuated by the slight entertainment of Jefferson trying to make some headway with the shy and retiring Alun.

The cop was managing to eat heartily and extremely slowly at the same time. "So, are you two relatives?" He waved his fork between Christos and Alun.

The poor Welshman turned round eyes on Christos, obviously unsure of what to say. "We are. By marriage, I suppose." Damn, no one had figured on this much scrutiny by allowing Alun to leave the house. It had seemed a small gift to let him have more freedom, given that he wasn't technically a prisoner, but secrecy was key and no one had created a backstory that would make sense. Christos had to do it on the fly.

Jefferson stopped chewing, his gaze on Alun's hand. "You're not married though?"

Alun twisted the fingers of both hands in front of him. "No."

"He's widowed." Now Christos wanted to kick himself. If he'd been smart, he would have concocted a story about a fiancé or something to get Jefferson off the scent. Alun wouldn't have gainsaid him.

The cop's face grew somber. "I'm sorry for your loss. Was it recent?"

Alun nodded, his cheeks getting a little redder. "Yes, but we weren't close, like. I'm not upset about it."

Christos bet that was something of an understatement. He wouldn't blame the guy if he did cartwheels of joy every night over the loss of the asshole shipmate who'd enslaved him. Interestingly, as much as all this attention must be bothering him, he didn't say anything to shut it down or give any indication that he was counting on Christos doing it for him. If anything, he was giving the cop every indication that he had a shot. Maybe enslavement in Dracul's castle hadn't sucked the life out of him after all. There was hope that he could recover and lead a relatively normal life.

Not with this guy.

"If you're finished, Sergeant?" He held out his hand.

"Oh, sure." The man gave him his plate, then went right back to chatting with Alun. "Do you live at the club? I think my friend Duncan said something about his fiancé living there with his family."

"It's the next door building, actually, and yes, I do, with my son," he added.

Ah, there we go. That will send the horny fucker running.

Jefferson grinned. "Oh, yeah? I love kids. I'm hoping to have a few myself one day."

Or not. Christ.

"How old is he?"

"He's a teenager," Christos chimed in before Alun could think of an answer that made sense. "And the kind that makes you want to run right into traffic. Sorry," he added to Alun.

The poor guy hung his head. "No, that's a fair assessment."

Jefferson remained undeterred. "Sounds perfectly normal to me. If you asked my parents, they would probably have described me in the exact same way. And look how great I turned out." He opened his arms wide while grinning broadly.

"I hope you're right."

Jefferson leaned on the counter and over the tray of candied carrots. "And I hope you'll give me your phone number."

Alun shook his head. "I don't have one."

That surprised the cop. "Really?" Undaunted, he recovered quickly. "Not even a landline at the house or at the club?"

Alun's heartbeat became rapid. Christos could hear the thudding, the racing of his blood and the harshness of his breathing. Matters had gotten entirely out of hand, right while Christos had stood there trying not to think about Mateo yet not doing anything helpful either. Alex depended on him to watch over Alun. It was an unspoken rule any time the changelings or the hybrids left home.

He bent to catch the man's eyes. "Alun, why don't you go see if Logan needs help?" He phrased it as a question, but the human understood it as an order.

Alun's relief was palpable. "Yes, of course. It was nice meeting you, sir," he said to Jefferson. "Craig," he amended with a flash of a smile.

Christos waited until the man had gone beyond anyone's line of sight before fixing Jefferson with a glare. "You've had your food. It's time to go."

The cop didn't move. "What's your beef? You don't like the idea of Alun getting back out there. Is his dead husband your brother or something?"

"Hardly. No one misses that asshole." Once again, he could have gone with something less truthful. When he'd told Mateo that he didn't like lying, he'd meant it. Doing so didn't come naturally to him. And in this case, perhaps more brutal honestly would be helpful.

"Alun has been through a difficult time. His marriage wasn't conventional or healthy for him. It's too soon for him to trust anyone."

Jefferson's eyes turned flinty. "The fucker hurt him? Are you sure he's dead?" When Christos nodded, the cop made a fist and cracked his knuckles. "Too bad. Look... I get it, believe me. I work with abused kids all the time. I don't want to make Alun uncomfortable and I wouldn't have come on that strong if I'd known. You'll let him know that?"

"Of course. Good night," he added when the guy didn't move.

With his gaze fixed on the point in the kitchen where Alun had disappeared, he said, "Yeah, sure. Thanks again for the food and the update on Mateo. Please let him know I was asking about him and that my door is always open if he needs me."

He won't. "Certainly."

He made sure the cop truly left and the atmosphere in the room changed into a noticeably relaxed and more raucous mood. Someone, Logan likely, cranked the volume on the background music that had been humming constantly. More kids came in, giggling and hungry. He served them without thought, then looked at the clock.

Damn, the hands had barely moved at all.

* * * *

Mateo peeked around the doorjamb to make sure the hallway was clear. Other than Harry, no one had come into his room for hours. He hadn't heard anything all day, either, but now with the TV off, there was a heavy beat audible from somewhere in the distance. He could hear a faint sound of music with his door open. Knowing that he was lodged above a club, that made sense. And given how much better he felt, lying around was getting boring. He felt antsy, and nothing kept his attention enough to entice him to stay in bed.

Seeing that the coast was clear, he stepped all the way out and looked at each end. To the left was an elevator and to the right a staircase. He stood scrunching his toes in the deep pile of the carpet, trying to decide what to do. While no one had told him explicitly that he had to stay in his room, he felt as if he were expected to anyway.

"Well, if that's the case, they should have had someone stay with me," he said softly to himself in case there was any chance someone was around to hear him.

What he really meant was that Christos should have remained with him—which was selfish and silly, but how he felt nevertheless. He knew the man was at *Our Safe Place*. That was a good thing. Street kids were already coming to rely on it as a place to find food and warmth, even for a little while. It took a lot of people to keep it open and Christos' willingness to help out was a testimony to how good a man he was.

"Except to me." That was more churlishness on his part. The man had been very kind to him. It was because of that morning shower that Mateo was confident he could leave his room without scaring anyone who saw him.

He'd thrown on clean pajamas, of which there now seemed to be an endless supply. Having looked in the bathroom mirror, he knew he was his usual jail-bait self. Maybe if he followed the music, he would see some of the club. And perhaps some of the club members would see him, and...

Hm-m, that wasn't as satisfying a fantasy as he would have expected. Weird how when he pictured getting nasty with some guy, it always ended with Christos' stern face staring at him.

"Forget him. Have a little fun," he said aloud to himself.

He headed for the stairs, because that seemed like the obvious source of the sounds. Plus, it was easier to race back to his room. In an elevator, he would be trapped. They'd told him that this floor was on lockdown for his sake. He still kept an eye out when he passed the other rooms. The idea of someone jumping out at him, even without bad intent, made him a little leery. When he reached the end, he found a sign on a brass pole facing the stairs that declared the area off limits.

Okay, that was to keep people out, not keep him in. He crept quietly to the railing and peered over it. The height made him a little dizzy, as did the bright lights all the way down on the first floor. The one directly below him was more muted in atmosphere. He could barely make out forms milling back and forth and some sitting along the wall. As his eyes adjusted to the change in brightness, he could see that men sprawled in big chairs while mostly naked boys gyrated on their laps. It looked like fun.

The activity on the first floor was more so. He caught flashes of boys dancing across the floor and men crowding a couple of small, round stages. If he leaned way over, he could also see the poles they pranced around. And the music had him tapping his own toes and wiggling his ass. Christos had mentioned something about a job. If he could get him hired as a go-go boy, how awesome would that be?

He squinted again at the middle floor, and yes, that looked like more than mere lap dances. Apparently, the boys could hustle as well. He bet this was a more lucrative gig in that sense than his street whoring. Safer, too. His dick stirred with real interest for the first time since he'd passed out. His sickness was on the wane and his body was ready to get back into action. Maybe it would be all right if he slunk to the next floor to watch. If he stuck to the shadows of the bannister, he might not be seen. And if a man saw him and mistook him for a disheveled go-go boy, would that be so bad?

With a half-formed plan, he crept to the head of the stairs.

"What the fuck do you think you're doing?"

The question was asked in almost a whisper, but Mateo jumped as if someone had shouted it in his ear. He stumbled forward and reached out to grab the rail and steady himself. He never got a grip because Christos wrapped one arm around him and hauled him backward. Mateo scrambled to get his feet under himself like a cartoon character, then gave up. Christos was effectively carrying him like a rag doll. He didn't let go until they were back in his room. And even that was to toss him on the bed.

Mateo bounced in the middle a few times before stopping in a sprawl. He glared at Christos. "What is your problem?"

The man stood with his arms folded and fury written all over his face. "Feeling better, are we?"

"Yes, as if it's any of your concern." He folded his arms as well, and tried to convey his displeasure with his own expression and icy tone. There was no fear, he noticed. Christos irritated him with his high-handed ways, yet the man didn't frighten him, which was surprising, given how big and strong he was. Mateo should have been scared shitless.

"You know damn fucking well it's my concern. You're here because I insisted on it and I'm responsible for your behavior."

"I wasn't doing anything. I'm bored and wanted to listen to the music. That's all."

"Really? You weren't thinking of making some extra cash from the club members on the lap dance and playroom level?"

"No, I was not," he huffed, although he wasn't sure he could pull off the not-quite-truth.

"Huh! Well, if you want to listen to the music, you can do so from your bed." Christos went to a panel on the other side of the headboard from where Mateo had been lying and fiddled with some knobs. Music filled the room.

"Oh. How was I supposed to know it was there?"

"You want to watch the dancing on the first floor?" Christos grabbed the remote from the bed without waiting for an answer, and after a few seconds of more button-pushing, the scene from the railing came on.

This was better than what he'd gleaned from his perch. He could see everything as if he had a front-row seat. There were four stages where boys in thongs gyrated away. Men milled about with and without other boys. He could see a bar with a very tall and bald black woman serving drinks. With the sound coming out in surround sound from the TV, Christos switched off the music on the wall. Nothing diminished the effect of the closed-circuit station. It was like watching a party — one he wasn't allowed to attend, obviously.

He slid back to his spot against the pillows. "I didn't know about that, either. Can we see —"

"No," Christos barked, anticipating his question. "The lap-dance area and playrooms are private spaces. The only cameras there are for security reasons, not for prurient viewing."

"From what I could see, it wasn't very private. Guys were giving blow jobs right in front of everyone, and I swear some kid was impaled on a man's cock."

Christos' tossed the remote on the bed. "I knew you were thinking of getting in on that action. You must be feeling very well to have those ideas."

"It doesn't matter how I feel. That's my livelihood and, like lots of people, I can't afford to call in sick."

"It's a stupid way to make money."

"That may be, but there are lots of stupid ways to make money." He thought of his time as a barista. "At least this one pays well."

"If it doesn't kill you first."

"It's not that bad and better than working in a coal mine or being on an oil rig, or…or working a crab-fishing boat. I saw a show once that said that's like the most dangerous job in the world."

Christos worked his mouth open and closed for a few seconds before saying, "This is a moronic conversation."

"I didn't start it."

"The hell you didn't. When I came home to find this room empty, that was when it began." He huffed. "I'm glad you're feeling better, but that's not a license to push yourself. It's been less than forty-eight hours since you started treatment. I bet you've caused your fever to return."

"I have not!" Because he did feel tired again, though, he stuck his legs under the covers. "Happy?"

"Deliriously." Christos stood by the side of the bed, watching the television while Mateo lay there doing the same. "I told you I'd see about getting you a job when you're well. If you're determined to make your living as a prostitute, you may as well do it safely."

"Don't pretty it up with fancy words. I'm a whore. It's all I've ever been." He refused to look at the man or feel sorry for himself. There had been another road, one where he'd pretended to not be gay and with the love and support of his family. He'd tried to walk it for a long time, until it had nearly made him dead inside. Being on the streets wasn't great but at least it was authentic.

"If you had a chance," Christos asked quietly, "would you pick a different way?" He knelt on the side of the bed. "I mean, if you could do something else that paid well and you liked, is there something?"

Mateo did look at him now. The earnestness in the man's face almost made him want to cry. "I honestly don't know. I've never had a chance to think about it. Survival has always come first."

"Then I would ask that, once you've recovered and have a secure place here at the club, that you do give it some thought. I would be happy to help you in any way."

Mateo stared at his hands. "I'm not a charity case. It was hard accepting the free food first from Father Ted, then at *Our Safe Place*. If it's money you're offering, I won't take it — not unless I earn it."

Christos sighed. "You are surprisingly stubborn."

Mateo shrugged. "Whores have pride, too, you know."

"A loan, then? Surely that would be acceptable to your sense of dignity."

Mateo shrugged. "I don't know. Maybe. I may not be a very good credit risk."

"I think you're worth any risk."

The vehemence in the man's voice had him looking into his eyes. "I can't imagine what would give you that impression."

"Then you don't understand yourself at all. But this is a weighty topic and, despite what you say, you must be tired. Let's lie here and watch television. How does that sound?"

Mateo tried to hide his glee. "I guess that would be okay."

"What would you like to watch?"

"This, of course."

Christos sighed again. "Why did I even bother to ask? You obviously find this entertaining," he added.

"Yup. I love the music and the dancing. It's positively captivating. Plus, watching it arouses me. Doesn't it do that to you?"

Chapter Six

"What are you doing?" Merlin hadn't intended for his question to come out in such an accusatory tone.

Alun jerked and shied away from him nevertheless. "I'm cleaning the kitchen." Looking away, he continued to scrub the countertop. "Everyone is so busy. I'm only trying to make myself useful."

Merlin put the bowl he'd been carrying onto that same counter, although away from all the activity. He was there to pop more corn, a surprisingly tasty treat and one that the Queen adored. "I didn't mean that," he said, opening the cabinet to take out another bag. "You were, like, singing." He put the popcorn in the microwave and pushed the setting. Operating this convenient contraption was his only cooking skill, which was as it should be. He was a warrior—or intended to be one—not a kitchen slave, although when he thought of Emil and even Damien, he had to admit that one could be a cook without being...well, Alun-ish.

"It's called humming. I know you didn't grow up with music, but surely you recognize it now that you've been exposed to it."

Anger over the insult exploded within him. He whipped around, his hand half-raised. Alun froze, his gaze downward, yet he wasn't cringing as he once would have when punishment was coming his way. They both stood unmoving for a few seconds and, in that time, Merlin saw his dead sire's hand at the end of his own arm. He also saw Annika's look of disapproval, even though she was nowhere near. She was with Mackie on the couch, watching a *Star Wars* marathon, which was way better than the princess movies she'd been binging on previously. Whatever happened in this kitchen would remain between him and his...father.

It was hard to think of this human in such terms. His alien sire had always used far more pejorative terms — cunt, slut, slave. He'd encouraged Merlin to do the same, to be scornful of everything that Alun was or did, to lash out with words, fists and feet whenever he felt aggrieved. And such behavior didn't only extend to this pitiful human who'd somehow incubated him until he'd been cut out and welcomed into a world in which the mighty lorded over the weak. Anyone who got in Merlin's way or on his nerves was fair game, so long as he won. He could do so now. Alun would never hit him back or tell on him, either, for fear of worse. No, that wasn't completely true. This man for whom he'd held nothing but scorn all his life had been protective of him, too, since the raid. He'd even lied for him when he'd done something wrong, taking the blame or saying it had been an accident. He acted like those fathers in Annika's movies did.

Why would he bother when now is his chance for payback?

He had no answer — or maybe he did — but it was too painful to explore. As the microwave dinged, he lowered his hand, realizing that they'd been frozen in this weird tableau for longer than he'd appreciated. He reached to remove the bag of corn.

"I know what humming is. I guess I was surprised to hear you do it. You've never done it before."

"Not in your lifetime, no," came the quiet surprise. "It's something I used to always do…before. We Welsh have a passion for singing and I've been told I have a fine voice."

Merlin shrugged and dumped the popcorn into the bowl. "Sure, whatever… I don't care what you do."

"I was humming because I was happy."

He gave the man the side-eye, not quite sure how to respond to that bit of information. "Yeah? Well, I'll leave so you can feel that way again."

He considered his words and actions very mature and considerate — or maybe not. There was a weird feeling in the middle of his chest, like a dull ache. His mind poked at him that he'd missed an opportunity to obtain something he really wanted, that by walking away to leave Alun to his own devices, he'd given up a chance to be happy himself. *No!* That was ridiculous. There was nothing he wanted from the man, nothing to be learned or gained by spending time with him. It was the Queen whose company he constantly sought, and it was the warriors who would continue his training so that he could execute her plans when the time was right.

"Oh, thank God!" Mackie said when Merlin returned to the living room area. "Now we can start

Episode VII and get that whole prequel trilogy out of our heads." He shuddered dramatically.

"I was gone for, like, five minutes. And here's *your* snack." The pregnant changeling had moved on from the puking-constantly stage to the eat-his-own-weight-in-food-every-hour stage. Annika and Merlin would be lucky to get anything from the bowl.

Not that any of that mattered. When Annika swiveled her head to smile at him, his heart lightened and that weird feeling in his chest eased. After scooping her dog into her arm, she patted the now-empty spot beside her on the couch, an invitation for him to get even closer. But just as he sat, the baby monitor on the coffee table squawked. *Damn!* Dafydd and his man were having what they called 'date night', albeit in the club for safety reasons. Annika had volunteered to watch Idris, which really meant Merlin was.

Mackie paused the movie. "Sorry, dude. We'll wait."

Annika put her hand on Merlin's arm, and the warmth of her touch sent a shiver through him. "He probably only needs the bathroom, and it's important for him to be potty trained." Yeah, he knew that, although he didn't know why. "He might be hungry, too, so bring him one of those soft cheese sandwiches that Emil has stocked in Mr. Dafydd's refrigerator. No bottle, no matter how much of a fuss he makes."

"I understand." He didn't, not really. Annika had a bunch of these rules that she seemed to press only when Dafydd and the other adults weren't around. It didn't matter. He did whatever she said because he trusted that she knew what she was doing, even if he didn't.

"And remember to get him to come to you."

He stood. "Don't worry. I know what to do. I won't let you down."

He took the stairs at a quick jog, needing to work off the excess energy he felt. Idris was standing in the far corner of his crib, his lips quivering in the dimness of his night light, obviously seconds away from crying over having to wait a couple of minutes for someone to heed his summons.

Instead of going around to pick him up, Merlin stood in front of the crib and held out his hands. "Come to me, Idris." When the baby didn't move, he repeated his soft command, "Come to me now, Idris." After another second of delay, the boy did as told, his chubby hands reaching for Merlin. "That's a good boy."

Merlin lifted him out of the crib, surprised at how heavy he felt from only a few days before when they'd gone through this little ritual. There didn't seem to be any bulk in his bottom, so as usual, Annika had been right. Idris was willingly going along with this potty-training thing. Merlin had no memory of having done this when he was younger, but he must have. And he did remember one father smacking a hybrid son who had leaked on his trousers. Nothing like that would ever happen in this place, yet Annika was very keen on Idris becoming diaper-free as soon as possible. She had such a sweet way of getting what she wanted, and no one argued with her.

He put Idris on his feet and pulled down his pajama bottoms and training diaper before balancing him on the toilet. This was totally disgusting work, not that Idris seemed to notice or mind. He sat there, kicking his legs and babbling about something unintelligible before finally letting go of his stream. Fortunately, it all went down where it belonged. It didn't always play out that way. Merlin jiggled him a little before taking him off, because he wasn't going to get any closer to the source of the pee than *that*.

"Are you hungry?" he asked, taking the toddler by the hand to walk him back to the crib.

"I want bottle!" The kid had a way of practically screaming his words, as if already anticipating a fight.

"No, Idris. You can have a sandwich." The boy's face scrunched and he looked ready to holler. "Annika says so. Remember how we always obey the Queen?"

Idris' expression fell and he sniffed back his nascent tears. "'Kay."

"Good boy." Merlin led him into Dafydd's sitting room, where there was a mini-fridge. Everyone had one, actually. He couldn't deny that his standard of living had increased a thousand-fold since coming to live under Alex's roof.

He took out a container of pre-cut tiny sandwiches and sat himself and Idris on the floor right there. "Here." He handed over one with cream cheese filling. Idris took it with both hands and started stuffing his face. "Careful... Don't choke."

Idris grinned at him, his teeth covered in food, reminding Merlin that after this, they'd have to go back into the bathroom to brush. He suppressed a sigh. How had his life turned this much? Things he never would have thought he'd be not only asked, but willing to do had become second nature to him. It all came back to Annika. Her dominion over him should have caused him resentment. And it had at first, his body responding automatically while his mind had rebelled. Now, the fight had fled, leaving him with almost a sense of inner peace. It was sort of like being under Dracul's rule, except this one felt...right, and there was no fear associated with it. He was sitting on the floor catering to a toddler and was content to do so.

He didn't want to lose this feeling, ever.

* * * *

Christos looked back with fondness on his time spent at the food shelter. He'd only thought it had been boring. Compared to watching the club in full swing, it had been captivating. This was excruciating. He simply couldn't understand the appeal of all that noise and the spectacle of mostly naked young men gyrating around, up and down poles. Sure, it had been impressive the first few times he'd observed it. Now, it was humdrum. And rich men making drunken fools of themselves held no appeal at all as a form of entertainment.

No, slinging food onto plates and seeing the effect it had on needy youth was far more satisfying and rewarding. In fact, the more he watched, the more he realized that the disparity in this world between the haves and have-nots hadn't changed much. Alex's club was Versailles by another name. At least Christos' mountain home had the benefit of restraint, although it also reminded him that he was sitting on a big pile of wealth himself and had done nothing meaningful with it.

Mateo, however, was obviously enjoying himself. A grin was plastered on his face and his eyes glowed from obvious happiness — and not only from the light cast by the television. He'd paused his viewing only long enough to take his meds and suffer a medical check-up by Demi. That hybrid was too clever by half, giving Christos a quick look that held the promise of untold horrors if he dared to hurt this vulnerable boy. He ignored the warning, if only because he would do worse to himself if he did what he wanted with increasing urgency.

That was the other reason why he was remembering his time spent at *Our Safe Place* with increasing nostalgia. Then, he'd had Mateo on his mind nearly constantly, like an unreachable itch that needed scratching. Now that he was in a position to satisfy that urge, it only made it worse. Lying next to the human was a whole other circle of hell. And that was true even if the kid hadn't tossed that verbal bomb between them earlier. *Watching it arouses me. Doesn't it do that to you?* Actually no. It was Mateo's proximity, his unbridled joy and the clear scent of his arousal that was driving Christos mad. They could have been watching *The Weather Channel* for all he cared and his cock would still be painfully hard. Thank God he'd had the good sense to toss the edge of the comforter over his lap. It hid the obvious, although given the sly glances from Mateo, he didn't think he was fooling him.

Needing a distraction, he asked, "Are you hungry? I can go get some food from the kitchen." He had a half-formed idea of jerking off along the way. *Yeah, like that's going to help.*

Mateo surprised him by rolling onto his side, facing him. "What if I said I had a taste for something else?"

Please don't say for my dick.

"Like your dick."

Ah fuck! He turned his head and gave what he hoped was a stern look. "You really need to learn a new refrain. This song of yours is getting old." He nearly took his words back immediately when he saw Mateo's expression.

The boy flopped onto his back again. "Why are you so mean?"

Affronted, Christos barked, "I am *not* mean."

"Yes, you are. You lie here with me watching all of this porn-light stuff then deny me any release."

He gaped with outrage. "First of all," he ground out when he managed to take in a breath, "this was your choice, not mine. I'd rather watch that princess crap of Annika's than the ridiculous bacchanalia going on downstairs. Second, we both know that you're only trying to get me to use you as a form of misguided payment. I will not be another exploitative man in your life. Which reminds me... Sergeant Jefferson was at *Our Safe Place* earlier, asking about you."

"Oh?" Mateo sounded alarmed. "What did he want?"

Christos regretted lobbing that information as part of his tirade. "Nothing bad," he soothed. "He was worried about you, that's all. He hoped to find you there and was pleased to learn that you were safe."

After a few moments, Mateo said, "That was nice of him. He was a good guy. I kept expecting him to hit on me, even when he said he was only trying to help. He never did. Maybe he's not gay."

"He's gay all right, because he was hitting on Alun, of all people."

"I have no idea who that is."

Christos cringed. Of course not. Mateo had so seamlessly integrated into his life that he forgot that he wasn't acquainted with the whole family or privy to their affairs. He needed to watch out that he didn't say anything inappropriate.

"He's a family member who helps out with serving the food. You would have run into him if you'd been there prior to that day we met."

"I see. Well, that's nice. Jefferson deserves to be happy, I guess. We all do."

"He is obviously a good man. Gay or straight, only bad people prey on the vulnerable."

"Which brings us back to…us."

"There is no 'us', Mateo."

The human blew out a breath. "Fine, be that way. If you think this is all about my rewarding you for helping me, you are being really insulting. I don't suppose it's ever occurred to you that I'm being the predator here."

Christos gave a short laugh. "That's ridiculous."

"You think so. Look."

Against his better judgment, Christos turned to give his full attention to the boy. The sight that greeted him dried his spit. Mateo had pushed the covers away and tugged the waistband of his pajamas past his crotch. His slender cock was fully erect, bobbing a few inches above his perfectly flat abdomen. A pearl of pre-cum glistened at the slit. Christos gaped like a landed fish. His balls cramped and his dick jerked like a dog straining at its leash.

"See how much better I'm feeling." Mateo practically purred. "Tell me your cock doesn't want to come out to play."

"Sweet Jesus, put that thing away."

"Why, because you think that's what's best for me? I bet I'd get a really good night's sleep if you fuck me, and everyone knows that sleep is the best medicine when you're sick."

The little brat actually fluttered his eyelashes at me.

Christos nearly swallowed his tongue. When he found his voice again, he said, "I'm not going to fuck you," with as firm a tone as he could manage.

"Oh." Mateo pouted, making those lips even more tempting. "If it's a matter of condoms and lube, I bet there's lots to be found in this place if you know where to look. I ran out of my stash and couldn't afford to buy more. That's why I was offering a blow job and not more when we first met."

That cold reminder of their situation was a blessing. It helped quench Christos' increasing thirst for the boy, although it did nothing to decrease his appetite for his blood. More enticing than anything else was the lure of that which hummed through Mateo's veins and the quick throb of his pulse. Christos couldn't help licking his lips at the thought of sinking his fangs into the human's neck.

And that was what gave him the perfect solution. He wanted Mateo yet didn't want to exploit him. If it were about serving his own sexual needs, there was no way around that problem. Seeing that the boy himself was aroused and obviously interested in sex gave him a loophole. If this became exclusively about Mateo's pleasure, then there was no harm in it. Christos would be only giving and taking nothing in return. *Okay, point of order...* Making the boy come would be immensely satisfying, but that was collateral damage. It couldn't be helped. It only took a millisecond for him to be convinced of the rightness of his actions.

Pleased with his plan, he surprised Mateo by reaching out and clasping the boy's shaft with a firm grip. The gasp he elicited was most gratifying. "When was the last time someone gave *you* a blow job?"

Mateo's eyes widened before slinking down to half-mast. "Some guys get off —"

Christos quickly put his finger on Mateo's lips to shut him up. "I don't mean as a transactional act. When was the last time someone sucked your lovely dick simply for the pleasure it would bring you both?"

The human shook his head slowly, as if to say there hadn't ever been an occasion when sex had been a mutual and spontaneous act. The idea that Mateo might never have experienced a sexual encounter that hadn't been for survival broke his heart. He'd thought giving him a safe job and place to heal was the best he could do for him. Maybe he'd been wrong. Pleasure for pleasure's sake might be a far better gift.

"Allow me to make you feel good. Everything is for you tonight, Mateo. I want nothing in return. I won't accept anything in return. Do you understand?" When the boy nodded, Christos took his finger away and maneuvered to loosely straddle Mateo's body. "Don't hesitate to tell me what you want, what you like, what you don't like."

Mateo nodded again, then said, "I would like you to kiss me."

Christos hesitated. Damn, that was not a good idea. It was too intimate and personal. This was supposed to be almost a clinical act, medical with a big dose of compassion thrown in.

"No one ever really has," the boy added.

That was probably a lie, although also true in the sense that no man had likely kissed him because it made Mateo happy.

In the end, his internal war was short-lived with an inevitable outcome. He leaned over and, bracing himself with one hand, pressed his lips against the boy's. He'd intended to make it light and quick. But the moment he felt that soft, warm skin against his own, he was lost. A quick peck, or twenty, was out of the question. A hunger for something more overcame him. He slanted his mouth to slide it back and forth, deepening the pressure with each pass. Mateo remained pliant under the gentle assault. When Christos gave in to the inevitable lure of tasting some of him, the boy didn't hesitate to open on a soft sigh.

The treat was oh so delicious, almost as good as blood. He worked his tongue around every nook and cranny of Mateo's mouth. The boy almost shyly entwined his tongue with Christos', leading to a slow wrestle that somehow left them both panting when Christos finally pulled back. He didn't go far, however. His self-restraint didn't hold. He peppered Mateo's cheek and jaw with kisses before descending to his throat and resting at the base of it. With closed eyes, he pressed his nose and lips against the jugular and simply breathed in the tantalizing scent that lay right beneath the thin layer of skin.

Mateo shuddered and his cock jerked within Christos' grip. "W-what are you doing?"

"Something wicked, more perverse than you can imagine," he confessed. Getting a hold of himself, he pulled back to sit on his heels. If he didn't create distance between them, the temptation to do more would test the limits of his strength.

Mateo looked at him with blown pupils and a provocative grin. "It didn't feel like it."

"You have no idea."

Because the impulse to do it again, and more, was strong, he forced himself to concentrate on what he held. Mateo's dick was hot and hard but also satiny smooth and almost alive in its vibrancy. Beneath the shaft, the boy's small balls curled up tightly. Christos used his other hand to cup and roll them. He was rewarded with a long, low moan from Mateo. Pleased with the results, he did it again while jerking the boy's dick slowly. How fortunate they were to have landed on a planet with beings with such similar biology to their own. He knew what to do with this treasure, how to make this experience satisfying for Mateo.

When he pulled the tight skin to the tip and ran his thumb through the slit, Mateo arched into the touch and fisted the sheet beneath him. Naturally Christos repeated the motion, over and over. He quickly learned this particular human's body. There were always individual differences and preferences to take into account with a new lover — not that he'd taken many. It wasn't hard to do this time around. Mateo gave away everything with an unbridled joy that delighted Christos. How could it not? It seemed that this boy was wholly sensual, his body open to lots of different touches. A stroke here and a pinch there elicited amazing sounds and movements. The underlying message each time Mateo moaned or twisted was *more, more, more*.

Christos was happy to give him what he wanted, appreciating every reaction, enjoying watching as Mateo's arousal ratcheted higher. Each time, however, when it appeared that the boy was on the verge of coming, he felt a disappointment that it was ending so soon. If he could, he would keep at it all night. He repeatedly gripped the base of the shaft hard, to quell the orgasm. The first time he did it, Mateo pounded the bed and grunted in frustration, so Christos eased back.

"Don't you like that?"

"I love it."

The sincerity behind the declaration was obvious to him, so he edged the boy a few more times with his hand before deciding it was time to get to the part he'd promised right from the start. Scooting back, he leaned over and took only the cockhead in his mouth. The salty tang of pre-cum hit his tongue, and now it was his turn to moan. It had been a long time since he'd had the treat of tasting that which reminded him of blood—salty with a hint of bitter. It wasn't quite enough to quench his thirst but it would do. He continued to work the shaft and balls with his hand while feasting on just that bit of cock.

Mateo thrashed his head. "Take me all the way down. Please!"

Christos wanted to prolong the pleasure for them both, but the boy had been terribly sick and still was. It wouldn't do to set him back in his recovery and have to explain to Harry the how and the why of it. So, he did as the human demanded, letting go of his grip on the dick and swallowing it down to the root. He pressed his lips against the boy's pubic bone and, once again, he inhaled what he could of the fragrance beneath the skin. Then he squeezed his balls at the same time he worked the shaft with the muscles of his throat.

Seconds later, Mateo cried out and bucked into Christos' face. There was no chance that the boy could dislodge him, even if he truly wanted to. Using his head alone, Christos kept him in place, riding out the orgasm until Mateo collapsed boneless beneath him. He let go of his balls but took longer to release his dick, slowly pulling back until only the head remained. And before he let go of that, he scraped his teeth against it and was rewarded when Mateo shuddered once more. A tiny bit of cum hit Christos' lips. He licked it like a cat with cream.

He sat back on his heels, satisfied to a degree that surprised him. As new as this experience had been for the boy, so too it was for him. Sex had always been a relatively quick, mutual release that was as selfish as it had been generous. He couldn't think of an occasion when he'd been intent on only giving without any expectation, or even desire, for something in exchange.

"There. Think you can sleep well now?" he asked.

"Ugh," was the only reply he received.

Grinning, Christos swung his leg over and grabbed the remote as he settled against the headboard. He turned off the TV, plunging the room into darkness that was only relieved by a light from the hallway shining under the door.

"Hey," Mateo said in a sleepy voice, "I was watching that."

"Not anymore. It's late and you're still sick. Cover up and go to sleep."

"Do I have to?" He sounded like a child, reminding Christos that he practically was.

"Yes." He made his voice firm, pleased that he'd been able to cater to the boy without compromising his principles.

Mateo rolled onto his side. "What about you?" he asked without opening his eyes.

What about him, indeed. Christos' dick was crying for attention like a petulant child. It helped to think of his male member like that, something with a will of its own and acting immature. And like a parent or a pet owner, he had control over the situation. It would get exactly what he chose to give it, nothing more, no matter how much it begged or whined.

"I'm fine," he replied gruffly. "Remember... That was for you, not me. I'm not a mindless creature that needs indulgence."

"Are you sure about that?" Mateo reached over with unexpected speed and without opening his eyes. He grabbed Christos' dick right through his jeans and gripped it like a vise, which wasn't hard to do, given the thinness of the material and the thickness of his cock. Mateo worked the shaft with strong and nimble fingers before Christos had time to react. His dick had no such trouble, getting with the program without hesitation. It jerked and his balls tingled with urgent anticipation.

And just like that, he was coming with a roar and bent over as if in pain, which he kind of was. The intensity sucked the breath right out of him, leaving him shuddering and heaving as his lungs struggled to restart. His balls emptied with a speed that left them cramping. His cock didn't care that it was constrained and managed to fill and kick out another climax before the first one had finished. Saliva pooled in his mouth and his fangs started to descend, keen to join the party. It took strength he didn't know he possessed to pull them back in before he did something entirely unforgiveable.

As opposed to the mostly unforgivable thing of coming in the first place... *Goddamn it!* Disgusted with himself and infuriated by Mateo getting the best of him, he twisted out of the hold. But instead of doing the sensible thing and escaping the boy's reach, he rolled toward him and covered his body. For a few seconds, he lay flush against him before he pushed up and braced himself on both arms. He glared down at the wide-eyed human. His breath was coming out in pants.

He wanted to yell at the boy, berate him for his persistence in creating something between them when there was nothing there at all.

Instead, he swooped in to take that pretty mouth with its kewpie doll lips into a punishing kiss that morphed quickly into insatiable hunger. He plundered that mouth as he hadn't before, laying waste to every corner. He dominated in a wordless assertion of his commanding position, reminding the boy that he was in control. On some level, he knew his intent was to frighten the human. It didn't work. Far from shrinking back or trying to push him away, Mateo wrapped his arms around him and gave as good as he got. By the time they broke for air, their bodies were entirely entwined and they were both hard again.

"Having second thoughts about that 'no fucking' thing?" Mateo's eyes shone brightly in the dark with passion and mischief.

Christos answered with a growl before going in for another kiss. This time, he humped the boy, regardless of whether he was rubbing his exposed dick raw and uncaring that he was going to fill his pants with yet more cum. It took a little longer to come the second time — or was it the third? Like...twenty seconds instead of five. As they both bucked and gasped, he dared to press his mouth against the human's jugular again, this time licking the skin and picturing the sweet pleasure of sinking his fangs through the flesh and tugging at the vein. His cock jerked at the thought, releasing what had to be the last of his stored cum.

He rolled over, taking Mateo with him, resting the boy's head against his shoulder. The pounding of both their hearts reverberated in his head. "If you relapse tomorrow because of this, I'm going to be very cross."

Mateo sighed against his neck. "That's fair. We should probably shower and maybe change the bedding or something."

"Yes, that would be the wise thing to do."

Neither of them moved, however, and soon Mateo's breathing evened out and his heart rate settled to a normal rhythm. Christos lay there, listening to it, mesmerized by the sound, completely satiated. Guilt threatened his peace of mind, but he batted it away. There was no point in wallowing in the past. That was something he'd learned early on this planet. He could only move forward and do better. This night was an aberration, a testament to Mateo's strength and his own weakness.

He had to do better. He would, because becoming involved with this boy was a mistake on so many levels. It wasn't only that he refused to be one more man to exploit Mateo's vulnerability. He mustn't lose sight of the precarious situation he was in. Alex had called him to Boston for a reason and nothing had changed. As time wore on, the danger grew closer. He would be damned to hell if he was going to embroil Mateo in that shit. Being on the streets would be safer, if it came to that.

His resolve reaffirmed, he relaxed and allowed himself this one pleasure of spending the night with Mateo in his arms.

Chapter Seven

"So, you and Christos, huh?" Demi dropped the not-quite-a-question as they walked to the elevator.

Mateo scowled. "There is no Christos and me." And wasn't that the sad truth. Two nights ago he'd fallen asleep thinking that they were an item of some kind. Yet the next morning, the fucker had acted as if it had never happened, shoving him alone into the shower while he stripped the bedding and put fresh sheets and a comforter on. Any time Mateo had tried to hug or even touch the man, Christos had deftly avoided him. When he'd tried to talk about what they'd shared, he'd shut Mateo down with a gentle firmness that had made him want to scream.

Demi pushed the call button. "The state of your linens says otherwise."

"Thanks for the reminder of the night that never was." He followed Demi into the car when it arrived and folded his arms. "Christos acts like we didn't come all over each other. Well, I came on him. He never took his pants off."

Demi raised his eyebrows. "Men can be amazingly dumb sometimes."

"Tell me about it." The doors opened and the sound of the club music increased. He got out and looked around. All he saw was a hallway. He worried that he was underdressed for the place. All he had to wear was his own ratty jeans, long-sleeved T and grungy sneakers. Demi, as usual, was wearing effectively the same thing, except his clothing obviously came with a much heftier price tag. Mateo envied him his wardrobe. But the guy had assured him back in the bedroom that he was fine as he was, so he tried not to worry that he stood out as the poor friend.

"This way." Demi motioned for him to walk to the left. "Don't pay any attention to what Christos says. He's completely hung up on you. Why else would he sleep in your room every night?"

"He does?" That bit of news lightened his step. "I never hear him come in and he's not there when I wake."

"He's very good at being stealthy."

"He must be ninja-like." The idea that Christos watched over him when he was sleeping was both weird and exhilarating. No one who didn't care would bother to do that. On the other hand, what kind of freak crept into another person's room then sneaked out again so he wouldn't be seen? Christos had to know that he wanted him there. What was his problem?

"It doesn't matter anyway," he added with a sigh. "He seems to be very stubborn and totally convinced that he's taken advantage of me. Any time I try to talk to him, to convince him otherwise, he nopes the fuck out of my room."

"He'll come around."

They entered the main room, the one Mateo kept watching every night on television. The images didn't do it justice. Even in the middle of the day with practically no one around, there was a vibrancy to the place that lured him in. He stopped by the end of the big bar and took in the whole three-sixty view.

"This is amazing. I really hope I can work here." There was pathetic longing in his voice but he didn't care. Finally, there was something he could really become passionate about.

"Of course you can," Demi replied, leaning beside him. "I mean, you've got the job if you want it."

"Really? Don't I have to audition or something?"

Demi shook his head. "Christos wants you to have the job and that's good enough for Alex. See that blond boy over at the far-left stage? That's Quinn. His audition was fainting in Alex's arms. He got hired on the spot."

"Well, if passing out into a man's arms is all it takes, I guess I'm good to go." Mateo watched as Quinn gracefully twisted to hang upside down. "He's really good."

"Sure, now. You should have seen him at first." Demi chuckled. "He landed right on his ass a few times. That was before he landed in Alex's bed. He's been there ever since. Alex doesn't like him dancing, too, but he knows better than to try to stop Quinn. That boy is sweet and biddable...until he's not."

"At least it explains why he didn't have to be a good dancer. I can't see my keeping this job if I'm not."

"The club members don't care very much. They like to ogle pretty boys. You've got that down already, right, with those Bambi eyes of yours. And some of them like to tie them up and beat them in the playrooms. Dancing skills aren't high on the list of qualities they're looking for."

Mateo swallowed hard. "Is that always part of the job, the stuff in the rooms?"

"Oh, no. Some of the club members have their own subs — submissives — that they bring with them. Only a few of the go-go boys are into that kind of shit. Honestly, whatever you do outside of the dance floor with the members — or not — is totally up to you. As long as everything is consensual, Alex is cool with it."

"What kind of cut does he take for, you know, the extra stuff?"

"None."

"Seriously? What pimp doesn't take money off the top?"

Demi smacked him lightly on the arm. "Alex isn't like that. He's just an employer who pays well with a great benefits package. The stuff guys earn on the side is their business, not his."

"Right, sorry." Mateo didn't want to argue the point, even as he found it hard to believe. Likely Demi didn't know the ins and outs of the club because he was a family member — and a young one at that. He probably was kept out of the loop on a lot of things. He'd have to ask some of the other boys for the real information.

Or maybe he could ask another certain person, if he could convince the man to stay with him long enough to have a conversation. "I guess Christos must be a part owner or something." That had to be it, otherwise his influence in getting him a job didn't make sense.

Demi shook his head. "Alex, Val, Emil and my dad Harry own it, I think. Or maybe only Alex. No one tells me much around here." He shrugged. "Not that it matters. It's our home, no matter what — or, it used to be. Now we live in the next-door building. This place was getting too small."

"And Christos lives there too?"

"Not really. He, ah, is really just having an extended visit. A lot of the family has come to stay awhile."

"For how long?" He'd assumed that Christos had relocated from somewhere to Boston. It hadn't occurred to him that he'd be leaving at some point.

Demi merely shrugged, looking uncomfortable. "Hey, Quinn's finished his set." He waved at the guy to come over.

Mateo wasn't done with his questions, however. "Where does he usually live? Christos, I mean." As if that weren't obvious.

"Uh, Greece, I think."

That explained his accent—and the fact that he spoke Greek. "Like Athens?" He'd read about that place from long ago. It was probably still a bustling city.

"No, more like the mountains, maybe."

"Oh." That didn't sound quite as fun, although it wasn't as if it mattered. The man was determined to brush him off. What difference did it make where he lived? When he left Boston, he wasn't going to take Mateo with him.

Quinn came to join them, his face flushed from dancing and gripping a bunch of bills in one fist. "Hey."

"Quinn, this is Mateo."

"I figured. How are you feeling?"

"I'm okay." His cough had subsided significantly and his fever had been gone for over a day. It didn't feel like someone was sitting on his chest anymore, either. "I was going stir-crazy in my room and Demi volunteered to show me where I'd be working—if I get the job," he added, because he couldn't quite believe in his good fortune.

Quinn laughed. "Of course you have it. It's up to Harry to give you the green light, which I'm guessing won't be for another week. This is hard. You have to be completely well."

Mateo twisted his fingers together. "I don't know why your man would agree to spend his money on me when he already has lots of go-go dancers."

Quinn shrugged and started counting his money. "Alex is filthy rich and doesn't care how much he spends on employees. This club is an amusement to him more than anything else."

"If he's so rich, how come you're dancing for a living?" Nothing about this made sense to him.

The boy paused and looked pointedly at him. "He's rich. I'm not. I am also not a charity case and I need to make my own living."

Demi grunted. "You could always accept his marriage proposal."

"I'm thinking about it. It doesn't mean I'd stop working. Do you plan on staying home like June Cleaver when you marry Trey?"

"Point taken. I'm engaged to be engaged," Demi said, holding up his left hand to show off his simple ring.

"Nice, but I get what you're both saying. If you have your own money, you can't be trapped." He looked closely at what Quinn had counted. "Wow, that's over a hundred bucks! And there's, like, nobody here on a weekday afternoon. How much do you rake in on a Saturday night?"

"Over a thousand—and that's me not doing anything *extra*, not even lap dances, because Alex's head would explode. And I don't want anyone but him touching me anyway."

Mateo was practically salivating at the prospect. A job here would mean real security for the first time since he'd been kicked out of his family home. "Oh man, I really want this."

"Want what?" Another boy loomed behind Demi all of a sudden—another family member, by the looks of him, but younger and with an accent that was different from Christos' and Harry's. This family really got around, apparently.

"Hey, Merlin," Demi said before sharing a quick look with Quinn.

"I want to be hired as a go-go boy," Mateo explained.

"Oh, that," the boy scoffed. "Isn't Christos pushing for you to be one? It's yours, then."

"Merlin," Demi interjected, "you're not supposed to be here. He's too young," he added to Mateo.

The kid made a face. "Like I'm going to be traumatized by the sight of naked boys and drooling old men. Annika sent me over to fetch Mateo, actually."

"What do you mean?" Demi demanded with an edge to his voice that Mateo had never heard before.

"I don't think I can say it any clearer than that." He huffed when Demi glared at him. "She wants him to come hang in the living room. There… Is that better?"

"That's the family's private space. We don't let employees go there. No offense, Mateo."

"Alex won't like that," Quinn interjected.

"Then he can go tell her," Merlin retorted. "Let me know if he does, because I'll want to pop some corn to watch that little show."

Quinn frowned. "Don't be such a little fucker, Merlin."

"I'm only the messenger, doing what he's told. I don't see the big deal anyway. Mackie is taking a nap in his room. It's just Annika, Idris and I watching *Sesame Street*, which frankly makes me want to jab a screwdriver in each ear. Now, doesn't that sound like fun?" he asked Mateo.

He looked from Merlin, to Demi, to Quinn and back again. There were some heavy-duty undercurrents that made no sense to him. All he could think of was to ask, "Who's Annika?"

The tension among the three boys ratcheted to the proverbial eleven. No one answered him at first. Finally, Merlin said, "A cousin. She's cool. You'll like her, just don't try anything with her." He had a menacing look and an almost-growl to his tone.

Mateo leaned away. "No worries, dude. I'm not into girls."

Merlin's expression turned friendly in an instant. "Great. We'll get along fine. If you two are finished with trying to kill me with your eyes, I'll take him over."

Some silent communication occurred between the two other boys before Demi said, "Fine. Take him through the garage. It's cold outside and he's still sick."

"Thanks. I would never have thought of that myself. Come on," Merlin jerked his head in the direction of the elevator.

"Sure, see ya." He waved at Demi and Quinn before following the kid. He was intrigued to see where the family lived and it beat going back to his room. "Are you sure it's okay for me to be near this Annika and

Idris? If they're watching Sesame Street, they must be pretty little. I don't want to get them sick."

"Don't worry. You won't. And only Idris is small, anyway. Annika is more my age."

"Oh." None of this made sense to him, but he was too excited about the prospect of maybe seeing Christos that he didn't make a fuss about it.

They went down and came out in a basement area filled with cars. No, not only cars. There were trucks and SUVs and two really awesome monster motorcycles. They were all so shiny. He wanted to reach out and touch the ones they passed, but he didn't dare. "Do you get to drive any of these?"

"Please... They barely let me out of the house."

"Your parents are strict, huh? Mine were too."

"It's the family, really. Alex and Val, in particular, make the rules. My father goes along to get along."

"What about your mom?"

"Don't have one. I never have."

"You have two dads?" He'd seen that sort of thing on TV, yet hadn't met anyone before now who'd been raised that way.

Merlin shrugged. "Yup. Had, actually... Past tense because one is dead."

"It must have been really hard losing one of them."

Another shrug. "Not really. He was an asshole. I don't miss the back of his hand, I can tell you."

Mateo's eyes swam with sudden memories. It wasn't only straight, homophobic parents who could be abusive, apparently. "With me, it was the belt a lot."

"I got that, too."

"But not with the dad you have left?"

"No." Merlin paused, his hand on the knob of a door on the other side of the garage. "He never hits.

Sometimes he looks at me like he's really sad and disappointed. It's stupid and it shouldn't bother me. It does kind of, though. Weird, huh?"

"I know what you mean. I used to get that from my mom. I wanted to please her, except I couldn't because she wanted me to be something I'm not."

"Yeah, I get that. Everyone wants me to change. I sort of want to and also resent it at the same time." He shrugged. "It doesn't matter. Annika's waiting. She's awesome. You're going to love her."

Mateo followed the boy into a land of wonder. It was like the club, bright and shiny. Unlike the club, it was also homey. The big, open room held vast amounts of furniture and the kind of games one would find in an arcade. In the middle, there was a huge sectional sofa with what must be an eighty-inch flat-screen suspended from the ceiling in front of it. A beautiful girl with white-blonde hair reclined in the elbow, a dark-haired, chubn'tby toddler sitting next to her and a fluffy white dog curled up in her lap.

She sat forward when she spotted them. "Merlin, you succeeded! Hello! You must be Mateo. Come and join us." She beckoned him and he felt drawn to her in some unnamable way.

"Hi, you're Annika, I assume."

"I am indeed. And this is Babette." She was like a China doll, with flawless pale skin and the brightest blue eyes he'd ever seen. Her dress was a frothy pale pink confection that came down nearly to her ankles. "Merlin, take Idris. I want Mateo to sit next to me."

The boy did as she'd asked—demanded really—plucking the little kid from his place and setting him on his hip. It was strange to see such a snarky guy play nanny. Maybe the toddler was his kid brother. Mateo sat gingerly near where the toddler had been, although not as close to the girl. That didn't seem right, given that they were strangers. She turned on her side to stare at him anyway, dislodging the dog, who wandered over on its tiny paws to sniff at him.

"How are you feeling?" she asked him.

"Um, better, thanks." He petted Babette, enjoying the animal's soft, springy fur. It looked at him with wet, brown eyes.

"That's good. It's important for you to regain your strength."

"I suppose."

"Dr. Harry and Demi are taking good care of you?"

He eyed her, wondering why a girl like her would be so concerned about his well-being. "They've been great, yeah."

They were quiet for a few seconds, then she said, "Mr. Christos is being very foolish, don't you think, in avoiding you?"

He blinked at her a few times, trying to figure out how she knew about that. Who would discuss such a thing with her? Then he decided it didn't matter. This was one weird family, but they'd been very kind to him and were offering him a brighter future than he'd had mere days ago. He rolled with the topic while trying to keep it as PG as possible.

"Yes, I do. I like him a lot, actually. I wish he'd trust me on that point."

Annika shook her head, and her elaborately braided hair swung with the movement. Someone must have spent hours getting that 'do' in place. "He'll come around eventually. You are meant for each other."

He raised his eyebrows. "I'm not sure I'd say that, exactly. I don't think we're, like, fated to be together or anything."

The girl's expression turned serious. "Oh yes, you are." She put her hand on his shoulder and the touch was oddly calming. "He will be there for you when you most need him."

"O-kay." He turned his head to look at Merlin, seeking a break from all that intensity. The dog shuffled back to its mistress, managing in the way of all dogs to press its little paws right where it hurt a guy most. He hid his grimace.

Merlin's attention was on the baby he held, anyway. He stared intently at him. "Who's your friend, Idris?"

A finger poked him nearly in the eye. "You!"

Well, that answered the question of whether they were siblings. It still seemed odd that Merlin would be the least interested in such a young child.

"It's very important that they bond," Annika whispered into his ear.

Before he could think of a response to that bizarre statement, two men came over from somewhere behind them. They looked like more family members, with their dark hair and pale skin, although the shades were a tad lighter and darker in both cases than Christos and the other men. Annika's different coloring stood way out. He wondered if there were more like her or if they were all like Christos. Was it a gender thing? He didn't think that was how genetics worked, but his home schooling had been hit or miss, especially when it came to science. There was a lot about the world that he didn't understand.

The taller of the two gave him an assessing look. "I'm Dafydd. You must be Mateo."

"That's right. I hope it's okay that I'm here."

Dafydd glanced at Annika. "I suppose, as it's not my call anyway." He turned his attention to the boys. "It's time for Idris' nap." He held out his hands.

The toddler clutched at Merlin. "No!"

"Don't be chopsy now, Idris. You can come play with Merlin and Annika when you wake."

"Be good," Merlin whispered into the kid's ear before tickling him briefly. He handed him over to Dafydd, who had to be the father.

"Thanks, like. I swear he listens to you more than me these days," Dafydd said, hefting his son on his hip.

"Idris and I understand each other. That's all."

"I dare say you do," came the cryptic reply. At least Mateo didn't get it.

When Dafydd left with Idris, the other man shuffled over to take his place. He kept his gaze cast downward and fiddled with his stubby ponytail. "Would anyone like some cookies? I just took a batch out of the oven."

Annika clapped her hands and bounced on her bottom. "Oh, snickerdoodles?"

The man smiled. "Yes."

"Then please do bring a plateful. And milk, as well…and treats for Babette?"

"Of course."

Before the man left, however, Annika looked around Mateo to Merlin. "Make the introductions, if you please."

The guy didn't seem to appreciate that command. Nevertheless, he nodded toward the man in front of him. "This is my father Alun."

This timid creature had raised the brash teenager? It made sense, he supposed. The dead father had been the ball-buster. He'd probably beaten his husband, too.

That was true of a lot of abusive men, although not of his own father. Perhaps because nothing had made the man angrier that having a sodomite for a son. Compared to that, his mother couldn't have done anything wrong that would have been as bad.

He gave the man a bright smile. "Hi, nice to meet you. Thank you for welcoming me into your home."

Alun looked surprised at that, but eventually said, "We are happy to have you." He never really stopped looking at the floor. *Poor man.*

Something clicked. "Hey, you're the guy Damien said that Sergeant Jefferson met at *Our Safe Place*." He wouldn't have thought this was the cop's type, except the man was lovely to look at like the rest of the people he'd met so far in the family. *Pretty* and available was every man's dream, after all. Alun was a hot widower — with money, probably. Except Jefferson didn't strike him as being greedy.

"Who's that?" Merlin demanded, a scowl on his face. It was a good thing this wasn't the father who hit.

Alun surprised Mateo by standing straighter and staring his insolent son down. "Someone I met, that's all. I'll go get those cookies, milk and dog biscuits," he added to Annika before leaving on quiet feet.

Mateo sat awkwardly between Merlin and Annika, the former still scowling with his arms folded and the latter fussing with the TV controls. "So, Merlin," he said into the silence, "I guess your fathers were really into the King Arthur legend, huh?"

The boy's expression didn't change. "No, we're just Welsh." As if that were answer enough. And apparently that was all Mateo was going to get.

He tried the girl instead. "So, what are we going to watch?"

She smiled brightly at him. "Have you seen the movies *Frozen* and *Frozen II*?"

"I snuck into a theater to see the first one when I was a kid, but I haven't seen the sequel yet." Movies were way too expensive to spend his hard-earned money on.

"Then we shall see both. I must warn you that sometimes I like to sing along."

"That's okay. I do too."

"Excellent."

Merlin muttered something like, "Shoot me now."

Mateo didn't care. It was fun to be with others, and if he stayed long enough, he might run into Christos. Then the man could see how well Mateo fit into his family and... No, wait. That was silly. He was thinking along the lines of forever when it was about having a good time, earning some coin.

He wasn't falling in love with the guy and Annika had been wrong. They weren't fated to be together. They weren't.

* * * *

"Christos, are you listening?"

Val snickered. "No, Alex, he's mooning over his boy."

From his perch in the corner of the couch, Christos glared at his shipmate. "He is not my boy."

"Really? Because you absolutely reek of the kid every day, so..." Val shrugged. "My mistake."

Christos turned to Willem. "Will, do you mind if I take your place in your weekly sparring sessions with Val?"

"Yeah, no, I'm not getting into the middle of this nonsense. And do us all a favor, Christos, and fuck the human already."

Christos rose. "Fine, I'll take you both. I could use someone to pound on. All this waiting around shit is driving me crazy."

Alex smacked his hand on his desktop. "Enough! Sit, Christos. And shut up, Val. Baiting him isn't helping any."

Christos sat again. "I'm sorry, Alex. I did miss what you said. Would you mind repeating it?"

"I was relaying our most recent conversation with Petru. He has given us fifteen potential locations where Dracul could be holing up. Of those, Val's satellite searches have eliminated ten as clearly lacking in activity."

"I don't understand, sir. I thought we were going to leave it to Dracul to come for us?"

"That plan never sat well with me, even though it seemed like our only choice at the time. This waiting game is dragging out too long. We're losing our edge and fretting over the safety of our families. And it can't be good for them to see us like this and to be constantly in training for a battle that may never come."

"And why wouldn't it?"

Val answered. "Petru has done the math and insists that Dracul is out of all but three men. And knowing them as he does, he doubts they'll be inclined to rally to the cause, not now that they've seen he's vulnerable. It's far safer and more appealing to live out their lives in anonymous comfort with the riches they've amassed."

"Not that we can count on the fucker being honest about that," Malcolm pointed out.

"That goes without saying, of course," Alex agreed. "Although his devotion to Annika does seem to be genuine."

"It had better be," Will interjected. "I won't hesitate to tear him apart if he so much as gives her the wrong look."

"Yes, Willem," Alex soothed. "We all know your fatherly ferociousness is not to be trifled with. But I did promise him safe passage so long as he plays square with us. I have to believe that, if nothing else, he has a strong sense of self-preservation.

"Which leads us back to whether to play defense or offense. Dracul's message to us may have been all bluster. He's outnumbered unless he uses humans."

"He's done that before," Emil reminded them all, before pushing a plate of brownies in Christos' direction. "Eat something. You've been working all day at *Our Safe Place*, yet Logan tells me you don't touch the food."

"It's for those kids." He took one of the gooey squares anyway because he was hungry. And maybe he'd take another one when the meeting ended and take it to Mateo. *Oh geez*, it had been maybe five minutes since he'd thought of the boy. It was why he'd missed what Alex had said. Damn Val for being right anyway. And it was happening again. He forced his attention back to Alex.

"Even if we locate him, I wouldn't dare mount a raid and leave our home and families underdefended."

"The hybrids and the changelings will never be able to fight on their own." The thought of it, of Mateo being caught up in some invasion mounted even by mere humans, made his blood run cold.

"I'm going to use drones," Val said, "to scope out the last five places. There's some activity in each of them, although it's hard to say what kind. It's possible that humans have discovered his lairs and taken them over. Petru says that he has large stockpiles of weapons, food, Krugerrands and other precious metals and jewels in each place. They're well-hidden, but even the ancient pyramids get discovered every once in a while. It's not impossible that humans stumbled upon some of them and stripped whatever was there, leaving it useless for Dracul."

"We're looking to outfit some larger drones with weapons, as well," Will added. "If we can find him, we may be able to do significant damage from a remote location without using all our manpower."

Tony waved his hand. "I've been experimenting for years on building a bunker buster that's a quarter of the size and weight of the kind humans use."

Christos grinned. "And here I thought you were raising reindeer or something."

"That too, although they mostly raise themselves and the winters are really long in Lapland. I had to find something to do with my time—or risk driving Mikko crazy."

"I told you to come to Tanzania," Claude chastised. "Nen would love having Mikko for company. And there's no snow there."

"Only bugs the size of elephants." Tony shuddered. "And, also, elephants."

Claude swatted him on the back of the head. "Who the hell doesn't like elephants?" He grinned at his shipmate. They had always been among the most congenial of them all. Christos was glad they'd found their happiness on this Earth and hated how they'd had to leave that for this shitshow of Dracul's making.

"Gentlemen, we are getting off topic," Alex rebuked mildly. "We need to remain vigilant while working this parallel plan of bearding the lion in his den. Christos, I'm giving you the lead on security here at the club. Val is too busy. Claude, you will be his right-hand man."

"Yes, sir."

"I know it may seem a mundane task, but we can't afford trouble with the human police and I won't give Dracul the satisfaction of forcing me to shut down the one place where many of us have found a measure of peace and joy."

"We're with you on that, sir," Malcolm spoke for all of them. "This is a fine place and lots of people depend on it for their livelihood."

"Yes," Christos echoed as he stood. "I don't take offense at the request, nor do I resent helping those homeless kids with Will and Emil. Being good citizens of this planet has always mattered to those of us in this room. If not, we would have thrown our lot in with Dracul ages ago."

Alex nodded once. "I appreciate the sentiment and what all of you have done. I swear to you that this is the end. We will stop this rogue drone once and for all. Then Annika can lead us to a brighter future." He smiled at Will as he said this last bit, reminding their shipmate that his ability to produce a Queen was welcome news. "Thank you, gentlemen."

It was a dismissal and they all knew it. They filed out of the office and scattered to their various tasks, except Claude, who stuck by him.

As did Val. "Do you guys need any help with the security? I ask because I promised Annika I'd give her lessons on coding. She's into computers and Will doesn't have the skills to train her."

Christos answered for both of them. "We're good. It's not that hard, because you've got everyone under tight control already. Although I would like to check in on Mateo before I head to the main floor. Don't say it," he added, putting his hand up in Val's face.

"You won't find him in his room." Quinn walked over on his way to Alex's office. "Merlin came to get him, at Annika's request. I would have said something to Alex earlier, but I don't like being a snitch and I really don't want Alex to go toe-to-toe with the Queen." He said the last word in a whisper, likely in case any human lurked nearby.

Christos didn't care who heard him. "That's crazy! Why in the fucking world would she do that?"

Quinn shrugged. "Don't look at me. I'm the reluctant messenger. I wouldn't have said anything, except I didn't want you to waste your time looking in the wrong place. Last I saw, which was like five minutes ago, he was on the couch with Annika and Merlin watching *Frozen II*. Just when we all thought we'd gotten her off that kick, they had to release a sequel." With that and a roll of his eyes, he continued on his way.

Christos smacked his forehead. "For the love of God, what am I supposed to do?"

Clapping him on the shoulder, Val sang, "Let it go!"

Christos glared at him. "If we didn't need you so badly, I'd rip your throat out."

"I'd like to see you try. Come on. Let's go get your boy."

"He's not my boy."

Val walked away. "Sure, Christos. Where have I heard that before? Oh yeah, Alex about Quinn, Emil and Jase, Will and Damien for sure...nd me. I used to say that about Mackie." He paused and looked over his shoulder. "And how did all that turn out?" He laughed his way down the hall.

Chapter Eight

Christos found Mateo right where Quinn had said, sprawled on the couch next to Annika. The other hybrids, except for Demi, were ranged beside him. They were focused on the big-screen TV, although, from the sounds of it, the movie had ended.

Perfect timing.

He passed Val in his haste to reach Mateo and had the satisfaction of the boy's eyes widening at his approach. Likely it was due to the harsh expression he knew he wore. But the reaction didn't last long. As he took the final few steps, Mateo's demeanor shift to something more coquettish, as if he were glad to be found where he was. *The brat.*

"Hello, Christos." He batted his eyelashes. "Have you come to watch movies with us? We were thinking of changing to *Star Wars*. I bet that's something you'd like, all that manly lightsaber battling and dog-fights in space."

Christos planted himself right by the boy's feet. "That just goes so show how little you know me. I'd rather watch a documentary on wine-making."

Mateo pouted. "I'd know better what you like if you deigned to speak with me once in a while instead of lurking in my room like a perv while I'm sleeping."

Christos waged a short war within himself before acting on his impulse. Reaching down, he grabbed Mateo and tossed him over his shoulder. "Speaking of that, you could do with a nap," he said over the boy's screech of outrage.

Mateo pounded on his back. "Let me go, you psycho. Isn't anyone going to help me?" he added when Christos walked away from the couch.

"Sorry, kid," Val said. "You're not in my purview."

"Goodbye, Mateo," Annika called out. "Come back to see me tomorrow."

"Thank you for the lovely day," Mateo shouted back at the same time as kicking Christos dangerously close to his balls.

He swatted the boy's rump. "Stop that."

"I will not. Let me go. You have no right to manhandle me like this."

"The hell I don't. I'm responsible for your conduct while you're living in Alex's club. I promised him I'd make sure you behaved."

"But I was! I didn't do anything wrong. Annika invited me. Can't she do that?"

It was a fair question and one that didn't lend itself to an easy answer. Annika did have a lot of power. It didn't mean that she always made the best decisions. She was still young, after all, Queen or not. What if Mackie had come into the living room? How was that going to be explained? Or one of the hybrids—Merlin came to mind — might do something inhuman and give the game away. Having Mateo stay in the club had been one of Alex's explicit requirements.

"Not really," he answered, because in a human world that was always the case. "Alex makes the rules...mostly."

"Well, that seemed to be an open question when Merlin came to invite me. If it's a problem, you should take it up with them, not me. I didn't do anything wrong. And being carried like this is making me dizzy and kind of pukey."

"Oh." Feeling guilty, Christos stopped on a dime while they were still in the garage. He gently set Mateo on his feet, although he kept a good grip on him. "Better?"

Mateo took in a deep breath and let it out slowly. "Yes." He glared at him. "For someone who insists there's nothing between us, you sure act awfully possessive."

He could hardly argue the point, so he fell back on duty. "You are my responsibility," he repeated, "until you're well."

"I'm fine now. I don't need to stay in bed and... I guess I should plan on leaving and finding somewhere else to live. Do you think Alex would give me an advance on my pay? Assuming I have a job at the club."

Because he couldn't stand the vulnerable look on the boy's face or the idea that he'd go back to the streets, he gentled his grip and cupped Mateo's jaw. "Of course you have a job, and Alex will advance as much of your salary as you need. I will guarantee it. Plus, there is no reason for you to leave yet. You should wait until at least you've run the course of antibiotics."

Mateo shook his head. "That doesn't seem right. It's too much of an imposition on your family." He gnawed at his lower lip, drawing Christos' gaze to that delicious spot. "Now, if we were sleeping together, that would be different. Then I'd be in *your* bed."

Christos hardened his heart and his voice, because picturing Mateo in his own quarters was far too tempting. "Don't start on that again. Come on. Let's get you dinner," he added, taking hold of the boy's hand. He practically dragged him onward.

"Are any of these badass vehicles yours?"

"No, although I can use them. I have a plane that I flew over and keep at a private airstrip nearby." He could have kicked himself for adding that information. What difference did it make to tell Mateo, though?

"Really? You're a pilot? That's awesome!" And that was why he'd said it, to hear approval in the boy's voice.

"Willem might dispute my calling myself a pilot, but I am licensed to fly various craft."

"You come from Greece, right?"

"Yes." He thought of his beautiful mountain home with its ancient vineyards and herd of goats that were being tended by others in his absence. God, how he missed it all. And he could picture Mateo there, his golden sun and dark hair against the backdrop of the cliffs and the Mediterranean below. The mere thought of it made his stomach flutter with an unusual sensation.

"I suppose you're going back there soon." There was a vulnerability in the tone of the question.

He paused before entering the club area and looked at the boy. "Not for a while yet." Not that his plans to stay or go should make any difference. Yet Mateo smiled at the answer. "We'll go see what Emil has available in the kitchen. There's no need for you to eat in bed if you're well enough to watch movies all afternoon."

"That works for me. I don't want to put anyone out by waiting on me, and I am feeling pretty good."

"That settles it, then." There wasn't really a reason to keep holding the human's hand, but he continued to do it anyway. Mateo didn't seem to mind and it was pleasant in a purely non-sexual way. He allowed them both that bit of comfort.

The kitchen was bustling with activity and filled with people, most of whom were human. It was a relief, actually. He didn't have to endure the temptation of being alone with Mateo, and the others were a constant reminder that his true nature was unknown to the boy. The thought of how Mateo would react if he knew what Christos was, the expectation that it would lead him to fear and hate Christos, also helped as a reminder to keep his distance. That would have been true, even if the human had not suffered at the hands of Dracul's whelp. That experience, however, was guaranteed to make him run in fear if he ever saw Christos in his natural state.

There is no future for us.

With that thought firmly entrenched, he maneuvered Mateo to the dining table that sat in one corner. He knew that Val and the others often ate there during their work shifts, so he was confident that they wouldn't be in any of the staff's way. "Have a seat. I'll go scrounge up some dinner for us both."

Before he could make good on his promise, Damien hurried over. "Hey, look who's returned to the land of the living. How are you feeling, Mateo?"

"Much better, thanks. Christos said it would be okay if we ate dinner here. I'm tired of being stuck in my room and there's no need for you to put yourself out by bringing me a tray."

Damien waved away that comment. "It's no trouble, but I'm glad you don't need that kind of care anymore. So, what'll be?" he asked, looking at them both. "I have stuffed pork chops with scalloped potatoes and homemade apple sauce. If that doesn't appeal, I can grill you a couple of steaks."

Christos answered for them both. "No need to go to extra trouble on our account. The chops sound delicious. If you lead me to them, I'll fix our plates."

"No, sir," came the cheerful reply. "Emil would skin me if I made a guest serve themselves."

"We're hardly that."

"In this kitchen, you're either staff or a guest. Unless you want to don some whites and get cooking, you're in the latter category. Sit. I won't be a moment."

Having been left with no choice, Christos eyed the chair next to Mateo and decided his resolve didn't need more testing. Going around to the other side, he sat opposite him with his arms folded on the table. "I trust the menu is acceptable to you."

Mateo propped his chin on his upturned palm. "Sure. If it's not fast food or something out of a dumpster, I'm totally down with anything."

That casual reminder of the life the human had been leading sent anger boiling through him. "You will never have to worry about that again."

"You seem pretty sure about that for a guy who isn't my boyfriend."

"Do I have to be that to care?"

"No, but I've learned to count on nothing that I can't assure myself." He raised his head and put his hand over Christos'. "Look... I know you mean well and I really appreciate your finding work for me in the club. But please don't make promises you can't keep."

Against his better judgment, Christos didn't end the contact. Instead, he flipped his hand to clasp Mateo's. "Who says I can't?"

"It's the way the world works. You'll head back to Greece sometime soon, and if you don't already have a guy in your life—"

"I don't," he interjected, once more missing an opportunity to cut off any notion that he and this boy had a future together.

"I don't understand how that's remotely possible." Mateo sighed and peered at where their fingers interlaced. "Anyway, it will happen at some point and you won't remember me."

"Impossible." He squeezed the boy's hand. "Nothing could cause me to forget you, not time or space or anything else."

Mateo rolled his eyes. "Space, huh? Are you planning on volunteering for the manned mission to Mars or something?"

"Why would I want to go to that desolate place? There are much better planets to explore and colonize." He could have kicked himself for giving an answer that no human would have. This was why nothing could become of his relationship with this boy. He'd never mastered the kind of filter necessary to exist incognito. He was much better off living alone on his mountain.

"Are you some kind of amateur astronomer or something?"

"No, that's more Malcolm's thing."

"I don't know who that is."

"I keep forgetting that you haven't met the entire family. It doesn't matter. My point is that I won't forget you, Mateo." Seeing Damien approaching, he reluctantly broke contact. There was no point in fueling the gossip mill any more than necessary. He ignored the look of disappointment on Mateo's face.

"Here you go, guys." Damien placed two large plates of food in front of them. "I figured if this is too much for you, Mateo, Christos will finish it. These Stelalux men eat a whale's worth of food every day. Can I get you something to drink?"

"Thank you, and I'll have water," Christos said. When Mateo nodded at that, Damien took off again.

"What kind of name is Stelalux?" the boy asked after his first mouthful.

"The family is originally from Romania. I guess it's from maybe Roman soldiers at some point." That was a lie, of course. He remembered well the moment Alex had made it up for them to seem more human. Then each of them had picked a first name for themselves to, again, blend in better with the human population. It had meant nothing to them at the time, yet was ingrained as part of their identity now.

"Mm-m. Thanks," Mateo said when Damien brought them glasses and a pitcher of ice water. "Isn't that where Transylvania is located?"

"Yes." Christos filled the glasses.

"That makes you a vampire, huh?"

He bobbled and spilled some of his water before recovering. "Um, no. That's all nonsense. We, ah, don't like it, actually."

"You all have the look down pat, though, don't you? The dark hair, the pale skin… You seem really strong and fast. I mean, I swear you were too far away to catch me when I fainted." He forked some more food and popped it into his mouth. "You're even kind of cool to the touch. And the way you practically inhaled my jugular that one night we got our freak on…"

Mateo's fork clattered onto the table. He stared at him wide-eyed. "You're not a vampire, are you?" Christos froze mid-bite as he struggled for a suitably strong denial. His hesitation itself was a mistake. Mateo leaned over the table. "Are you?"

Swallowing hard, he shook his head. "Don't be ridiculous," he choked out. "There's no such thing. It's…it's a racist stereotype. A micro-aggression." There, that ought to end this nonsense. Mateo struck him as a woke kind of kid.

The boy settled back into his chair and picked up his fork. "Sorry. I know it's silly. It would explain a lot," he added under his breath before fixing a bright smile on his face. "This is delicious, don't you think?"

"Indeed."

The rest of the meal was blissfully either silent or filled with small talk. They were both hungry enough to plow through their meals relatively quickly. Damien had been right, as well, that Christos had to finish Mateo's serving, although there wasn't that much left on the plate. It made him happy to see the boy eating heartily. He was too skinny.

Dessert was brownies, reminding him that he'd intended to take some from the meeting to give to Mateo. He was glad there were more left, especially when the human's eyes lit up with obvious joy. They ate as they returned to the bedroom. Mateo wanted to go hang out in the club's main area. Christos nixed that idea. It was too soon in the boy's recovery, plus he wasn't ready to see the members circling him like fresh bait. Fortunately, Mateo didn't argue the point. His loud yawn helped cement the plan anyway.

When they entered the room, they found a dose of medicine waiting on the nightstand. Mateo didn't need to be prompted to take it. As he did, Christos eyed a mound of colorful material lying on the bed.

"What's this?" He poked at it with one finger. There were scraps of cloth with waistbands and leg holes and… "Fuck me."

"Is that an invitation, finally? Ooh!" Mateo jumped on the bed and started pawing through the heap. "Demi said he'd drop off some excess thongs the boys keep in their dressing room." He held up a scrap of midnight blue shiny material. "I love this."

Christos sputtered. "That wouldn't cover one of Annika's dolls!"

Mateo blinked back at him. "It's the perfect size for me. As you well know, my dick isn't all that big and my waist is tiny—as is my butt, thank you very much."

"There's nothing there to cover that part of you, so it hardly matters how big it is. And your cock is the perfect size."

Mateo turned coy. "You think?"

"Stop fishing for compliments. You know how beautiful every inch of you is."

The teasing look fled. "Actually, I don't. All anyone has ever been interested in is my two holes, which are both basically one size fits all." He shrugged and picked up a red thong. "It will be nice to be admired for something more, even if it is still surface deep."

"Jesus, Mateo, you have a way of flaying me wide open."

The boy snatched the rest of the clothing and went to shove it into a dresser drawer. "I honestly don't mean to. I'm not looking for a pity fuck. If you don't want me, you don't want me." He shrugged. "I hope the club members feel differently. I know I can make a lot simply by dancing, but I bet the real money is in the lap dances and the playrooms. Demi said Alex doesn't take a cut, which is great. I can earn enough to — Hey!"

Christos felt as if he were having an out-of-body experience. He could see himself leaping over the bed and grabbing Mateo by the arms. He knew that it was a mistake, that it betrayed what he was feeling for the boy. He knew, too, that his super-human speed would only add to the crazy idea that he was a vampire. There was no power on Earth that was going to stop him, however. Certainly he'd lost all self-control.

He pulled Mateo to his tiptoes and eyed him nose-to-nose. "I won't have other men's hands on you. There will be no lap dances or blow jobs, no tying you up and fucking you. None of that, do you hear?" He shook him a little in emphasis.

Mateo didn't flinch. His expression turned mulish. "You don't get to say that, to demand that or control what I do or don't do. You're not Alex and I'm not Quinn, because you have insisted that there is nothing between us, even after you made me come harder than I ever had before and kissed me like you meant it."

The boy's breath hitched and a frightening sheen filmed his eyes. "You treated me like a stranger after what we shared. You treated me like a *whore!*"

Aghast at the accusation, Christos pulled back, although he didn't let go. "No, I didn't. I did the opposite. I gave you space. I didn't presume that you would welcome more or that I had a right to it. Damn it, Mateo, I will not be like every other man who has used you for his own pleasure. You deserve better than that."

"Yeah? Then prove it." He leaned into Christos' embrace. "Don't fuck me. Make love to me. I hear there's a difference."

"There is," he said quietly, although he couldn't say he'd ever experienced that himself. On this world, he'd only ever known the transient release of casual sex.

"Prove it," came Mateo's breathless reply.

Christos licked his lips, his gaze whirling while he pondered the right response. He went with the truth. "I'm afraid I'll screw it up."

"Impossible." Mateo closed the distance between them, setting the whole thing in unstoppable motion.

The moment the boy's lips touched Christos', he was lost. His control snapped and he tugged him into a fierce embrace. Their tongues clashed as they wrestled, chasing each other from one mouth to the other. Mateo leaped up to wrap his legs around Christos' waist, saving him the trouble of scooping the boy into his arms. They were both hard, and their straining cocks rubbed fruitlessly together.

Christos tumbled them onto the bed, humping with gusto as he ripped at the boy's clothing. Everything came off in shreds, regardless of his need to be careful. Even Mateo's sneakers ended in tatters. No matter... Christos would buy him an entire new wardrobe. Nothing would be too good for his boy. *Yes, my boy.* Val had been right. Everyone had. Why had he fought the attraction? His concerns burst into dust with his growing quest to get inside his lover. There was no reason to hold back. No one benefitted from whatever stupid nobility he'd talked himself into. All that mattered was their flesh touching and finding their releases together.

When he had Mateo naked, he abandoned the boy's mouth to go exploring. There was so much tantalizing flesh to touch and lick, suck and tweak. He started with his face, over to the boy's ears, then raced to his nipples because his throat was too tempting. He didn't trust himself not to scrape or bite him there and tug the sweet blood coursing through Mateo's veins. The way the boy moaned and writhed from the sucking of his hard nubs spurred Christos to do more and better.

Anything his lips didn't latch on to, he roamed with greedy fingers. All that silky-smooth skin was a delight to pet. Mateo was incredibly sensitive. From the sounds and movements he made, everything gave him pleasure. This was no act, either. Christos had no doubt that the reaction was genuine. He wanted to give the boy everything. And Mateo wasn't merely lying there soaking up the attention. His small hands did some exploring of their own. He tried to feel Christos' back under his shirt and cup his ass under his jeans.

"No fair," the human muttered under his breathy moans. "You've got too many clothes on. I want you naked."

"As you wish." He lipped the taut skin of the boy's belly while he tore off his shirt and his pants then kicked his boots to the floor. Nothing survived entirely intact. As if he cared.

Soon there were no barriers between them, only hot skin brushing and rubbing. They mashed their cocks together, causing them both to groan. Christos nearly spent right then and there. But that wasn't how he wanted this to go. And he wasn't going to give in to the temptation of taking Mateo's cock in his mouth again.

Been there, done that. Tonight, he would pull out all of the stops and claim his boy completely.

He straddled Mateo's slender body, taking the base of the boy's cock in a firm grip, and demanded, "Tell me what you want."

Mateo shuddered, his eyes barely open. Yet his answer left Christos in no doubt. "You. Inside me. Now!"

Christos chuckled. "As you wish. Damn, condoms, lube." He frantically fought to think of the nearest place to find such things. Body wash might work to slick the way, but that was only half the problem. Not that Mateo needed protection from him, but the human didn't know that and Christos wouldn't give him a moment's worry about it.

Mateo smiled. "Check the top drawer of the nightstand. They were there the whole time."

"Thank God." He let go in order to lean over and yank open the drawer.

It was a matter of seconds before he'd covered and slicked his cock and added another dollop or two to his fingertips. He slung one of Mateo's legs over his body in order to more easily gain access to his hole. The boy helped by curling his legs and opening them wide, then holding that position by clasping his knees. With a slightly shaky hand, Christos went exploring. He found the exposed hole with ease and circled it to spread the lube.

"You don't have to be gentle."

Christos stopped what he was doing, holding his fingertips at the entrance to Mateo's ass, his heart feeling as if it were being squeezed in a vise. "That's where you're wrong. There is a time and place for a bit of rough play, perhaps. This isn't it."

He massaged in slow circles until the puckered ring softened and opened for him. Then he slid his fingers slowly inside. Mateo sighed and relaxed more, easing the way. Christos entered as far as he could go before thrusting with long, easy strokes. Mateo's channel gave way, even as it wrapped his fingers in a warm, wet sheath.

Christos maneuvered to kneel between the boy's legs, pressing them wider with his thighs as he continued to prep him. With his other hand, he worked that lovely cock—not enough to get him off, merely to stoke his arousal. He rubbed the boy's prostate with each pass, simply for the pleasure of seeing Mateo jerk and whimper. Any time he thought Mateo was getting too close to the finish, he clamped the base of his shaft again until he settled down.

Mateo thrashed his head back and forth. "No fair. Stop teasing."

"Do I have your permission to enter you?"

Mateo giggled. "I'm not some Victorian miss. Fuck me already."

"Gladly." He'd made them both wait long enough. His own cock leaked and throbbed. He longed to free it from the condom, but his wishes were irrelevant. This was for Mateo.

Taking more lube for both his shaft and Mateo's hole, he readied the boy as best he could for what he knew would be a strain. His dick was long and wide, while Mateo's ass was small in all meanings of the word. He wouldn't hurt him, no matter how torturous it was to go easy.

Satisfied that he'd prepped enough, he positioned his cockhead at the puckered ring. It took little pressure to coax it to fully blossom for him. He eased his dick past it and slowly slid it in until his balls hit Mateo's ass. They sighed in unison, a silly, sweet sign that they were in perfect sync. He stayed where he was, clasping Mateo's knees for him so that he could relax his arms. It felt so utterly perfect that he didn't need to do anything more, not on his own account. Mateo had other ideas.

The boy squeezed his sphincter tight and said, "What are you waiting for? Fuck me!"

Mateo had meant what he'd said but hadn't expected Christos to obey with such utter abandon. No sooner had the words left his mouth then the man began to drill his ass with long, fast strokes. Each pass of that huge dick goosed his prostate. The girth of the shaft stretched his channel to a point that was just shy of pain. He could barely catch his breath with the pounding he was taking. Then Christos leaned over and robbed him of what little he had.

He clung to the big body with both his arms and legs, wanting more—closer, harder, deeper. Nothing Christos did was too much. Mateo's body molded itself to the man's, opening as much as he needed to take him as far inside as possible. There didn't seem to be any limit to what he could take or any amount sufficient to satisfy his need. He dug his nails into the big man's back and reveled in the shudder that he brought on.

When Christos broke the kiss to scrape his teeth along Mateo's jaw, he said, "Give me more, Christos. Give me what no other man can." He wasn't even sure what he was demanding. There was something there, lying beneath the surface. He'd sensed it from the first, especially when Christos nuzzled his neck.

Instinctively, he turned his head to expose that part of him, understanding that Christos wanted to press his lips there. And he was not disappointed. The wetness from the man's tongue tickled the straining tendons. He raised his hips to open himself wider, to let Christos slam far inside him. His cock bounced between them, aching for attention, the climax not quite hitting from the fucking alone. Christos wiggled his hand in place and took it in a firm grip. It took only a few tugs before Mateo was coming. He arched into the grasp and cried out.

"Do it! Whatever it is you want. I'm not afraid."

The cock inside his ass swelled and pulsed as Christos climaxed a second later. As foolish as it was, he regretted that he couldn't experience the sensation of all that cum coating his insides. Then a razor-sharp pain lanced his neck before a languid feeling stole over him. There was a rhythmic tugging at the side of his neck and his dick jerked again. Cum splashed onto his stomach and his ass spasmed around the dick that stretched it even more now. He felt as if he were floating, then he felt nothing at all.

Mateo thought maybe he'd passed out for a few seconds, but when he managed to open his eyes, Christos sat on the side of the bed, staring at him. He was tucked under the covers and felt refreshed with all the residue of sex seemingly having been washed away. Only a sweet, dull ache throbbing through his ass proved Christos had fucked him. He brought his hand up to touch his neck and found a little scab there.

He smiled shyly at Christos. "Did you bite me?"

"Are you all right?" the man answered with a question.

"I'm fine. Awesomely so. Did you *bite me*?"

Christos looked away. "I'm sorry. I got carried away. I, um, scraped you with my teeth."

"Is that all?" Mateo felt the spot again and wished he had a mirror. It felt as if he'd bled, although not much. "You have a blood fetish, huh?"

The man's Adam's apple bobbed on a hard swallow. "Yes. Yes, I do." He looked at him again. "I am sorry."

Mateo reached out to touch his arm. "Don't be. I asked you to, remember? I knew there was something you had a kink for, and with all that stuff about vampires, it made sense."

"You made that connection. I am *not* a vampire."

Mateo rolled his eyes and giggled at the same time. "Of course you're not. There's no such thing. Honestly, I don't mind, although I hadn't expected to, like, faint or anything. I guess I'm not as well as I thought I was."

"Here... Drink some water." Christos produced a bottle from beside his feet.

Mateo did feel thirsty and drank half of it straight off. "Thanks." He lay back against his pillows. "Did you wipe me down while I was out?"

"Yes. I wanted you to be comfortable."

"I am that," he agreed, burrowing into the covers more. Then he yawned. "I guess that's it for me tonight. Sorry."

"There is nothing for you to apologize for."

"Okay. I figured a guy like you would be up for more." He patted the spot next to him. "Why aren't you lying beside me?" His face fell and his heart stuttered at the obvious answer. "I guess you'd rather just go now that you know I'm okay."

"No!" Christos practically jumped onto the bed. "Don't think I'm done with you now that the sex is over with. I want to hold you. I wasn't sure of my welcome."

By way of answer, he held his arms out wide. Before he could blink, Christos was snuggled beside him, with his arm anchoring him to his large, cool body. With a sigh, Mateo threw his own arm over the man's chest and lay his head against his shoulder.

"I like cuddling. I never got to do it much."

Christos squeezed. "We will stay this way all night if that is what you want."

"It might make sleeping harder, but I'm game. You sure you're not just doing this because you feel guilty?" Insecurity made him ask. It didn't seem possible that anyone would want him for something other than sex. All the men he'd slept with before had rolled over and gone to sleep, forgetting he was even there unless they woke up wanting to fuck him again.

"No one has ever assured you of your worth, have they?"

"Not really. Is that a thing? Do parents and lovers normally do that?"

"If they are any good, they do."

"I always thought my parents and other family were good people. Good Christians, you know, with a capital C. They went to church every Sunday and brought food to neighbors when they had a baby or got sick. We all did volunteer work to help the poor."

"Those are excellent things to do. But their charity didn't extend to you, did it?"

"No." It made him not only sad to say it, but embarrassed too. Christos would judge his family harshly for how they'd treated him and he wished he had a better story to tell, one that he could be proud of.

"They forced you to leave your home?"

"It's more that they made it impossible for me to stay. I didn't have much money and had no idea what

I was going to do. I only knew that I couldn't stay because lying and pretending had become impossible. Sometimes I wonder if I'd stuck it out, maybe they'd have come around in the end." As he said the words, he figured it was wishful thinking. The brutal treatment from his father in particular didn't make it likely — or even desirable.

"Perhaps they would. I cannot say. If you want, once you're more settled, you could try contacting them to see if they have had a change of heart. It's possible. And if they haven't, I promise to be there for you to give you the love and security that you deserve."

Mateo lifted his head to look at him. "You don't have to promise me forever. It's enough that we are together now and enjoying each other."

Christos tucked strands of hair behind Mateo's ear. "*Agápi mou*. My love, my heart is not so inconstant. When I entered you, it was because I wanted *forever* — not that I expect you to feel the same way. In fact," he added quickly when Mateo tried to open his mouth, "I don't want *you* to promise anything. First, get well. Then start work, albeit without the lap dancing, etcetera, if you can possibly indulge me in that restriction."

"I can...and happily so."

"Excellent. We'll see how you feel once you're established. Besides, I need to get a few things done for Alex. I may be distracted from time to time, but please don't read that as my changing my mind or pulling away."

Mateo lay his head back down, keeping his face toward Christos', ignoring the awkwardness of the position. He liked looking at his...boyfriend? Yes, he dared to think of the man in those terms, if only inside his own head. "I get it. You have family obligations. Don't you also have to get back to Greece, though?"

"There is no timetable on that. And I do hope to show you my home there before you make any long-term decisions." He paused and, for a moment, it looked as if his eyes reddened. "I would ask one more thing of you. Please stick close to the club until you are more settled. I worry about you," he added.

"I can take care of myself, you know."

"I'm sure you can, and I only mean please take ride share instead of the T and stay in groups as opposed to wandering around on your own. In fact, if you want company shopping or something, I'm happy to go when I'm not needed in the club."

"Okay, if it will make you feel better." He couldn't stifle a yawn. "I'm not used to someone worrying about me these days. It's…nice."

Christos put his hand on Mateo's head. "Get some sleep. I promise I'm not going anywhere."

With that assurance making him feel warm and wanted, Mateo let himself drift off.

Chapter Nine

"Use the pole like a prop," Quinn advised. "It's not necessary to do any dramatic tricks with it, not until you're comfortable. It's enough to swing around it as you would a partner while you dance."

"Yeah," Demi chimed in. "The members appreciate a good show, but really, your face and ass are the money shots."

Mateo stood by the stage, feeling a little awkward yet excited. Harry had declared that he would be fit for work in a few more days. And Christos had already taken him shopping — on Newbury Street, of all places. He'd only ever dared to stare at the window displays there before, knowing he could never afford to buy anything. Christos hadn't blinked an eye at the prices, and he'd insisted on purchasing far more than Mateo figured he'd ever need. Plus, he'd bought him a suitcase for it all, because, as the man had said, he wanted Mateo to feel as if he could move out of the club at any time and leave nothing behind. Everything had been purchased with cash, too. Christos said he preferred the old ways. Mateo had never seen a fatter wad of bills in his whole life and pictured Christos' mattress stuffed with mounds more.

He rubbed his palms down his new, distressed jeans. They were soft and molded to his body, so he felt that he could practice dancing in them. He didn't yet have the balls to prance around the room in only a thong. "Do your fathers actually let you dance here?" he asked Demi. For someone training to be a doctor, the kid seemed to know an awful lot about being on the pole.

"Only when Trey is here to watch, and that's mostly because they leave it up to him to set limits for me."

Mateo frowned. "That sounds controlling. You are an adult, after all."

Demi shrugged. "Barely, and I like doing what Trey says. I trust him."

Quinn snorted. "You'd never know how much Demi has changed in the last year. He hated being told what to do when I first met him."

Demi stuck his tongue out at the other boy, proving that he was not as mature as he looked. "Show him an easy routine." He turned to Mateo. "Have I ever told you about how Quinn fell on his ass when he was first learning?"

"Ha, ha," Quinn retorted. "We all fall at the beginning, except for Demi." He added that with a frown. "Oh good, this is a perfect song."

The Jonas Brothers' *Sucker* started playing. Quinn wiggled his hips in time to the music and took rhythmic steps around the pole while holding it with one hand. He put a sultry look on his face and tossed it around to the mostly empty room. Given the time of the day and day of the week, there were only a few members sitting at tables, eating and socializing. The other stages were also occupied by go-go boys, so they had plenty of entertainment to choose from. Mateo hoped that they would ignore him as he began his lesson. Of course, he could have used the one in the family home, but Annika was there and that didn't seem right. He wasn't sure how old she was, but there was something almost pure about her, regardless. She didn't need to witness his sexy gyrations. Did she even understand what went on in the club? He hoped not. Whereas he'd been forced to grow up fast on the streets, he still wanted other kids to have a slower transition into adulthood.

As the song morphed into the chorus, Quinn used his other hand to pull up on the pole, opening his legs wide as he whirled around it. He stopped with a knee holding him in place and bent backward, his hands spread wide, fingers beckoning the audience.

Holy crap, I'll never be able to do that.

After jumping off the pole onto the stage, Quinn waved him over. "Come on. Try it."

Mateo licked his lips and glanced at Demi, who nodded in encouragement before joining Quinn. The boy moved aside to give him access to the pole. It was cool to his touch and slippery, given his sweaty palms. He wiped them again on his jeans and took a firm hold before daring to dance around it. Remarkably, it wasn't as hard as he'd feared. Quinn had been right that it was like dancing with a partner—a very skinny one. If he put the men in the room out of his mind, he could imagine that he was goofing around with friends.

Concentrating on the music, he put a wide swing to his hips and added in a head toss or two. Soon it was easy to get into a rhythm. He even dared to grab with both hands and pull his feet off the stage for a few seconds. His recent sickness had taken its toll, however, so he couldn't do it for long. That was okay. As the song ended, he bucked his hips against the pole with his eyes closed, picturing himself riding Christos. That was a position they'd yet to try and he resolved to do it soon.

When he stopped, he was met by a smattering of clapping. Opening his eyes again, he saw that it wasn't only Quinn and Demi offering him encouragement. One of the members had come over and was grinning at him while he showed his appreciation. Mateo smiled shyly in return. "Thank you."

The man stepped closer, pulling a bill out of his pocket. "I know you're in training, but here's a little something to encourage you to finish up quickly and come join the fun this weekend." He waved the money at him.

Mateo let go of the pole and reached for the tip, being sure to bat his eyelashes and give the man his best come-and-get-me look. It was only make-believe, after all, a nice change from what he'd done while on the streets. The man raised the bill beyond his grasp at the last second, forcing Mateo to stand on tiptoes to snatch it. He didn't mind the game, knowing that lots of guys got off on the power exchange. His ego had learned to take a back seat to survival.

Holy fuck, it was a hundred dollars, and he hadn't done anything more than make brief love to a brass pole to get it. "Thanks, Daddy."

"Don't forget where it came from, precious."

"I won't," he said, stuffing the bill into his pocket.

"There's plenty more...for the right kind of attention." Now the guy leered at him, and while that sort of behavior would have been welcome in the past, it made him a little uncomfortable now. He understood what was being implied. The real money was in the personal attention. He wasn't going to forget what he'd promised Christos, however, nor jeopardize their budding relationship.

"Sorry, Daddy. I'm only going to be working the pole."

The man's grin got wider. Powerful, successful men weren't put off easily and didn't give up without a fight. "We'll see. I can be very persuasive." With that, he walked back to his table, his Master of the Universe swagger full on.

He turned to the other boys. "I can't believe I made a hundred dollars for doing that little work!"

Quinn patted him on the shoulder. "That's one of the great things about being a go-go boy here, and don't let a guy like that pressure you. Anyone crossing a line you draw will feel the wrath of Val."

"You got that right," Demi confirmed, "although I don't think Val is going to get a chance to before that guy intervenes." He jerked his thumb toward the bar.

Christos was there, his hands gripping the edge of the thick wooden table. Kitty, the nice woman who ran that part of the business, stood polishing a glass, her gaze fixed on Christos and shaking her head slowly.

Mateo worried his lower lip. "He looks mad."

Demi slung his arm around his shoulder. "He looks jealous. I'd say the lesson is over for today. Go reassure your man that his cock is the only thing in this world that you crave."

Mateo couldn't help but giggle at the dramatic suggestion. He took the advice anyway. At least, he sauntered over and hopped onto the bar stool opposite from where Christos was leaning. "How'd I do?"

When Christos simply stared at him, he turned to Kitty. "May I please have a Coke? I can pay." He pulled the bill out of his pocket and put it on the bar top. It made him happy to be self-sufficient again. Well, almost. He'd bet that just the food he'd eaten in this place cost more than that.

Christos pushed the bill back. "Keep your money. I pay for your needs here."

"Both of you keep your money, because Alex pays for everyone's needs here," Kitty interjected. Shaking her head again, she filled the glass in her hand with a lot of ice and Coke. She topped it with a slice of lime, which was way cool. It made him feel sophisticated, even though he was only drinking soda.

"Thanks." He beamed at her before slurping a big amount of the sugary drink. "Dancing is thirsty work." He couldn't say why he was baiting Christos in this manner. Maybe it was because he liked it when the man gave him those hungry, possessive looks, like now.

"You are done for the day?" When Mateo nodded, he said, "Good. You look tired."

"I feel fine and there's enough sugar in this drink to boost my energy."

"If you say so. When you're finished, I'm taking you to your bed."

Exasperated, he asked, "Why? I don't need a nap. Didn't I just say that I felt good? Even my cough is gone."

Christos let go of the bar top. "I'm glad to hear it, because I intend to fuck you."

Mateo's heart stuttered at the bold declaration. Then he downed the rest of his drink and went to hop off the stool. Christos beat him to it, coming to his side with dizzying speed before hefting him under his arms.

With a giggle, Mateo latched on, wrapping his legs around the man's waist and reveling at how easily he could carry him. This was someone with truly raw power and he was using it to coddle him, not hurt him.

Instead of going to the elevator in the back hallway, Christos headed deeper into the main room. As he passed the table where the man who'd tipped him sat, he stopped. "I beg your pardon, sir," he said with a confidence that made clear the courtesy was a mere formality.

When the guy looked away from his companions, his eyes went wide from whatever he was seeing in Christos' expression. "Do I know you?" His gaze flitted to Mateo and back again.

"Not in the least. My name isn't important, either. I simply want to be sure you understand that this is *my* boy."

The guy looked annoyed. "Wait a minute... He's a go-go boy and I'm a paying member and...I... Sure, whatever," he added hastily when Christos continued to stare at him.

"Excellent. Please enjoy your meal. Forgive the intrusion, gentlemen," he said as he strode off.

Mateo hid his face in the crook of his boyfriend's neck and thumped him on the back at the same time. "Oh my God, that was *so* embarrassing!"

"Was it? I didn't notice." Christos took the stairs that led to the lap dance floor two at a time.

Mateo thumped him again, although without any real anger behind it. "Yes, you did. You were acting positively medieval, like a possessive jerk, too. I have to make my living pleasing guys like him and he's already given me a hundred bucks, remember? I can't afford to piss off any of the club members."

"You didn't. I did."

"Ugh! You're not hearing me. If you give every guy who tips and propositions me the glare of doom, I won't make as much money. I know Alex pays a great base wage, but I need more than that. Wait? Where are you going?"

At the top of the stairs, Christos didn't walk through to the hallway that housed his room. Instead, he carried him around the perimeter of the second-floor area until he reached the far back corner. Then he sat in one of the wide, plush chairs with Mateo straddling his lap. The furniture was designed for exactly this configuration, and up here, the music and the lights were lower, lending the area an almost-romantic atmosphere.

Christos removed one hand from Mateo's hip and used it to cup his face. "I want to make sure you don't feel cheated out of any experience. This is nice, isn't it?"

Mateo smiled. "Yes, it is." He looked around. "Everything is so...pretty, I guess is the right word. It's like being in a movie or something."

"The rich like their comforts and Alex knows how to cater to them. And I'm sorry I embarrassed you, but I wanted to establish the right boundaries. A man like that one is used to getting his own way. He'll push and push until he does. Simply saying no isn't going to work with him."

"Demi and Quinn say Val—"

"Is a last resort. He comes in after the problem has already started. I want to cut it off at the pass, as they say."

Mateo rocked back, liking the feel of Christos' hard dick pressing against his ass. He liked, as well, that his man was worried about him. "I am not that easily intimidated. I said I wasn't going to do more than dance on stage. Don't you trust me?" He jutted his chin.

"With my life." The solemnness of his answer was a little too heavy.

"I don't think it will come to that," he teased to lighten the mood. "Anyway, what's up with all this, exactly?"

"I thought you might like being able to pretend with me. Treat me as if I'm a club member. Give me a lap dance, then let me fuck you in this position." He frowned. "The idea doesn't bother you, does it?"

Seriously? The idea was mega-sexy. By way of an answer, he closed his eyes and concentrated on the music being piped through the area. He got into the rhythm of the song as he'd done on the stage, gyrating his hips and letting himself imagine that it was his first night on the job and Christos was a club member.

"How do you like this, Daddy? I just started as a go-go boy and don't have any experience giving lap dances. I'm little nervous that I'm doing it all wrong." He peeked through his lids to make sure his manner of role-playing wasn't upsetting Christos.

The man was staring at him with an intensity that sent shivers down his spine. He could swear, too, that Christos' violet eyes had darkened. "I wouldn't have guessed. You're very good at this. You are a natural, I would say."

Christos slid his thumb across Mateo's mouth before keeping it there and pressing. Mateo got the message and parted his lips only enough to pull in that digit. Then he wrapped them around it and sucked, using his tongue to work the thumb as he would a dick.

Christos' breath stuttered. "Your lips are beautiful, like the rest of you. I bet your mouth would feel exquisite wrapped around my cock."

Happy that they were on the same page, he sucked harder while picking up the pace of his gyrations. He kept his gaze on Christos' eyes, telegraphing how much he was enjoying himself without using words.

Christos pulled his thumb out. Mateo didn't make it easy on him, wanting it to continue as long as possible. It passed his lips with an audible pop. He was compensated for the loss by Christos instead placing his hand loosely at the bottom of Mateo's neck. That wet thumb was right against his jugular, which thrilled him. He liked that Christos had this fixation. It was something new and different that he shared with this man alone.

As the song changed, getting more raucous, he humped against Christos' bulging fly. He knew well what lurked there and couldn't wait to free it. Not yet, though. He wanted to play some more. Moaning, he ran his hands along Christos' massive shoulders.

"You're so big and strong, Daddy. It makes me wet thinking about what you could do to me. *For* me. I'm hard for you already. Can you see?" he asked in a breathy voice.

"I see all of you always," came the husky reply, Christos breaking the scene temporarily. Mateo didn't mind. The sound of the man's voice sent another shiver through him and his hole clenched in anticipation of what was to come.

Mateo pressed closer to his man, nuzzling his face and twining his fingers in his hair. As usual, it was tightly tied in a ponytail. He pulled the strands free and arranged them around Christos' beautiful face. And that was exactly the right way to describe it. The man was like a classical statue, perfect and symmetric. He could stare at him all day. For the first time in his life, he regretted not being an artist. Drawing this face would mean having it to look at whenever he wanted.

"I like your hair this way," he murmured, rocking his hips against that hard ridge between his legs.

Fine tremors ran through Christos, testament to the effect he was having. It made Mateo feel powerful in his own right. Christos could carry him around like a rag doll, but he could make the big man come undone in return.

Leaning in, he scraped his teeth along the man's earlobe. "Tell me what you want, Daddy. I'll do anything for you."

The hand that had been loosely around his hips tightened, taking hold of Mateo's ass with an almost painful grip. "I want in you."

"Oh yes," he murmured. "That's exactly what I was hoping you'd say." He broke away reluctantly, causing the hand on his throat to fall.

The low, round table next to the chair had a drawer. And inside, he found what he'd expected. He waved a condom in front of Christos' face. "May I do the honors, Daddy?"

A quick nod was all he got for an answer. He wiggled back to allow himself better access to the man's fly. It was hard to unzip, given the straining dick pressing against it. Mateo gnawed at his lower lip in concentration. Knowing that his boyfriend went commando, he didn't want to cause any injuries that would put a stop to their party.

The cock, hard and already weeping with pre-cum, lurched free before he'd even managed to get the zipper all the way down. He grabbed it, held it, ran his fingers along the shaft, loving the hot smoothness of it. An annoyed grunt told him that his delay was not appreciated, so he tore open the condom and slid it over the dick. The fit was tight because his man was extra-large, but he covered the whole thing then gave it extra slickness with lube. He pulled off his shirt, uncaring about the mess, and was rewarded when Christos cupped his pecs. He flicked Mateo's nipples with his thumbs, making him moan.

"I love it when you do that."

Christos' next move was to pinch them. "Don't make me wait any longer."

"Yes, Daddy. I mean, no, Daddy."

The next part was tricky, making him regret chickening out earlier and not practicing only in a thong. He had to reluctantly slide off Christos' lap in order to wiggle out of his jeans. Unlike his man, he was wearing underwear, the sexy kind, having wanted to get used to what he'd eventually be dancing in. Of the costumes Demi had brought him earlier, he'd chosen the red one because it was the sexiest. As he stood, feeling a little shy, the look of hunger that crossed Christos' face made it all worth it.

There was no chance to get fully naked. Christos grabbed him with snake-like speed and hauled him back onto his lap. Then, grabbing the lube, he greased two fingers. His gaze never wavered from Mateo's. There was so much unspoken promise in those eyes. And yeah, they were nearly black now. Maybe it was the lighting, but he didn't quite think so. Christos slid those fingers past the string on the thong and down the crevice of Mateo's ass. He found his hole and slid both digits in without warning.

Mateo hissed at the burn before relaxing. He began to rock, fucking himself on those fingers, undulating his hips in time to the music. Between them, his own dick stood stiff and eager, the head peeking out from the waistband of the thong. It bumped against Christos' larger shaft. Each bit of contact sent shocks of pleasure straight to his balls. He thought he could come from this movement alone, except it wasn't enough. He wanted more, to be stretched to the limit.

He clasped his man with one hand while clinging to his arm with the other. "Let me ride you, Daddy."

After a moment's hesitation, Christos withdrew his fingers and placed both hands on the arm of the chair. He trusted Mateo to do the work. It took no time and little effort to get himself where he wanted to be — impaled on Christos' cock. He sat on it all at once, again relishing the burn of being stretched quickly. Then he began to post, slowly at first. He wanted to make this last, even knowing that neither of them was good at holding out for long.

"Help me, Daddy. I want to feel your hand around me."

Christos pried one hand from the chair's arm to give his boy what he'd demanded. At that moment, he couldn't deny him anything, least of all what he himself also truly wanted. This giving up control was new to him. He liked it and so did his dick. Mateo wasn't hesitant, riding him with confident, fast movements. The scrap of cloth between him and Mateo's cock was dealt with in a second. He let the ripped front sag to one side and took the boy's dick in his grasp. He didn't need to jerk it. Every time Mateo rose and fell, he fucked Christos' hand as surely as his boy was using his cock to fuck his own ass.

This fucking in a public place was surprisingly erotic, as well. His idea had been to give Mateo something he might enjoy after his high-handed, yet totally unavoidable, reaction to the club member. He hadn't expected to like the experience himself. Although, truth be told, he was glad that no one else was actually around to see him. He'd been surprised to realize how hard it was for him to see others appreciating Mateo. It made him wonder what kind of madness had compelled him to get him a job like that to begin with. No matter... Mateo obviously loved the opportunity. The delight on his pretty face as he'd held up the money for all to see had been heartbreaking. It had out-shone his reaction to all of the clothing he'd bought for him, and Christos understood why. Accepting gifts wasn't nearly as satisfying as earning his own money. Christos would give him anything and everything that he could to keep that smile on his face.

The tension built quickly, as it always did when he was inside this human. He wanted to make it last for Mateo's sake, yet found himself grunting and jerking as his cock swelled and filled the condom. Damn, he longed for the chance to feel his boy without that barrier. A second later, Mateo came, his warm cum spilling over Christos' fingers. The boy tossed back his head and groaned loudly. Christos continued to work the shaft until Mateo collapsed against him.

He wrapped him in a tight embrace, uncaring that he smeared his back with the sticky spending. So what if they got dirty? That only meant using the shower again together. That process had become routine now, even though Mateo didn't need the help. It was fun and led to wonderful things, like mutual blow jobs while hot water sprayed them.

The sound of voices coming up the stairs roused him. He suddenly felt very possessive, and using slightly less than his normal speed, he rose with Mateo still impaled and raced him out to the hallway. He didn't stop until he had them in the bathroom.

Mateo lifted his head and peered at him with sleepy eyes. "You're awfully fast."

He pressed a kiss to the boy's nose. "I'll try to fuck you slower after the shower," he said, deliberately misinterpreting the observation. "That's assuming you can get me off again while we wash, using that bratty mouth of yours." He grinned to make it clear that he was kidding. "Otherwise, I'll be too eager and come quickly like a teenager."

Mateo gave him a lazy smile in return. "You're insatiable, but I'll see what I can do."

* * * *

"Are you trying to make Petru jealous, then?"

Christos gave Malcolm a confused look. "What? Why would I want to do that?"

The man shrugged. "No reason. And if not, you should try to wipe that well-fucked look off your face. It's making me long for my own boy, to be frank."

"Fuck you," he said without heat, because he *was* well-fucked and nothing was going to take that glow away, not even talking to the Asshole-Formerly-Known-As-Petru.

Val sighed. "I should do this on my own. You two are a major distraction. Plus, I'm not fucking my husband currently, due to his condition, so I'm not particularly interested in hearing about your respective sex lives."

Malcolm's expression grew somber. "Sorry, laddie. Is there something amiss?"

Val opened the door to the old weapons room. "No, Harry has cleared us for gentle stuff, but it freaks me out. I keep thinking I might be poking the kid or something."

Malcolm laughed at that. "I don't think that's a real concern."

"My mind gets that, but my dick shrivels at the thought. The only way I can pacify Mackie is to give him a blow job—which is great fun, don't get me wrong—except," he added with a shake of his head, "then I get this weird feeling that the kid is watching me."

"You're a head-case for sure, Val, my lad."

"Don't I know it. A few more months and this whole problem goes away—if things go well."

"Then it will be diapers and feedings that get in the way of sex," Malcolm reminded him. Which was better than letting Val start to swirl around the drain of doom.

Christos got how his shipmate felt about the sex, however. In a totally unscientific way, it made sense. It didn't help that among their kind, breeding females lost all interest in sex until their babies were weaned. It was one of the reasons males tended to turn to one another for release. His shipmates were in unchartered territory when it came to procreating with humans. That led to thoughts of what it might be like to be in Val's position. What if Mateo didn't run screaming from him when he learned about his true nature? Would he agree to take his blood and become a changeling? And how would it feel to see his son growing inside his lover's body? Of course, there was always the chance that he might turn out like Will and be the one to become pregnant. The idea made him shudder. It would be an honor to produce a queen, but still, he liked his innards just as they were.

This is all too soon. He and Mateo had barely started their relationship and there would be no future for them at all unless they put a stop to Dracul for good— hence this little confab.

Petru was lounging on his hard bed, reading as usual. It was a good thing he enjoyed the activity so much, because there was fuck-all else for him to do. Alex didn't allow any electronic devices, including a TV, for fear that the guy would find a way to either contact Dracul or break free of his confines. Petru straightened and put the book aside when Val opened the door. "The Queen?" The look of anticipation on his face was both creepy and reassuring at the same time. If his devotion to Annika was faked, he was giving Tom Hanks a run for his money.

"Yeah, yeah," Val said. "She sends her regards and all that. Plus"—he pulled a piece of wrapped parchment paper out of his pocket—"snickerdoodles." He tossed the gift onto the guy's lap with obvious disgust.

Petru, on the other hand, was delighted with the treat, likely because his Queen had thought of him. He immediately stuffed one into his mouth. "Hmm." His moan was practically orgasmic.

Val glared for all of them. "If you're done coming from your sugar fix, I need to go over the last five sites I'm monitoring to find Dracul."

Petru didn't look happy, but he didn't press the point. He put the rest of the cookies to one side. "How may I be of assistance?"

Val lifted the tablet in his hand and showed the screen to the guy. "I got these images for the one located in the Niger Delta. As you can see, there are a lot of men milling about in red berets. What do you think, mercenaries that Dracul has hired?"

Petru took the screen, stared at the images, then shook his head. "No, these are definitely local militants. They fight for ideology as well as money. That's the last kind of person Dracul wants to deal with. Devotion to wealth, he understands. The rest?" He shrugged. "It's a distraction that he won't permit his soldiers. And this particular location wasn't that well-stocked, as I recall." He handed the tablet back. "I think you can cross it off your list of possibilities."

Val grunted in response. "That's what I thought too. It's something, I suppose."

"I am at your service," came Petru's smug reply.

Christos' hands itched with the desire to slap the guy silly. His post-Mateo-fucking buzz was getting killed by being in this fucker's presence. There had to be more to this visit than this. "So far it sucks. You must have something more and better for us to go on."

Petru gave him the once-over. "Hello, Christos. It's been a pleasure seeing you again. You're looking *relaxed* today, I must say."

His hand fisted and his nostrils flared with the compulsion to use it. "I'd be even more so if I pound your face into a bloody pulp."

Petru lounged against his wall. "Hm-m. I see that living with goats all these years hasn't made you better company." He lifted his hands. "What do you want from me? It's not as if I was privy to his Plan B. I don't think he had one, not really. We never thought Alex would have the balls for a direct assault or that the castle would be overtaken, regardless. All these other sites have been dormant for years and a reflection of Dracul's greedy nature more than anything else. Why have only one of something when you can have a hundred?"

Christos ground his molars in frustration. "That may be, but once he had to make a decision about where to run, he would have gone with what pleased him most. Tell us what he likes."

"Beating pretty boys while he fucks them raw."

"Not. Helping."

Petru rolled his eyes — proof that he was more stupid than any of them thought, because he was so begging for a punch to the face. "Very well, let's go with his perverse nature and how he always fancies himself the smartest person in the room. Which to his credit, he usually is."

"And what's that supposed to mean when it's at home?" Malcolm asked.

Petru sighed. "I don't know…that he'd go to the least likely place. We all hate how hot this planet is, right, and gravitate toward colder places for the most part? So you'd think Dracul would want Siberia or Nepal. But I would focus on Syria and Mexico next, merely because they are less obvious choices."

Christos hated to admit it, but the fucker had a point. He himself had made a home in Greece in part because he didn't expect Dracul to go looking for him in such a warm climate. The heat and bright sun were easier to get used to than dealing with endless war. Claude had headed for the African continent for much the same reason.

"It does have some logic to it," Christos said. "The fucked-in-the-head kind, of course. Still…"

Petru smiled. "There you are. You will tell the Queen how helpful I've been?"

"Sure," Val said. "I'll make sure she knows you've been a good little narc."

Petru sneered. "There's no need to be rude about it. I am trying to reform in her service." He paused and lost much of his bravado. "Ask her to come visit me?"

"That will be up to Will."

Something sly crossed Petru's face. "That goes without saying."

"I've had about as much of this as I can stomach," Malcolm said, turning to leave.

Christos gladly followed him, waiting only until Val had secured the door before crossing the room. "Shall we go see how Tony is coming with his projectiles?" Although he wanted to race back to Mateo's bed, he worried that he was overtaxing the human. It was best to keep busy with other matters.

Val shrugged. "Sure, why not?" The experiments were going on in Harry's lab across the narrow hallway. Within seconds they'd crowded in.

Harry looked up from where he tinkered with some chemicals that hissed and popped. "Gentlemen… Is there anything new with our incarcerated friend?"

"He might have actually given us more useful information," Val replied. He headed to a bench in the far corner where Tony was doing his own fiddling with mechanical components.

"I do trust you are being careful with my patient, Christos," the older man said pointedly in his direction.

Pausing in his tracks, Christos tried not to squirm. He was doing nothing wrong. "I'm being very mindful of his recent sickness, if that's what you mean."

"It is. But also remember where he comes from. Survival sex has become second nature to him."

It was like a fist to his gut, raising his own worries. But he stood tall and looked the man in the eye, because he had thought of little else before and after he'd bedded the boy. "This isn't some means of passing the time, Harry. I am committed to doing what's right by him. I, ah, love him."

Jesus, that had been hard to say to anyone other than Mateo and he wanted to take the words back as soon as they'd left his mouth. He didn't. The world didn't crumble around him and the more he sat with the public acknowledgment, the more natural it felt. It helped, too, that none of his shipmates laughed or dismissed his claim as implausible.

Malcolm slapped him on the back as he passed by. "Breathe, laddie. Being in love with a human won't kill you. There's a lot of that going around these days, and thank fuck for it."

Harry smiled. "Well, that's an entirely different matter. Hang on tight. You're going to have a bumpy ride," he said, using his best Bette Davis impression.

Christos grimaced and decided to change the topic. "How is it coming, Tony?"

"Pretty good." He held up some tubular contraption that was obviously a relatively small, short rocket. "This is the delivery mechanism."

Christos got closer to inspect it, jostling Val and Malcolm for space. "Hard to believe that can hold enough explosive to penetrate an underground bunker."

"It's all in the mix, gentlemen." Tony grinned. "I've been using some of the seeds from our ship that we saved to find something that packs more of a punch."

"I bet Emil would be helpful in that regard," Val interjected. "Marius tried much the same…the motherfucker," he muttered.

Christos might have been out of the game for a long while, but he had stayed in the loop. He knew all about Marius' bombing of Boston and how Emil had found a way to stop him. "Then we know we have something to neutralize it if it gets out of hand."

"Exactly," Val agreed.

Tony looked affronted. "It won't. I know what I'm doing." He eyed Val in particular. "You just have to give me a place to try it out on."

Val sighed. "Working on it." He turned to Christos. "I'm going to hunker down in my office tonight and focus on those sites that Petru mentioned. I trust you and Claude have the club covered?"

"*Naí.*" Mateo had been invited to spend time with some of the hybrids in the family living room and Christos said as much. "Monitoring the club activities will give me something to do. I don't share his enthusiasm for video games and movies," he added. He didn't care about having the duty, boring as it was. It beat hanging around waiting for Mateo to come to bed.

Putting his device away carefully, Tony stood. "I'm going to hang over there, myself. The boys are pretty good and behaving, especially around Mateo. They understand to act like normal human boys and are used to doing that back home. There's no harm in my keeping tabs anyway, though."

"Thanks for that. I appreciate it." Eventually, if things continued on their current path, he'd have to tell Mateo the whole truth. But he wanted to control the when and how that information got conveyed. God help him if it slipped out in some other way. Mateo might not recover from the shock.

His friend smiled. "We all like him, you know. Annika's approval in particular is a good sign. Don't wait too long bringing him into the fold."

Christos scowled. "It's far too soon for that. We have to finish with this nonsense first." He didn't add that he was concerned that Mateo might never accept him as he was.

But that was a worry for another day.

Chapter Ten

"It's a pretty quiet night, all things considered," Claude shouted into Christos' ear. That was the only way to be heard at this point. The music was at full volume as some of the boys went through a routine on the dance floor that had the members out of their chairs and throwing money.

"It depends on your definition," he yelled back. He turned away from watching them because it made him picture Mateo doing the same thing in the near future. Plus, him ogling others made him feel as if he were being unfaithful, as silly as it seemed. He hadn't appreciated in a thousand years how much of a one-man kind of guy he was.

Then he nodded in the direction of the entrance and wandered over there. Claude followed. In the dark hallway between the front door and the main room, there was a measure of peace and quiet. At least here, he didn't have to raise his voice as much.

"Val and Alex have this place operating in a well-oiled fashion. These rich men know how to behave, even when they're liquored up. Alex hasn't tasked us with a hard job."

Claude scuffed the toe of his boot against the carpet. "I know. I feel guilty that we're not doing more."

"Being in a holding pattern doesn't give us much choice. Our talk this afternoon with Petru may have yielded some useful information. It doesn't change the overall problem of whether we attack or wait."

"Neither choice is ideal."

Antsy, Christos found himself longing for a smoke. "Is your man over at *Our Safe Place* tonight?"

"Yeah, he and Mikko put their collective small feet down and demanded some time out doing something useful. Willem and Malcolm and their boys are with them, so I'm mostly okay with it. I hear they've hired a bunch of humans to get in more staff anyway, so this may be one of the few chances left for them to help out. Plus, Val has already picked a security company to discreetly monitor the place. It's not about Dracul. Humans are predators enough and those kids are easy targets."

Christos tried to imagine Mateo out where he couldn't lay eyes on him within minutes, and he fisted one hand. It would make him nuts. As Claude had said, forget Dracul. This world held plenty of horrors for the weak and unsuspecting. Not that any of the men and boys he and Claude thought of or worried over could be called that, exactly. They weren't children and, in the case of Nen and Mikko, were humans with enhanced abilities and some combat training. There was only so much coddling they could do. And yet, he was glad that Mateo was in the family home, playing games with Matti and Yaro. He was safe, at least for this night, including from the pawing attention of the club members. That would have to be sufficient for the time being.

God, Christos hoped he would keep his shit together once the boy started working. He didn't like the idea of anyone else so much as looking at him. And his display of jealousy earlier didn't bode well for the future. Of course, it had also yielded an afternoon of hot sex in various locations, so there was *that*. He would have to work hard to ignore the leers and the money being thrown at him for more. Mateo was his boy and knew it.

My boy. Yeah, that felt right, even though they were in the middle of a war and the future was uncertain. When had it been any different? One thing he'd appreciated about humans was their resilience and ability to carve out some kind of life, regardless of the circumstances. It was a good lesson to learn from the usually lesser-evolved beings.

One of the go-go boys, Shawn, sauntered by. "Hi, guys," he waved. "I'm going to take over on the door unless you have any changes to the schedule."

Christos shook his head. "No. Whatever Val has established stays. Think of us as new and out-of-place decorations."

Shawn winked. "Naw, you two fit right in." With that, he wiggled his cute ass to the door.

Claude hummed. "Makes me eager for Nen to get home."

Christos snorted but, for once, he had someone who would welcome him into his bed and his body, too…if he could wait that long. *Shit*, how many times had he come already that day and he was still hard merely by thinking of the boy? He sighed. "Mind if I go outside for a smoke?"

Claude shrugged. "Not a problem. There's nothing happening here anyway. I'm sure I can handle it if one of the club members gets out of hand."

"Great, thanks."

He wondered if his smoking bothered Mateo. It hadn't come up and it wasn't as if he did it often. It was at most something to pass the time and gave him a mild comfort. Humans had been doing it for eons but had recently realized that it was very bad for their health. Many found it a disgusting smell and Mateo might be one of them. If so, he would give it up. In the space of a few days, nothing had become more important to him than pleasing that boy.

He smiled at Shawn and the boy whom he was relieving and went out to the sidewalk. It was blessedly cool and quiet out there, the only sounds the usual ones from traffic and the occasional revelers. It was early enough for humans to still be hopping from one form of entertainment to another, although this part of the city wasn't as congested. Taking out a cigarette and matches, he lit one and leaned against the building with a boot propped flush against it. This was how Mateo had first seen him. What had he thought at that moment? The resemblance to Cadoc must have given him pause, yet he'd propositioned him anyway. It was a sign of how desperate he'd been. Harry's warning came to mind. Was the human really in a position to consent to a relationship at the moment?

Damn, he could drive himself mad second-guessing his decisions. He only knew that resisting the attraction had proved futile. And the beauteous feeling inside him when he thought of a life with Mateo was too tempting to resist.

A group of scruffy young men caught his attention. They were laughing and weaving in a tight group. They weren't likely to be club members and there wasn't really any place for them to find fun on this block. Maybe they didn't understand that this was a private form of entertainment. They seemed overdressed, given the temperature. It was cool, but not freezing. Every one of them had on a long, heavy coat and he instinctively checked to see if they were armed. It was impossible to tell at this angle and distance.

Flicking his butt away, he straightened, intending to ward off whatever mischief they might be intending. He didn't know true alarm until the snick of a gun hammer caught his attention. He whirled around to find four men sneaking up from behind him. One was pointing a gun at him and had already fired. Christos was gone from his spot before the bullet left the gun, rushing at full speed to meet his attackers. He had the guy's arm up and away when he heard a scream and the pops of more gunfire. From the corner of his eye, he saw dozens of human men rushing from alleyways and around corners toward the club.

There was no chance for him to chase after them. His personal assailants had to be dealt with first and they weren't making it easy. As he twisted the arm in his grip right out of its socket, he kicked the face of another who was trying to get off a shot. He heard the screams of his opponents and felt the sting of a bullet scraping his thigh. The sounds, along with the scent of blood, sent him into a frenzy. He smashed a third one's head into the concrete, leaving it a flat, pulpy mess that slid lifeless to the ground. The fourth one's neck snapped in his one-arm embrace while he made sure that the first two were down for good by stomping on their chests.

Done, he roared his rage then grabbed the four guns lying around, slipping two into his waistband. He ran to the club entrance and almost stumbled over Shawn. The poor boy was lying face-up with blood spattered over his chest. His lifeless eyes confirmed that there was nothing to be done for him. There was no time for even a second of mourning, either. Inside the club, a battle raged with rapid firing and male screaming. The scent of even more blood hit his nostrils. The club was already awash in it. He could only hope that some of it was the attackers'.

He raced unheeding into the fray. The music pounded and the strobe lights pulsed, amping the nightmarish quality of the scene he'd entered. Tables and chairs were upended everywhere. Bodies littered the floor, although whether they were all dead, it was impossible to tell. The combatants hid around the room, exchanging fire. Christos took out two more as he dove for cover behind the table where his kills had been hiding.

Their guns and ammo became his and got stuffed wherever he could manage to find room in his jeans. He searched the immediate area to see who else he could eliminate. From where he crouched, he saw Kitty pop up from behind her bar and get off a few good shots before a spurt of red burst from her shoulder and she fell back again. The mirror behind her shattered, raining glass shards. Fuck, he barely knew her but said a human prayer that it wasn't a fatal wound. When the fucker who'd lobbed the shot lingered too long from his hiding place, Christos gladly dispatched him. Emil sprinted from the back over to the bar and slipped behind to minister to the woman.

A familiar sharp whistle caught his attention. He craned his neck around the table to find Claude a few feet away. He gave hand signals that they hadn't had to use in decades. Christos understood and nodded. Claude jumped from his position behind a wide load-bearing post and fired across the room. When the inevitable return fire occurred, Christos was able to locate more targets. He rushed toward them, firing with both hands, then slid behind their bodies and lay as flat as he could manage. He jettisoned the spent guns and grabbed two more from his pants.

Now he was closer to the dance floor, which was slick with blood. Members and boys alike lay in twisted positions, some moving, others not. Quinn was at the far end, sprawled over another boy, covering him as much as he was able. There was blood on him, too, although whether it was his or another's was impossible to tell. His eyes were open, however, and he quivered as a few of the attackers moved toward him and took aim. He could have used the speed that Alex's blood afforded him to escape, but he stayed where he was, protecting his colleague. As focused as the assailants were on Quinn, they must have been targeting him in particular.

Alex's boy. If there had been any shred of doubt about who had sent these killers, it was gone now. Dracul had always been good at finding someone's weak spot. Christos couldn't let this happen. His life was expendable. Alex needed his Quinn, while if Mateo lost Christos, he would get over it. There had been no declaration of love from his boy, and now he was glad, although he hated the idea of not being the one to rescue Mateo from his hard life. No sacrifice was too great for his captain, however. He owed his life to the man ten times over. And really, other than finding Mateo, this world had never appealed to him. Death would almost be welcome.

Just as he got set to launch himself between the advancing men and Quinn, an unholy roar shook the room. Alex flew in from the back hall, catapulting from one of the stages and careening into Quinn's stalkers like a vengeful god. One man fell from a well-placed bullet, thanks to Val, who followed, armed like twenty men. The others disappeared into a scrum that spewed blood and body parts as Alex literally tore the men apart.

Christos took the opportunity to head to the second floor. There was more firing from there…and screams. Obviously the lap dance area and perhaps even the playrooms were under assault. It had been impossible to note the number of humans in Dracul's army. He found a couple of the fuckers methodically moving from chair to chair, looking under and around for those hiding and shooting them. Christos roared to get their attention and took great pleasure in delivering double pops to their faces before they could get a shot off.

He found a man and a boy cowering near the hallway. "Have any gone down there?" He had to repeat the question when they both stared wide-eyed at him with fear. Finally, the boy shook his head. "Are you sure? Then go. Lock yourselves into the first room you find open. Now!"

The humans scrambled to obey. He found a few more live ones, including those who were wounded. The mobile ones helped the others and cleared the area while Christos covered their backs. When they were gone and he was sure there were none left to save, he peered down into the main area to see where he could be of most help. There were more bodies littering the floor, although now they included only those of the attackers. They were easy to spot compared to the well-dressed members and the scantily clad boys. Slowly, the battle was coming to an end.

Quinn remained where he was, only now Alex covered him and Val was nearby laying down suppressive fire. It was a dicey situation, one that couldn't last much longer. Alex and his boy, as well as Val, were exposed, and it was only a matter of time before one of the mercenaries Dracul had hired got lucky, especially as it was clear that those who were left were focusing on those three in particular.

Then it all changed. From the back hallway, Logan emerged, a gun in each hand. Emil made an attempt to grab her when she passed his location behind the bar. She deftly avoided his grasp and kept her eyes front. Both guns bucked as she fired her semi-automatics with endless sprays of bullets. A round of returned fire hit her in the chest, just below her right shoulder, kicking her back a half-step. And still she fired. Another hit her leg a moment later. She barely flinched and stepped onto the dance floor. Her march into the middle of the concerted assault against Alex continued with a steady pace and a deadly barrage of rounds — in both directions. There was no fear in her expression, only determination.

When she ran out of ammo, she tossed her weapons and pulled two more from her waistband, losing only a second of time. Her side bloomed with red, and she redirected her fire in response. Emil yelled and emerged with both hands gripping his revolver — and his fangs descended. He shot past his friend, giving her some cover. Val stood as well, drawing fire toward him.

But Logan didn't back away or falter. She kept coming until she stood right in front of Alex. Two more hits to her torso and she went down, still firing until she landed on the floor.

Grabbing the railing, Christos vaulted over and down into the fray. He whipped his head around, looking for targets, even before his feet hit the ground. A few assailants bolted, heading toward the front door. He gladly shot them in the back, as did Claude. There were more to ferret out, but hopefully not many. This part of the last battle with Dracul would end soon. A bullet missed his ear by a whisker, reminding him that it was still ongoing. As he dove for cover, a sound made his heart stop.

An explosion, faint but clear to his hearing, grabbed his attention. An alarm blared, mixing with the raucous noise of the music that continued to blast through the club. It was the alarm for the family building. It had to be. This attack in the club had been only part of the plan. The most vulnerable of them were under attack. "Mateo!" he yelled and lurched toward the door. Fire pinned him down and he howled with frustration. Then he took a page from Logan's book, stood and fired at anything human that moved.

* * * *

Mackie sat forward on his bed as much as his belly would allow. "What was that?"

Merlin hopped to his feet, certain of the answer. "An explosion." The alarm went off right after that, proving that the house's security had been breached.

"We're under attack!" Mackie cried and tried to get up.

Annika held him back with her free hand, showing greater strength than she had ever done. She managed to contain both the boy and her dog, which whimpered and struggled against her hold. "No, you need to stay here, and so must I."

"But I think only Tony is home for protection. Whatever's going on, the others need our help."

"There is nothing we can do except get killed or captured." Annika's expression turned fierce. Her dog whimpered some more, obviously reacting to something it sensed from its owner. Annika shushed it with a kind of impatience than she'd never shown the animal before. Her obvious stress added to Merlin's own.

Mackie struggled to get free. "I have a gun and know how to use it."

"Do you think whoever has broken in does not?" She shook her head. "There will be too many of them and you will be killed, having sacrificed your child for nothing. You would do that to Mr. Val?"

The reminder of his husband did the trick. Mackie gave in and collapsed against his pillows. Tears leaked from his eyes.

Annika's gaze steadied on Merlin. "You know what to do. It's all right to be afraid."

He swallowed back his protest that he wasn't, because she would know he was lying. "I won't fail you," he said instead and bolted from the room.

"Wait!" Mackie called. "Take my gun at least." He pointed to a dresser.

Merlin glanced at Annika before saying, "I won't need it."

Out in the hallway, the sounds of chaos were more obvious. There was gunfire from the first floor and screams. Idris wailed, telling him that the baby was already in their attacker's sights. That was good. At least maybe they'd have no reason to search the upper floors. Dracul wanted his son. Hybrids and changelings wouldn't matter to him. A Queen, though, would be a different story, and there was no telling whom he'd sent and whether they would recognize Annika for what she was. At a minimum, she would be at risk, simply because she was female.

The alarm thankfully cut off, leaving only the sounds of sobs and crying, which was bad enough. Creeping to the head of the stairs, he peered down and saw human men with large weapons milling about. He clutched at the bannister and took a deep breath for courage before slinging his leg over it and sliding down. He landed right in the middle of the fray.

A half-dozen humans with big guns were corralling everyone toward the couch where Dafydd already sat, clutching Idris to him. Mateo cowered beside him, a bewildered look on his face because, of all of them, he was the only one who truly had no idea what was happening. Tony lay on his back mid-way between the living area and the kitchen, his arms outstretched and his chest covered in blood. Matti was on his knees nearby, sobbing, Yaro's arms around him in an obvious effort at comfort. Alun lurked near the dining counter, and seeing that his father was alive and unharmed gave Merlin a surprising sense of relief.

Dracul's men wasted no time pointing their guns in Merlin's direction. He lifted his arms in surrender and pasted a look of non-aggression on his face. He knew how to do this. His whole life had been filled with dangerous, heavily armed males with hair-trigger tempers. He had learned the way to navigate these waters, had mastered the technique practically in infancy. Brutal men would find nothing to worry about in his expression or actions. Hiding his fear was second nature, too.

"Can anyone join this party?" As he walked by, he kicked the gun lying near Tony's hand out of his reach. He knew the guy wasn't dead because he hadn't turned to ash, but he was betting these humans had been told nothing about alien physiology and thought the man was gone. Otherwise, they would have already taken this precaution. It wouldn't help matters if the honorable idiot came to long enough to reach for his weapon and become really dead as a consequence.

Merlin sneered at Matti. "What's the matter? Can't you even manage to cry over your dead father's body?" He darted his eyes to Tony and hoped his meaning got through. A moment later, Matti, with Yaro still clinging to him in support, crawled to Tony and threw himself over the man—putting pressure on that wound, Merlin hoped.

One of soldiers barked, "Stay right there!" to Merlin.

He stopped and smiled. "I'm not your enemy."

"Shut the fuck up! We're wasting time," he said to his companions. "We need those two," he added with a flick of his free hand at Dafydd and Idris. "Come over here, cunt, and shut that brat up."

Dafydd didn't move other than to shake his head. "I'm not going back to him. I'd rather die."

"Nobody said you could speak, cocksucker. And if that were an option, believe me, you'd already have a hole in your head. Get over here *now*!"

Merlin took a half-step forward. "Dafydd, don't be the stupid cunt Dracul always said you were. Do what the man says. Have you forgotten your place already?

You belong to Dracul and so does Idris. If you don't obey this man, they'll knock you out and take you both anyway, except then Idris won't have you to care for him. I know how much that matters to you." He sneered.

"Listen to the emo wannabe, cunt."

Dafydd hesitated only a second more before rising from the couch. One of the men grabbed him by the arm and tugged him toward the door. Idris cried even harder, clearly irritating the men. And while Merlin figured they were smart enough not bring the boy back to Dracul harmed, there was no telling what humans would do under stress. They didn't always act in their own best interests, and their scents told him that they were far more stressed out at the moment than they should have been, given that they were in control. All it would take was one stupid hair-trigger move for this whole thing to end in a blood-bath.

This was when the many interactions he'd had with the child paid off. Merlin leaned to intercept them. "Be a good boy, Idris. You know how."

The baby stopped crying with a hiccup and, sticking his thumb in his mouth, laid his head against his father's chest. Dafydd raised his eyebrows at Merlin but otherwise said nothing and let himself be contained by the doorway without further protest.

"We've got one more to grab," the lead soldier said, looking around.

Before the man could explain himself, a figured dropped behind Merlin from the second floor. The only warning was a whoosh of wind that caused him to turn in time to see it. Demi crouched with fangs bared, hissed, then lunged toward the man holding Dafydd's arm. Before he could get far, Merlin put his training to good use. He whirled around, raising one leg in a roundhouse kick to Demi's face. The connection jarred him to the bone and he almost winced at the sickening sound. Demi fell to the floor with a grunt and tried to get up before passing out.

"Nice move, kid. What's your angle?" the head soldier asked with a sneer of his own.

Merlin straightened. "I want to come with you."

What the fuck is going on? Mateo was frozen to his spot on the couch. He didn't understand any of this. An explosion had caused the front door to bang open before these strangers with guns had burst in. The home invasion had stunned everyone into inaction except for Tony. The guy had pulled a gun from a holster in his waistband that had been hidden by his shirt. Mateo had watched in shock as the brief shoot-out had occurred. It had been so surreal that he'd felt as if he were still watching a scene from the *Star Wars* video game that he'd finished playing an hour ago.

Poor Tony hadn't stood a chance against the six armed men who'd invaded the cheery home. It had been over in seconds, with Tony obviously dead and Matti having to now live with the horror of seeing his father killed in front of him. And that hadn't been the end of the surprises. Apparently robbery wasn't the point of this evil madness. They wanted Dafydd and the baby for God-only-knew what reason. No, that wasn't true. Dafydd understood and, whatever awaited him, death was preferable.

Now Merlin, who had practically flown down the stairs, wanted to go with them. He'd always thought the kid was kind of a jerk, but this made no sense. Why attack his own family member to join these murderous assholes? At least Demi wasn't dead. Demi...who had leaped from the second story and landed like a cat that had more than nine lives to spare. How had that been possible? And had those been fangs he'd seen protruding from the boy's mouth when he'd uttered a sound that was nothing human? He'd looked and sounded like a B-movie vampire before Merlin had knocked him out. It wasn't possible, though. That was terror playing tricks on his mind. He reached for the spot on his neck that still had a bit of a scab. *Is it?*

It hardly mattered, because the reality of the situation was that Dafydd and Idris were being kidnapped. There wasn't a damn thing he could do about it except sit there and watch it happen and hope that the fact that none of these men were wearing any masks didn't mean they intended to kill all the witnesses. He felt helpless and longed for Christos. Except no, when he thought about it, he wanted his boyfriend to stay as far away from here as possible. Otherwise, he'd surely end up as dead as Tony.

"We're not the foreign legion, kid," the man who seemed in charge of the invaders said. "We don't take recruits."

Merlin smiled. "But I'm one of Dracul's soldiers. I've been held here against my will and have been looking for a way back to him. He'll want me and so will you. I'm like him," he added, jerking his head toward Demi. "Only, you know, *better*. Obviously."

"Merlin, no." Alun left the spot he'd been rooted to since the invasion had begun. He approached his son with more courage than Mateo would have thought possible. "That's not who you are anymore."

"A fucking lot you know, slut. You were never anything more than a convenient hole for my sire to stick his dick in." The men laughed.

Alun's head jerked as if he'd been slapped. Then he took a visibly large breath, threw his shoulders back and continued to walk toward Merlin. "You will not go with them."

Without any warning, Merlin leaped at his father and, grabbing him by the neck, propelled them both across the kitchen area. Given the distance they covered, it looked as if they'd almost flown, one more indication that these were not humans. It was almost not shocking at this point. The thud when Alun hit the far wall made Mateo wince. Merlin pressed his lips close to his father's ear and, although they moved, Mateo couldn't hear anything. The next instant, Merlin banged Alun's head against the plaster. The poor man cried out before sliding down to the floor. Merlin released his hold before his father had landed and walked away with a satisfied grin on his sick face.

"Sorry about that," Merlin said with a shrug. "Shall we go?"

The leader gave him an assessing look. "Maybe you can come, but I still need one more package for Dracul." He eyed Mateo. "This one looks like he fits the description. A Welsh kid. You're Brenin, aren't you, pretty boy?"

Having the attention on him sent a new wave of terror coursing through Mateo. He shrank into the cushions, unable to form a response. He had met Brenin and understood the confusion. There was a superficial resemblance, he supposed. Thank God the boy was with his man at *Our Safe Place*. Hopefully, these men would leave without him—or even better, linger long enough for help to arrive. No one had had the chance to call the police. It had all happened so quickly and there were too many pairs of eyes keeping watch to try it now. Surely someone had heard the explosion and maybe the burst of gun fire. Although the more he thought of it, the more he wondered why no one had come yet. Surely, even if they hadn't heard anything else, the sound of the alarm going off for a few minutes would have reached the club. Maybe not. The music was loud and the sound-proofing in both buildings was excellent.

"Answer me, cocksucker!" The demand was punctuated with a gun being pointed right at Mateo.

"No, he's not," Dafydd called out before Mateo could deny it. "That's not Brenin."

The man pulled his gun back and swore. "Fuck yeah? Well, we'll have to search the rest of the building, because my balls are on the line if I don't bring him along. Get those two out," he added to the one holding Dafydd.

Merlin's eyes went wide as the man headed for the stairs. He caught Mateo's gaze and shook his head only slightly. Then he started humming, low under his breath. *Let It Go.* Mateo got the drift. Annika was up there. What would these men do to that beautiful young girl when they found in her in a quest for someone who wasn't even there? Mateo nodded at Merlin, giving him approval to sacrifice him, because if it came down to his own safety versus that of another child, he'd take the hit. It was the easiest decision he'd ever made in his life.

"Wait," Merlin called out. "He's lying. This is Brenin all right."

With a grunt, the man turned and marching back to the couch, grabbed Mateo and hauled him to his feet. "Is that true? Are you the Welsh kid I'm looking for?"

His heart lodged in his throat, but he dug deep for a courage he didn't know he possessed and nodded. "I am, yes." He tried to mimic that accent he'd heard the Welshmen use.

It must have been good enough, because the man dragged him to the door. "That's it. We're out of here. The diversion next door won't last forever." *Oh God, what does that mean?* "Okay, kid, you've been useful," he said to Merlin. "You can come. Give me any trouble and I'll plug you right between the eyes."

"Yes, sir." Merlin dutifully fell into step with the others.

As Mateo was hustled outside, the sound of gunfire met his ears. It was coming from the club and Mateo nearly doubled over from the sudden understanding of why Christos and the rest of the family members hadn't come to their rescue. Two SUVs with tinted windows idled at the mouth of the alley.

"Aren't we going to wait for the others?" one of the men said.

Shoving Mateo into the back seat of the first vehicle, the leader replied, "Naw, they're already dead. They were never going to make it back. We were the real mission. They were a distraction. More Krugerrands for us, huh, boys?"

They all laughed at that as they climbed into the vehicles. Mateo was forced to scoot over to allow Merlin to sit next to him with Dafydd and Idris in the far back. Instinctively he turned to put his seat belt on, and that was when he saw Christos. The man was running out of the club toward them. His mouth was wide open with teeth bared and he was moving with a speed that almost made him blurry. He held guns in both hands. Mateo clutched the back of his seat and silently called out to him.

The SUV lurched into motion, however, and Mateo knew that all was lost. No way could Christos keep up with them. He didn't even want him to. The odds were now eight to one, counting the two drivers who'd been waiting outside—and an SUV with four men weaved between the one he rode in and the pursuing Christos. With everyone armed, those guns Christos carried wouldn't mean anything. Mateo craned his neck to get the last glimpse of his man through the sea of passengers and glass before they were separated, perhaps forever. Surprisingly, Christos was still on their tail, his legs pumping like pistons, his mouth remained wide open, as if he were screaming. A faint roaring sound reached Mateo's ears.

Then he watched in horror as the men in the second vehicle lowered their windows and fired. "No!" he screamed and tried to scramble over the seat, as if there were anything he could actually do to help.

Merlin grabbed him by the shoulders and forced him to turn back around. "Knock it off, *Brenin*. You're not doing yourself or anyone else any favors."

Mateo balled his hands into fists, but the look on Merlin's face was not unkind and he'd let go of him. So he settled for twisting his head to get another look at what was happening instead of hitting the boy. Christos was gone and the men had pulled their heads and arms back into the vehicle. He strained to see if a body lay on the street but he couldn't tell.

Holding back tears—because he would not give these motherfuckers the satisfaction of crying—he turned his face to the front again. As they raced through the city, cop cars and emergency vehicles passed them. God, the man had said 'a diversion'. And with all that gunfire he'd heard, it must mean that they had attacked the club in force. How many were dead? At least Christos had survived that battle. Was he lying dead anyway in the fruitless effort to save Mateo? He had to believe his man wasn't, that it was lack of speed that had finally caused him to drop back. Anything else was intolerable. The hope that his boyfriend still lived would have to satisfy him, even if his own life was forfeit — or maybe not. He might simply be on his way to some foreign brothel.

And who in the world is this Dracul everyone keeps talking about, anyway?

He jumped and let out a scream when a large object landed on the front of the SUV. No, not a thing, a man. Better than that...*Christos!* The man clung to the hinge of the hood, his teeth bared as before, except now Mateo could see the fangs. And Christos' eyes were red as he stared directly at Mateo. The driver swerved back and forth to fling him clear. Nothing doing. Christos never lost his grip, even when his legs swung off for a few seconds.

"Come on and shoot the fucker," the driver yelled at his boss.

"I've got a better idea." So saying, the man twisted to point his gun directly at Mateo. He held up the other hand in front of the windshield with three fingers showing. "One." He bent a knuckle. "Two." He did the same to a second one.

He never got to three. Christos leaped off the SUV and disappeared into the night. A quick look around confirmed that he hadn't resumed his chase of the vehicles. *Thank God*. If he had, surely someone would have fired at him by simply lowering a window again. This way, at least Mateo knew Christos was alive, and Christos knew the same about him. It would have to be enough — for now.

The man in the front seat grinned before pulling his gun away from Mateo's face. "The boss was right. These guys have a soft spot for civilians. Head directly to the landing strip, but don't speed. You got to figure most of the Boston cops are busy dealing with the carnage back there, but we still don't want any trouble."

Mateo curled away as best he could from Merlin, not sure of what the kid was up to and wanting as much space to himself as he could manage. His brain was misfiring from all the shocking information he had to process. There was no question now that all of that teasing about where Christos had come from and being a vampire hadn't been so funny after all. It hurt to think that any of this was real. Maybe he'd been sick all this time and was in some kind of weird coma-state or something. He pinched his arm, just to see if it hurt.

And fuck yeah, it did. This was actually happening, and the sooner he accepted that and started making plans on how to get out of it, the better. He'd survived worse. Well, maybe not worse, but bad stuff had happened to him and he knew he was tough. These men with guns were just that — men. He knew how to deal with them.

Gathering his courage, he said, "So where are you taking us, Daddy?" He put as much Welsh-sounding sugar in his tone as he could and silently asked Christos for his forgiveness.

This was about survival, and he bet that like Hawkeye in *The Last of the Mohicans*, Christos would find him, no matter what. He'd called Mateo 'his love' and he had to believe his man had meant it. He also wished he'd mounted the courage to say the words back. It had seemed too soon to make such a commitment, to agree to return to Greece with him and give up the only life he'd known, shitty as it had been. So he'd kept quiet, while making plans that might never occur now. There was nothing to be done about that, and his only job at this point was to stay alive to be there to greet Christos when he found him.

The leader turned his head and sneered. "Pretty cunts need to keep their mouths shut or I'll find something to stuff it with, and it won't be my cock." He nodded at a spot behind Mateo's head.

A slap sent him reeling against the window a second later. He got the message.

* * * *

Christos leaped from the roof of the building that housed the family and landed in the alley between it and the club. He'd been forced to go vertical to make his way back as quickly as possible without arousing suspicion. He still seethed at how he'd failed. All he could do now, though, was see how bad things were, both in the home and the club. The emergency vehicles had already begun arriving. It seemed as if every cop and ambulance in Boston had been dispatched to the scene. He quickly ducked and headed to the family building, scared to death of what he would find.

They have Mateo was all he could think, though, as he pursued his terrible duty. Although it made no sense to him. Dafydd and Idris, whom he'd glimpsed in the first SUV, were obvious choices. Dracul wanted them back because no one took his toys away. It didn't take much analysis to get why Merlin had been among them, either. That hybrid had always been a wildcard. Apparently, Annika's influence hadn't been as great as they'd thought, and he fervently prayed that it wasn't because the Queen lay dead. The boy was obviously returning to his sire's fold. The fact must be devastating to Alun…if the man still lived.

Demi stumbled out of the side door before he reached it. The boy's face was bruised, but at least he was alive. It gave Christos hope that others were as well.

He held out his hands to help the boy. "Jesus, Demi, are you all right?" There didn't seem to be any wounds on him.

"I'm fine. Just a bruised jaw, thanks to Merlin. The fucker joined Dracul's goons."

Putting aside that detail for the moment, he asked, "How bad is it in there?"

"Dafydd, Idris and Mateo have been taken."

"I know. I gave chase, but…" He shook his head.

"There was nothing you could have done. I'm glad to see they didn't kill you. The rest of the family are alive and unharmed, except Tony's been shot. He needs my father. Harry," he clarified. Then, Demi clutched Christos' arm. "*Are* they alive, my fathers? What happened at the club?"

He ignored the last question because there were no words and there was no time to describe what had gone down. "I think they're both fine. Lucien is probably somewhere safe over there. Harry would have made sure of that, and I didn't see him in the thick of the fight. I'll get him. Go back to the others."

Dumping his weapons so the cops wouldn't see them, he bolted to the side door of the club and headed for the main room. He immediately ran into Lucien.

The changeling grabbed him much as his son had. "Demi?"

"Alive," he wasted no time confirming. "Just a little banged up. Tony needs Harry, though. Where is he?"

"Helping with the wounded." Lucien made a face. "He made me shelter in place with the kitchen staff once the shooting started. I have to get home, no matter what he says." He paused and licked his lips. "How many casualties over there besides Tony?"

"Demi says none."

Lucien closed his eyes. "Thank God."

"There's more." He told him about the ones who'd been taken, his voice stuttering as he said Mateo's name.

"We will get them back," Lucien said fiercely before taking off.

The reassurance was oddly comforting. He pressed on to the one thing he could do for the moment, however. When he arrived at his destination, it was as horrific as he'd remembered it. People lay moaning or sat on the floor, shell-shocked. Police and other first responders were milling about. The dead were where they'd dropped. Val and Claude were careful to keep their unarmed hands were they could be seen by the cops as they assessed who were the bad guys and who were the victims. All the weaponry was in piles on the ground. Christos raised his hands, too, as he approached his friends.

"Yaro is fine," he called out to Claude before finding Harry. The man was on his knees, holding a compress to Kitty's shoulder. "Harry, you need to get to Tony quickly. Demi says he's been shot."

Harry popped to his feet. "How is my son?"

"Bruised, that's all. Now go. Lucien is already over there. I'll look after Ms. Kitty."

"I'm fine," she ground out. "It's Logan who needs help." Her voice hitched and tears streamed down her face.

Harry shook his head once before taking off. *Aw, Jesus, no.* Christos looked at the dance floor and saw Emil kneeling there with Logan in his arms. His white jacket was covered in blood and gore. Jase clung to him, crying quietly. With his hands still raised so as not to alarm the freaked-out cops, Christos approached the scene. Logan wasn't dead. Not yet.

"Hang on, damn you," Emil was saying. "The EMTs are here."

Logan managed a weak grin. "Like they can help when Harry can't," she rasped. "Sorry. I was hoping to make it to the last dance, you know?" She coughed, pink foam leaking past her lips. "You gave me back a whole year of my life when I thought I'd already lost it, so no mewling about this. Just get the fucker for me."

"I will," Emil vowed. "*We* will. It won't be the same without you."

Logan coughed again and her eyes rolled back. "Fuck yeah, it won't."

Emil held her tight to his chest and rocked her body back and forth while Jase sobbed loudly now. Christos left them to their private grief and caught Alex's eye. The man sat on the floor with Quinn on his lap, a cloth already tied around the boy's arm. The boy Quinn had been shielding was near them, curled into a ball and weeping silently. Quinn was holding one of his hands in quiet reassurance, even though his own eyes were glassy and unfocused. For the first time ever, Christos saw an expression of utter devastation on his captain's face. It was too painful to look at.

It was a relief when he focused on the entryway to see that among the many people swarming into the place were Duncan and his partner, Anderson. While he didn't know either of them well, he knew they were dedicated allies and a good buffer with the other humans, who would be asking tough questions very soon. The blond cop ran straight to Kitty and pulled her into his arms while calling for an EMT. Duncan headed toward Christos, who met him halfway.

"Demi's all right," he said before the cop could ask, because of course, that would be first on his mind.

Duncan staggered for a moment. "Thank Jesus, Joseph and Mary."

"But you need to try to cut off any investigation into next door. They blew the front door and took Dafydd, Idris and Mateo. Someone is bound to notice the damage and tie that in to what happened here. We can't afford for anyone to see something they shouldn't, like Tony dying and turning to dust." Damn, his heart ached at the thought of losing someone else.

Duncan's look of terror subsided when the news about Demi sank in more fully. "This isn't my case officially. Karl and I heard it over dispatch and confirmed we were going in to help. I'll do what I can, though. And who the fuck is Mateo? Wait! You mean that kid who helped bring Cadoc down? Why in the hell was he even here?"

Christos got into his face. "Because he's my boy, that's why."

The cop backed off. "Okay, okay, sorry. I didn't know and I'll take care of the mess next door. Then I'll help you get Mateo and the others back. I am so done with this Dracul shit. It's time for him to die and stay that way."

Before the man could leave, however, another familiar face came storming in. "Fuck me, what's *he* doing here?" Christos muttered.

Jefferson scanned the carnage before homing in on Christos. "Was Alun here? Is he hurt?" he called out as he made a beeline for him.

"How the...?" Duncan rounded on his colleague. "Jefferson, this is a homicide matter."

"Fuck that! This shitshow is being screamed all over dispatch and I recognized the club's name." He swiveled his head around. "It's a fucking war zone. Answer my question," he demanded of Christos.

"He's fine and not here." Then he made an executive decision, because someone had to take charge and Alex was too caught up with Quinn. "Do you trust him?" he asked with a nod toward Jefferson.

Duncan nodded. "Yeah, I do."

"Take him with you. Damage control is going to be a bitch, and the sooner we recover from all this, the faster we can rain unholy justice on Dracul's head."

Grabbing Jefferson by the sleeve, Duncan said, "Come on. If you're going to be here, you have to be useful. And you can see Alun, too, although how and why you care is something you and I are going to have a little talk about."

"Fuck you, you're not my mother. And who the fuck is Dracul?"

"That's right, Craig. Exercise that F-bomb good. You're going to need it."

Christos stood watching them go, feeling drained and oddly numb. The fury was there, bubbling beneath the surface, but he felt more cold than hot. Well, the Italians always said that revenge was a dish best served cold. He was going freeze Dracul's skin off his body, bit by bit, if it was the last thing he did on this Earth.

"Sir?" He glanced at a young woman wearing an EMT uniform. "Do you need medical attention? Are you hurt?" she persisted when he said nothing.

He shook his head slowly. "Not in a way that you can help."

"Are you sure? Your leg appears to be bleeding."

Looking down, he said, "So it is. It's nothing. A scratch." He put a hand to his chest and rubbed a spot that oddly ached far more than his leg. "Please do not concern yourself. I am beyond human help and have always been so."

A stretcher was carried past him with a crying boy strapped onto it. Christos turned in a slow circle, taking in the sadness and the misery, and mentally slapped himself. *Time to get to work.* Mateo was counting on him.

Chapter Eleven

"The top story this morning continues to be the horrific mass shooting at the private gay nightclub Lux. The official casualty toll remains at forty dead and twenty-seven wounded, some critically. That number includes an estimated two dozen assailants, whom our sources on the police force are unofficially saying were white supremacists intent on waging war against homosexuals. There is no word yet on whether any of the dead or wounded are the owners of the club, who are no strangers to controversy and are associated with other tragic events of the last year. Among those killed was former Marine Gunnery Sergeant Karen Logan, who is being hailed by many as a hero who defended unarmed club members and employees without any concern for her own safety. The President has ordered flags in federal buildings to be lowered to half-mast in her honor."

Christos grabbed the remote and turned off the TV. No one needed to hear anything more. They'd lived through it and the only concern was what kind of spin was being given to the event. They had the answer now. He looked at Jefferson, who sat on one of the many chairs that had been moved to the living area. At any given time, the whole space was crowded with family, allies and lovers. They all seemed to need the comfort of being together. Christos was no different. Being in his bed without Mateo was an impossible thought. That was true even given that they'd never actually spent time in that particular room together.

"Was that your doing?" he asked the cop.

Jefferson nodded. "Given that I wasn't part of the official investigation, I had time on my hands after helping to hide what happened here. It was easy enough to whisper in the ears of reporters milling about, to plant the idea. It helps that so many of the fuckers looked like skinheads and actually had fascist tattoos. I think the story will stick."

"I'll jump on various message boards and give it more legs." This from Val, who came in with Alex.

"Are the cops done with you?" Christos asked. They'd all been questioned, but as the owner of the club and the head of security, Alex and Val had been pulled aside a few different times. Even the fucking FBI was involved. Duncan had weighed in on thorny issues like who owned the various weapons that had been recovered. Thank God, Val had sanitized all the identifying marks from the guns long ago, and no one seemed to question the idea that most of them belonged to the attackers.

Alex nodded. "They're done with us for the time being. The CSI people are also almost finished. There's plenty of evidence, even without the security footage."

"Yeah," Val drawled. "Shame about that shorting out earlier in the day. Lucky for us, too, that the members abide by the no-mobile-phone-use-inside-the-club rule. Most of them didn't even have theirs on them to video the firefight, even if they'd thought to do so. There's no visual evidence of our more otherworldly feats, and given the chaos and fog of war, no one's going to believe that they saw what they think they saw, either."

"Come get something to eat," Emil called out to them.

The room was littered with food of all types. Emil and Jase had cooked and baked non-stop ever since Logan had been pried from them. The activity was obviously their way of coping, but no one had much of an appetite.

Neither man took him up on his offer. Instead, both went to where their boys sat on the couch and, picking them up, settled in their place with the boys on their laps. Quinn's arm injury was mostly superficial and a feeding from Alex had done wonders to help the healing process. Mackie was entirely untouched — thanks to Annika, apparently.

The Queen was quiet and unusually somber, her hand repetitively petting the fluffy head of her ridiculous dog — although she was not alone in her melancholy, that being the watchword for them all at this point. There was little to do except mourn for the time being. Christos itched with the need to go do...something. As there was no clear direction to chase, he had no choice but to sit and ponder what to do.

"I'll run all of this over to *Our Safe Place* later," Malcolm said, waving at the food. "With the front door fixed, I have time on my hands."

"I'll go with you," Val volunteered. "I want to check out the human security team I've hired for it. They and the staff that has been vetted recently can take over the running of the place so that none of us have to worry about making the time."

Emil came over, his arm tightly wrapped around Jase. "That's just as well. Our presence makes it an obvious target, but I don't want to shutter it. It was important to Logan, and we can't leave those kids in the lurch."

"We'll take care of everyone, including our employees here," Alex vowed. "How much severance is enough, do you suppose? A year, certainly. It doesn't seem sufficient somehow. Five, I think, and I'll keep track of them all, in case they need more help later."

"You're closing the club?" Mackie asked with a quiver to his voice.

"Well, of course. With a dozen prominent men murdered, I doubt the city will allow it to re-open, and even if they did, who would want to risk returning for a repeat? Besides, I should have done so when Dracul first resurfaced. If I had, none of this would have happened. How did I not see this coming?" Alex's devastated expression hadn't really left since Christos had first seen it at the club.

He wanted to reassure his captain, a strange reversal of roles. "You couldn't have known, sir. None of us thought he'd go this route. And if you hadn't had the club, he would have found some other, equally violent action to divert your attention. When has he ever done anything else?"

Alex pressed his face against Quinn's head. "I should have killed him from the first. The moment he started questioning my actions, I should have eliminated him."

Christos shook his head. "That's not the kind of man or leader you are. And if you had, it wouldn't have stopped there. He was the first to rebel, but others would have done so, too, even without him. Petru comes to mind."

Val snapped his fingers. "Damn, I haven't been able to slip into the basement yet. I don't want to call attention to it. Because the crime scene is in the main room and lap dance area, the cops don't have a warrant to search the entire building. He's going to have to go hungry a while longer, I suppose."

Christos bared his teeth. "Let him starve to death. The fucker hasn't been much use so far."

Annika leaned forward. "No, Mr. Christos, Petru has a role to play yet in all of this."

He didn't have a chance to dare to gainsay her. Duncan and Dr. Paz came in at that moment. He didn't think the cop had slept, like much of the rest of them, although for a human, the deprivation was more noticeable. The doctor looked the way Christos felt, weighed down by the heavy grief and worry that came from knowing that the man he loved was in the clutches of pure evil. For Paz, it was doubly so, because he'd obviously come to think of Idris as his son.

Paz headed straight for Emil. "I'm sorry," he said gently, "Logan's family has claimed her body. I know you wanted to give her a more personal send-off."

Emil nodded grimly. "They didn't care when she was on the streets, but I guess a dead hero is better, heh? That's okay, Doc. We said our goodbyes to her already." He hugged Jase tight as the boy started crying.

Paz turned to look at Mackie. "No one has claimed Shawn yet. The other two have family on their way."

Mackie swiped at a tear. "I'm not surprised. Shawn was literally an orphan. No one will see to him."

"We will," Val declared. "Whatever you think he'd have liked, that's what we'll do." Mackie nodded and curled into the man's embrace. Val placed his large hand on his husband's baby bump and left it there.

They were all quiet for long minutes, each lost in their own thoughts. Christos' were on Mateo, naturally, although he tried to banish images of his boy being hurt. That wasn't going to help anyone. Besides, the human had survived the brutality of Cadoc and he had the street smarts to stay alive, no matter what it took. The idea of Dracul or others forcing themselves on him, into his sweet body, made Christos want to smash whatever he could get his hands on. He would have to settle for waiting until they found Dracul's lair. He would take it and everyone lurking there apart, piece by piece.

Harry came down the stairs, his every step a testament to his fatigue. Claude trailed him, looking much the same. "Tony remains stable." That news sent a wave of noticeable relief through the group. At least they weren't going to lose another shipmate. "Mikko and Matti are staying by his side until he's strong enough to leave. Tony is against the idea, needless to say, but Mikko is adamant and I concur. His wounds are healing in the natural way of our kind, but they are also extensive, and he won't be at full strength for some time to come."

"I'm sending Nen and Yaro with them back to Finland," Claude added. "Their homestead is more isolated and more easily defensible than mine. Even at less than full strength, I trust Tony to protect my family if Dracul does bother with them." He focused on Alex. "I'm sorry, sir. I don't believe this is the best place for them anymore."

"I understand. You should go with them. I'm sorry I brought you back into the fray."

Claude's eyes turned flinty. "No, sir. I'm in this 'til the end. We can't know how many other humans Dracul has recruited. You need the manpower."

"Your family—"

"Understands my duty. We've discussed it and made a unanimous decision. The fate of this world and their lives depend on our wiping that fucker out for good. You need me, and I'm staying." He looked at Emil. "I need to fill a tray with food for them as they pack, as well as for Mikko and Matti, because they won't leave Tony's side. Will you help me do that?"

Emil smiled wanly. "Of course. We both will." With that, he and Jase uncoupled and headed back to the kitchen area.

Christos sighed and ran a weary hand down his face. "He's not wrong about needing him," he said to Alex. "We all know how cheap and easy it is to buy soldiers, even after you sacrifice a couple of dozen. Mercenaries always think it's the other guy who's going to get killed, while they survive and get rich."

"Yeah," Val agreed. "We could be facing a fucking legion of them."

"Plus, he has at least one hybrid on his side now, too." *Damn Merlin to hell and back.* Showing mercy to everyone who had been left in Dracul's castle had turned out to be a mistake, in his estimation. The other hybrids may have been very young children, but Merlin had been of fighting age.

"No, Mr. Val, you are wrong." Everyone stared at Annika as if she had two heads, including himself. "Merlin is our ally."

Malcolm spoke for all of them. "Och now, lassie, I know you like to see the good in everyone, but that boy is lost to us. We have to consider him our enemy now."

She gave him an indulgent smile. "I assure you that is not the case. He is what you'd call a mole. Did I say that right?" she asked no one in particular.

"She's telling the truth." This from Alun, who'd been lurking outside the circle of people for some time. Now, he stood close to Jefferson's chair, a curious fact that Christos didn't bother to ponder. There were bigger issues to worry about at the moment, and with the cop now privy to the truth, there was nothing to be concerned with anyway.

Alun stared at the ground for a few seconds, playing with strands of his hair in his usual shy way. Then he lifted his chin and faced everyone head on. "When he...attacked me, he whispered something." There was a long pause. "He said to trust him, that he knew what he was doing and that he'd find a way to communicate with us as soon as he could. And... he apologized right before he knocked me unconscious by slamming my head into the wall. He's never said those words to me before without Annika's prompting."

Christos barked out a laugh. "And you believed him? After everything you've been through, surely you know that no one influenced by Dracul can be trusted."

"Dafydd can," Paz declared hotly.

"He was a victim," Christos explained. Surely his point was obvious. "Merlin was raised by a shipmate who instilled in him the monstrous ethos of them all. Why would he change at this point?"

"Because of me, Mr. Christos. I am a far stronger force than Dracul could ever be. Merlin belongs to me, not that wicked drone." Annika punctuated her statement by placing kisses on the top of her dog's fluffy head.

He couldn't argue with the Queen, not when she looked down her nose at everyone with righteous certainty. *Dare I hope that Merlin is the key to finding Mateo?* Just thinking it made that spot in his chest ache more. He rubbed at it. "How will he help?" He heard himself ask.

"When he can manage it without arousing suspicion, he's going to send the information about their location, strength of numbers and any security systems to Mr. Val's server. I gave him the access codes, which I ferreted out during one of my lessons."

"Fuck me," was all Val said.

Alex narrowed his gaze. "It would seem, my Queen, that you've been a few steps ahead of us all along. How much further do your plans extend?"

Annika didn't answer. Instead, she added, "It will be very hard, but we must be patient. Dracul will not trust Merlin right away. We can't know how long it will take him to find an opportunity to contact us."

Christos rose. He couldn't help it. If he sat any longer, his head would explode. "In the meantime, he has Mateo. What's Dracul going to do when he sees the boy and realizes they didn't take Brenin after all?" That had been the nagging question in the back of his mind all along.

"Make another attempt to get him," Malcolm spat out. "And heaven help them if they try." He pulled Brenin to his side and hugged him tight enough to make the boy grunt.

Christos rounded on his friend. "I mean to Mateo! What's to stop him from killing him on the spot?" *Oh God.* This was the thought he'd been trying to keep out of his head, that Mateo wouldn't even have a chance to stay alive.

"And he has Dafydd," Paz chimed in. "Idris is who he wants. Dafydd is who he wants to *kill*. We can't afford to sit around waiting for some kid to shine a fucking bat signal for us."

Jefferson cleared his throat. "Excuse me, folks. I know I'm new to all of this. Frankly, I'm not sure I'm not in a padded room somewhere hallucinating. Anyway, from what little I understand about this Dracul fucker, he's a sadist, right?"

"Genocidal maniac is probably more accurate," Duncan said, "but, yeah."

"So, he's got this guy — Dafydd, is it? — who crossed him, and he wanted our guy, Brenin, here, too for the same reason. Right?" When everyone murmured an assent, the cop continued. "Okay, so this isn't exactly comforting, but if I were him, I wouldn't want to, you know, end the fun too soon. Do you feel me?"

"He'll torture Dafydd. Is what you're saying." Christos understood the logic. When Paz made a wounded sound, he added, "As awful as it is, the man has a point. Killing Dafydd right away would be merciful, to Dracul's way of thinking. And the asshole has none."

Brenin pulled away from Malcolm to go hug Paz. "Dafydd is strong, Ric. You know that, and I've seen how well he managed to survive that abuse. We have to believe he will do so again. He has everything to live for now…you and Idris."

Paz nodded as he clung to the boy. "You're right. He can hold on, and I'll be there to help him when the time comes. I'm not going to be left behind," he added fiercely to the room at large.

"Of course you won't," Alex assured him.

"And what does that mean for Mateo?" Christos could easily imagine that Dracul's fury over the mistake could spill onto his sweet boy.

Once again, Jefferson interjected with reassurance. "Look... We've got a murderous sexual predator on our hands, yeah? He'll be mad that it's not Brenin, but come on... Mateo is pretty and sexy."

Christos hissed at the implication.

Jefferson barely blinked. The man had accepted a lot of hard truths in a short amount of time. Perhaps it was because he was in shock. "And Mateo's savvy," the man said. "You must know that. Why would this fucker do away with someone better suited to be put to his own use?" The cop leaned forward as Christos fought not to slam his fist through the coffee table. "I know this is hard, but doesn't it make more sense for him to keep the kid as a toy and take his anger out on the guy who made the mistake of grabbing the wrong boy?"

Now Christos did give vent to his fury, bringing his fist down like a hammer and splitting the large wooden table in two. Hearing his own thoughts said out loud didn't make him feel any better and he simply couldn't contain his fury and frustration any longer. Cups went flying and platters of food careened into each other and onto the floor. He stood staring at the damage, his chest heaving as he fought to regain control. The dog jumped out of its mistress' arms and tackled some nearby ham. At least someone was enjoying themselves.

"Yes," he finally choked out. "Damn you, yes. He'll keep Mateo for his own pleasure, and the boy knows how to survive. He'll make himself indispensable."

Gesturing to the mess, he added, "Sorry… I'll clean this."

Alun started gathering the cups. "It's all right. I'll do it. Being at loose ends doesn't suit me, so I'm happy with the mindless distraction. No one was eating anyway, and I can salvage most of the food for the homeless children."

Too tired to argue the point, he nodded and murmured his thanks. "We can't rely solely on Merlin." He looked at Alex, who turned to Val.

"Have we made any progress on surveilling those five possible sites?"

Val nodded. "We're down to four, thanks to Petru."

"With leads to the most likely site among those remaining," he added. *God*, had it really been a mere twenty-four hours since they'd questioned the man and made jokes about the efficacy of Tony's explosives?

Has it only been a day since I admitted out loud to others that I love Mateo?

He rounded on Val. "Show me how I can be of more help, and for fuck's sake, let's get Petru out of his cell and on the job, too. He's been doing the bare minimum so far. If we're worried about him running, I'll tie him to my waist if I have to." And a thought occurred to him. "Surely we'll see if there's been any recent activity at any of those sites in the last forty-eight hours. Maybe we'll even see them bring our people in."

Val nodding. "Fucking A, you may be on to something. They must have left by way of a private airport, but they have to land somewhere and transport their prisoners to the final destination somehow." He placed Mackie gently on the sofa before standing. "Let's go see if we can sneak past the CSI people who are left."

Duncan and Jefferson also got to their feet. "We can help you there."

"Excellent." Christos pounded his fist in the other hand. "Because I'm not going to sit around while my boy is out there. We're going to bring this fight to Dracul again, and this time, he won't survive."

Hang on, Agápi mou, *I'm coming for you.*

* * * *

Mateo had lost track of the time. He didn't have a phone and wouldn't have been able to keep one regardless, given the thorough search his captors had performed once they were airborne. It was predictable, really. Whatever rules these fuckers were operating under, they'd still managed to cop some heavy-duty feels. His balls still ached from the squeezing. And they'd done the same to Dafydd, who'd weathered everything with a stony expression that spooked him a lot. Merlin had hissed and bared his fangs at them when they'd tried it on with him. Not surprisingly, their captors had backed off fast. Weird how something like vampire teeth seemed almost commonplace to him at this point.

Even Idris had been searched, his diaper ripped open and tossed aside. Mateo had worried that they were all in for a whole bunch of pee and poop, given that the idiots hadn't brought any baby stuff with them. The toddler surprised him by being able to hold it and use the toilet, when they were allowed such courtesies. Food wasn't readily available, either, and it was rather atrocious when it was given, but the baby was able to eat that, as well, and with a lot more of an appetite than the rest of them had. He was too young to understand just how completely fucked they were.

Small mercies.

They had changed planes at least once, although even in the daylight, he couldn't tell where they were...somewhere desolate and chilly. The clothing he'd been wearing didn't offer much protection against the cold. By the time they deplaned at their final destination, the sun was setting. He didn't see much except desert before being hustled none-too-gently into a large truck. The flap in the back was lowered, leaving them mostly in the dark. He leaned toward Dafydd, because the alternative was one of the men who was particularly handsy when given the chance. Merlin sat opposite them, being quiet and mostly compliant at every step. Mateo still couldn't figure out the guy's angle. Regardless, he couldn't afford to trust him.

The ride was long, bumpy and nauseating. The only relief from the boredom was trying to help Dafydd amuse Idris so that the kid didn't start screaming. It was remarkable how calm he'd been, especially as Mateo himself found it hard not to bawl his eyes out. Finally, they first slowed then came to a stop. The back flap opened to reveal the leader of the men silhouetted by a dingy backdrop. They were all dragged out and marched through a set of large wooden doors. There was a smell of mustiness, as if the place hadn't been aired out in years.

Sand littered the floor of the hallway they walked down before a set of stairs sent them even lower. They were greeted by more men with guns, all of whom looked as if they'd answered the same casting call for anyone who naturally looked like a mercenary. There were a lot of shaved heads and beady, soulless eyes —

and cammies, so many cammies, like they'd cleaned out the local Army Navy stores. The dress code would have been the envy of most ten-year-old boys. The men didn't scare him as much as they might have, because his boyfriend put them all to shame in the badass arena. Plus, they weren't vampires, so that was a clear disadvantage in his mind.

Dafydd shook beside him, subtly yet obviously. Unlike Mateo, he knew what they were heading for. It obviously wasn't good, and notwithstanding the men around them, he had to assume that this Dracul character was a vampire, too. It was in the name, so...*yeah*. He couldn't help wondering if he was in for a Bela Lugosi type or one of the more modern sexy incarnations. It didn't matter. Regardless, Mateo would do his best to keep himself alive by amusing the creature. And of course, the moment he thought it, he realized where *the Creature* had come from. This was undoubtedly the undesirable relative of whom Christos had spoken. A shiver ran through him before he steeled his spine. There was no room for that kind of nonsense. He could do this.

Another corridor led to a final set of doors that opened soundlessly in the middle when pulled by two men stationed on either side of them. The room they entered was something out of the Arabian Nights, with plush Persian rugs and silk wall hangings. Some kind of spicy incense permeated the place. At the far end sat a man on a chair that was almost throne-like. As he got closer, Mateo noticed that the guy fit none of his expectations.

This guy was *ugly*. His black hair was choppy, as if it had been pulled out in hunks, and his face was marred by scars, as was his chest, which was on full display because he wore only an open silk robe over loose pants of similar material. Keeping this guy happy wasn't going to be a picnic, but he could have been Adonis for all it mattered to Mateo. He wanted Christos and no other man.

Beside him, clad in a thong, was a beautiful boy with striped hair. On closer inspection, he had mismatched eyes as well. There was something definitely not quite human about him. His expression brought the definition of smug to a whole new level — except when he caught sight of Mateo, it turned flinty. The main man, Dracul, didn't so much as glance at him, however. His gaze was fixed on Dafydd. A tremor ran through the poor guy and his arms tightened around Idris.

Dracul gave him a toothsome smile. "My dear Dafydd, back in the fold. How wonderful it is to see you again." The tone was gag-worthy, oily and menacing in equal measure. It was amazing that Dafydd had the strength to stay upright.

"Nothing to say, cunt? No matter… I'm sure I'll manage to tease some kind of sound out of your traitorous mouth soon." His eyes widened. "And you've brought me my son. My, isn't he a big, strapping boy? Bring him to me," he barked at the striped boy.

The guy slunk toward Dafydd with his hands extended. "Come here, sweetie. I'm Andri, your new daddy."

Dafydd took a half-step back, but with the armed men standing in a semi-circle behind them, there was nowhere to go. Idris clung to his father, his face buried in the crook of the man's neck. Andri grabbed hold of his little waist and tried to pry him out of Dafydd's arms. The tug-of-war raged for a few tense seconds before Merlin stepped in.

"Here, let me." He actually hip-checked Andri out of the way and put his own hands on Idris' small body. "Idris, you know me. Let go now."

The toddler only hesitated a second or two before releasing his grip on his father and twisting to hold his arms out to Merlin. Dafydd didn't let go right away, however. Some look passed between him and Merlin before he handed his son over. Then he covered his mouth to stifle a sob.

Merlin smirked at Andri. "See how easy it is?" Ignoring the boy's efforts to take Idris from him, Merlin instead approached Dracul. "Master." He somehow managed to bow low while still holding the baby.

Dracul's eyes narrowed. "I know you. Your sire was loyal to the end, for as much good as it did me. He was an idiot." He shrugged. "Then again, they all were, so I suppose I can't hold that against you. Why are you here?"

"To serve you, Master. I was taken against my will and held captive by those who betrayed you." He actually spat to one side before rubbing the moisture into the carpet with his foot.

"Hm-m. You might prove useful. Give me my son."

Merlin didn't hesitate to hand over Idris to Dracul, who beamed as he sat the kid on his lap. Idris stuck his thumb in his mouth while staring at...*his father?* The parentage situation was confusing as hell. There had been no chance to ask any questions during their journey, but Mateo was curious as to how this double-father thing had occurred. He had a sickish kind of feeling that adoption or surrogacy was not part of the equation.

Dracul laughed as he regarded the kid. "What a strong lad you are, hm-m? Of course, my son would be so, although one worried what harm was being done to you living among all of those weak-willed dogs. No matter... I will teach you what it means to be a true warrior."

He switched his attention to the mercenaries' leader. "Has he been fed properly?"

"Yes, sir. He ate some of our MREs."

Andri rounded on the man. "I gave you formula!"

The man shrugged. "I didn't see any. It must have been with the other group's supplies. The kid did okay with regular food."

"Huh. He probably needs changing." Andri reached to take Idris.

"No," Merlin interjected, "he's toilet trained." By his tone and expression, it was clear that he was enjoying his role of bursting Andri's parenting bubbles.

"Let me take him from you, Master. I'll settle him into his new room."

Dracul waved him away, his focus suddenly and uncomfortably on Mateo. "Who the fuck is this?" His gaze swiveled around the room. "And where the fuck is that other Welsh slut?"

The mercenary leader stepped forward with obvious trepidation, hidden behind bravado. "This is him, sir." He pointed at Mateo.

Dracul's face twisted in rage. "You think I'm incapable of recognizing the hole I stuck my cock into for months?" He switched his gaze to Mateo before the guy could sputter out an answer to that clearly rhetorical question. "Who are you, cunt?"

He wanted to curl into a ball and suck his thumb, much like Idris was doing. Instead, he thought of Christos and drew power from the image. Putting his hands on his hips, he said, "I'm Mateo, Daddy." The saucy reply seemed to mollify the man some.

The mercenary was too stupid to stay quiet. "That guy said he was the one you were looking for." He fingered Merlin as the fuck-up.

The boy didn't seem fazed by the accusation. He shrugged. "One slut looks much like the other. He was the toy of one of your enemies, though. That much I can promise you. So, that's kind of fun, don't you think, Master?"

"Hm-m." Dracul didn't look entirely convinced. "I suppose it will have to do. I assume you know what to do with my dick to encourage me to keep you alive?"

Swallowing his fear back, he said, "Yes, Daddy. You won't be disappointed."

"I'm sure I won't. If so, I'll throw you to these dogs."

Mateo was careful to pout as if the idea only disappointed him instead of him being terrifying.

Andri sidled closer to Dracul. "You don't need him, Master. I can give you the pleasure you crave."

"Shut up." Dracul casually back-handed the boy while continuing to dandle his son on his knee.

Holy shit, is this guy a complete psycho?

Andri stumbled, yet went right back to where he'd been, and there was both anger and excitement shining through his eyes.

"I suppose I'll have to be satisfied with the limited success of the mission." Dracul eyed the mercenary. "Count yourself lucky that I need all the men I have at the moment or you'd be my lunch. Here… Take the boy and get him settled," he added, shoving Idris at Andri.

The boy was delighted with his charge. Idris less so. As they left the room, the toddler set to wailing. With a whimper, Dafydd curled in on himself, his fist pressed against his mouth. He didn't stay in that position long. Dracul hissed and sprang from his seat. He had Dafydd by the hair in a millisecond and slapped him, sending him to his knees.

Mateo gasped. He was afraid to look away because he didn't want to show weakness. Dracul would exploit any he could find. Yet watching the abuse was horrifying and he also wanted to give Dafydd a measure of privacy as he struggled to survive it. The man deserved that respect. It was Merlin, in the end, who took the choice out of his hands. He pulled Mateo against him and covered his eyes with his hand. Now, he couldn't see, but he could hear. And that was nearly as awful.

"Did you think you could escape me? You are mine and you don't go until I say so. I'm going to enjoy teaching you lessons all over again before I drain you dry."

"I'm going to enjoy seeing you turned to dust." Dafydd's defiant statement was rewarded with something that made him scream.

"Get him out of here. Where is that new slut?"

Merlin took his hand away and shoved Mateo forward. The force of Dracul's stare was temporarily blocked by the sight of a bloody Dafydd being dragged out of the room by two men. Mateo had only a moment to feel pity for the man before he had to focus on his own problems.

Dracul crooked his finger as he returned to his chair. He shoved his waistband past a hard and mangled cock. Being an abusive asshole turned him on, apparently. Dracul pointed at the thing. "Show me how much you want to live, cunt. We'll start with your mouth and see how that goes." From a nearby table, he grabbed a goblet and stared at Merlin over the rim. "You may stay and learn something... What is your name?"

"Merlin, Master."

He took a sip of his drink. "Really? How utterly unoriginal. I am waiting, slut."

Now that the time had come, his instinct to survive warred with his bone-deep fright and revulsion. It took a discreet push from Merlin to get Mateo's feet moving. *I can do this.* This was just another trick. He would get the guy off quickly and take his reward. Maybe he'd be allowed to rest and eat something hot, even tend to Dafydd. This was nothing new to him. Except now he'd experienced the wonder of Christos. He'd known decency and even found love. It was hard to go back to the life of a street rat after that.

As he sank to his knees, he reminded himself that this was all in service to getting back to that wonderful place — back to his love.

* * * *

"Here... It's fruit juice. It will clear the taste."

Mateo pushed up on one arm and accepted the cup Dafydd had offered. The drink was room temperature, which was to say warm, but sweet, and it eased his dry throat. "Thanks. I should be helping you, not the other way around. He didn't beat me, after all."

Dafydd carded Mateo's hair away from his face. "I'd rather take the beating, truth be told. It's only pain."

Mateo grinned at him before lying down on a pretty, soft rug and pillows. As prisons went, this wasn't so bad. A bit stifling perhaps. That was the worst of it. There was a commode and a sink in one corner, complete with both soap and toilet paper. It was much better than the rat-invested hellhole he'd been expecting when they'd dragged him away from Dracul. He was also pathetically grateful to be roomed with Dafydd. He'd been afraid they'd be separated. Misery was easier to handle when he had a friend with him.

"And I'd rather be skull-fucked than punched," he replied. "Lucky us... We're both getting what we want." Even as he said the words, he knew he'd gotten off lightly for the time being. Worse would come later.

Dafydd put the cup back on the small table, which held a pitcher. "Anything is preferable to having Idris taken from me. I know he's being cared for, because Dracul's ego demands it. Still..." He coughed out a laugh. "It's hard to believe I once rejected him. Now I can't stand the thought of not being with him."

"I think that Andri jerk is probably doing a good Mary Poppins imitation, for his own sake. He knows he's on thin ice if he fucks up."

"You're right, of course. And there's Merlin. Whatever else he's up to, he seems to care for my son. I guess I don't want my boy to see me like this anyway," he added, touching his swollen face.

Mateo ran his finger along his upper lip, which had split from the force of Dracul's attention. "Do you...?" He couldn't bring himself to finish the question.

"What is it? Come on. You can trust me."

"I know," he was quick to assure his companion. "It's just that I was wondering if Christos is still going to want me after this." His fantasy of his boyfriend scouring the planet to rescue him faded in the face of what he'd done.

Dafydd scoffed. "Don't be daft, mun. He loves you. Nothing Dracul does will change that, the same way my Ric's feelings for me won't ever be diminished by what I do to survive."

Mateo beamed at the reassurance, which made his lip bleed again. "Damn, this is going to suck," he said, patting the sore with the tip of his finger.

"I sympathize… Believe me, I do. I heal quickly, though." He frowned. "At least I used to when I was being fed his blood. I'm not sure what happens now that I've stopped."

Mateo wrinkled his nose. "I don't understand most everything that's happening or has happened—like how you and Dracul both fathered Idris and what their being vampires is all about. Will you please explain it to me?"

Dafydd settled down beside him. "I will, yes. God knows we've got time on our hands. It all started, you see, a thousand years ago when a ship from another planet made a navigational mistake…"

Epilogue

Craig Jefferson entered his duplex apartment in Jamaica Plain and headed straight for his bed. He'd been on his feet for nearly forty-eight hours, and if he didn't get horizontal soon, he was going to pass the fuck out where he stood. That was his plan until he heard a very angry meow, reminding him that he didn't live entirely alone. He might not have a lover at the moment and couldn't have a dog, given his erratic hours. But he'd longed for some kind of companionship and, like lonely people everywhere, he'd gone for something self-sufficient. Well, mostly self-sufficient. His cat didn't hesitate to make herself known any time her needs were not being met...like now. She even dared to wind through his stumbling legs, nearly leading to a bad ending for them both.

"Damn it, Coretta, are you trying to kill us?" In response, the cat turned her green eyes on him and let out another indignant yowl. She normally paid little attention to him when he was home, so her greeting was momentarily surprising. Then, his over-tired brain did the math. "Oh, I get it. You want food." He sighed. "Sorry. I guess that's more important than my getting to sleep in the next thirty seconds."

He staggered into the kitchen and crouched to pull out one of the cans of cat food in the lower cupboard. His lack of sleep got the better of him then, causing him to lose his balance and land on his ass. Too tired to worry about it, he popped the lid off the can and dumped the smelly contents into Coretta's food bowl. With another dismissive meow, she dove in as if she'd been left unfed for days, something he knew wasn't true. One of the reasons he'd dared to get any pet was because his brother lived in the other unit with his family. They made sure Coretta was never unattended.

He watched his cat devour her food, which would keep her until the evening. A quick glance confirmed that her water bowl was full. She didn't need him for anything further, so he could focus on his own needs again. All he had to do was get to his feet and go to bed. Instead, closing his eyes, he slumped against the cabinetry.

"What are you doing sleeping on the damn kitchen floor, and why are you feeding a cat that I fed not one hour ago?"

Craig pried open his eyes to see his brother Dante walk in from the back door. "She insisted that had not happened," he told him.

"Uh-huh. She's got you wrapped around her little…whatever it is that cats have."

"Feel free to take the dish away from her."

"No way, man. That is one evil cat. I don't care if she gets fat, and I don't need the scratches." He peered at him more closely. "Damn, you're a mess. Catch a tough case?"

Craig closed his eyes briefly but opened them again when all he saw was broken bodies. That didn't bode well for sleeping. "Not really. I was helping out with the mass shooting at Club Lux."

Dante winced as he leaned against the counter. "I heard about that. The whole fucking country has. A bunch of skinhead white boys working off their anger at not being supreme leaders of the world anymore, huh?"

Craig thought about the lie he'd made up on the spot and had spread to deflect from the truth, a truth that he still couldn't quite believe. "Something like that," he replied.

"Sweet Baby Jesus, I just don't understand some people. Who wakes up one day planning on massacring folks, especially knowing that it's not going to end well for you, too? Guess they didn't expect gay guys to shoot back, huh?"

With what Craig knew about the situation, he could guess that was exactly what the mercenaries had been told — that there would be no return fire. Nothing else made sense. These were not ideologues willing to die for a cause, not that he could share any of that with his brother. "Something like that, I guess."

Dante shook his head. His brother was a good man, with not a mean bone in his body. Not that he was a pushover, and he'd kill to protect his family, but this kind of evil was incomprehensible to him. And that was as it should be. "How come you got involved in a homicide case?"

A fair question, and one that he had a ready answer for. "It was a blood bath and extra hands were welcome." That wasn't strictly true, so he added, "And an old friend was working the case. I wanted to help him."

"You're talking about Duncan."

"Yeah."

"You thinking of getting back with him? He was the best thing that ever happened to you. I told you not to fuck it up."

Craig sighed. Dante's kind nature extended to unwavering support of his little gay brother. He'd bloodied a few boys in school over it. "So you did, but no. Trey has moved on. He's engaged, actually, to a relative of the club owner, as it happens. They're all…in shock. I've been lending a hand where I could."

Dante frowned. "That's too bad—about Duncan being taken, I mean. The other stuff is fucking insane and I can't think of anything to say about it that would help in the least. Seriously though, after you get your beauty rest, you really should get back out there dating. You're getting too old for all these one-night stands. Mama's worried about you and wants to see you settled, maybe with a family."

This was not what he needed right now. "Mama worries because she breathes. My settling down isn't going to change that problem. She'll find something else to fret over. Besides, she has you and LaKeisha and the girls to dote on. I'm just the gay son."

"She has *never* thought of you like that."

That was true. Dante had understood Craig's nature early in childhood and had become an ally long before anyone else in the family knew. When Craig had been nineteen and sick with worry that his parents would shun him for being gay, Mama had been the first to hug him tight and tell him how much she loved him. Daddy had taken a little more time, but he'd come around, too.

Craig hadn't worried that he'd be completely alone regardless, because Dante had always had his back. He couldn't have hoped for a better brother. And having him living downstairs was the perfect situation, and not only because it meant he didn't have to worry about Coretta. Any time he returned, worn down by the tragedies he witnessed on a daily basis, his brother and his family were always there to remind him that life could be wonderful.

"I promise I'll get right on finding a husband as soon as I get some sleep." Even as he made the snarky remark, he couldn't help thinking of that pretty, pale man who was something not quite human anymore. *Alun*, with his singsong accent and shy demeanor… He'd pushed all Craig's buttons the moment he'd first seen him at *Our Safe Place*. The whole fantastic alien vampire angle was surprisingly not a deal breaker for him. Knowing the guy had suffered abuse was a bigger problem, but he'd spent years working with people like that. If anyone could help Alun recover, he'd like to think he could do it. And maybe that teenage son of his—who might or might not be a traitorous fuck—would benefit from a good dose of Mama in his life. That woman knew how to keep wild boys in check.

Not that he said any of that to his brother. Even if he'd been well-rested, there were too many secrets for a meaningful conversion. And planning for the future was particularly pointless now that he knew there was a danger in the world that transcended petty human politics and even global warming. If his new friends didn't eliminate this Dracul creature, everyone was in for a fuck-load of pain. Knowing that he was now helping to wage some kind of apocalyptic war freaked him out. There was no way for his mind to process it all until he got some rest.

"You want me to bring you a pillow and blanket so you can sleep here?"

Craig managed a smile. "No, I only need a few more seconds and I'll drag my tired ass to my bedroom." As he said the words, his eyes drooped shut and he slid farther onto the floor.

A few moments later, his head was lifted and placed on something soft. Warm weight covered him. The last thing he heard was Coretta's irritated meow and the quiet closing of the door.

Want to see more from this author? Here's a taster for you to enjoy!

Alien Blood Wars: Final Dance: Part Two
Samantha Cayto

Excerpt

Alun bolted upright in bed, a scream stuck in his throat. It fought to escape, but he held it back, his mouth wide open in silent horror. He'd learned early in his slavery to never disturb his alien master with something as irrelevant as his own terror. That mistake had only led to punishment and the hideous pain that accompanied it. It was better to trap it all inside and push it down deep where even he didn't dare look. With his heart pounding, he clenched the bedding while fighting to regain control. It had only been a nightmare, nothing real, except it had contained bits from his actual life as a slave. The fact that he no longer lived in that world of misery didn't help. The remnants of his excruciating past hung around his neck as surely as the chains Jacob Marley had forged in life. The image from that book he'd been allowed to read long ago stayed with him as the perfect representation of his own life. There was no escaping what had been done to him, what he'd survived. And now it threatened to repeat itself in a new and unfathomable way.

"Merlin." He dared to whisper his son's name. There was no one to hear. He practically swam in the huge, luxurious bed afforded him in a room that was bigger than the tiny house he'd lived in with his family — before his world had been upended by a creature without mercy or morals who had used him as a toy and an unnatural breeder of his unholy spawn. At least, that was how he'd viewed his son in the beginning.

He pried the fingers on one hand to clutch at the simple gold crucifix that Lucien had kindly given him. The comfort of his religion had been denied him for so long. It was strange and miraculous to regain it. No one in this household would care about his wearing this symbol. Many of the aliens wore something similar, except they weren't believers — not really. It was only one way in which they'd sought to blend in among humans. For him, it truly meant something, a rebirth of his belief and hope that God had not forsaken him. He hid this sign beneath his shirt to keep it private as he slowly regained his faith.

Tightening his grip, he dared to say a prayer for his son. "Please, God, keep him safe. Forgive me for ever denying him my love and protection." It had been hard to accept the squalling bundle that had been cut out of him and impossible to protect him from the brutality of the alien who was his sire. When Merlin had started to abuse him as well, it had almost been a relief. It had given him a reason to harden his heart and turn away from the violence visited upon him with such casual cruelty.

That carefully constructed shell had begun to crack. His son was not who Alun thought him to be — or he'd changed with the right influence, something Alun had never possessed. When Dracul's army of mercenaries had invaded, Merlin had looked into Alun's eyes and expressed his sorrow over his violence. That had been the first real connection between them. Alun had seen actual regret and a softness of feeling that was purely human. At that moment, he'd found something of himself in his son and had known hope. But with that discovery came other, more frightening emotions. Now, he worried about Merlin. Was he truly safe? Was he even alive? Could he manage to deceive and betray Dracul without paying the ultimate price of losing his life? For the first time, Alun prayed for his son to live.

"Mary, Mother of God, please watch over him." He brought the crucifix to his lips, a reflexive action that helped calm the last of his nerves.

He released his grip on the bedding, as well, and lay back against his mound of pillows. Really, the luxury he lived in was almost as disconcerting as his captivity in Dracul's castle had been. He didn't know what to do with it. In his early life, he'd shared a small bed with two brothers. As a slave, he'd confined himself to a narrow strip of a bigger bed that he'd been forced to sleep in with his master. That arrangement had been about convenience, not kindness. His master had wanted him handy for his pleasure. Alun would have preferred sleeping on the cold stone floor than lying near his torturer. As he lay in the middle of his enormous mattress now, he felt just as small and insignificant as he had for those long decades of captivity. Little had changed, other than he could be sure that only his own thoughts would disturb him here.

He sighed and stared up at the pristine white ceiling. The muted light seeping past the edge of the curtain told him that dawn was breaking, and while no one expected him to be up with the sun and toiling away anymore, experience told him that trying to go back to sleep would prove impossible. Giving into reality, he shoved aside the bedding and got up. It was easy to head to the bathroom, because the light in there had been on all night. Since his 'rescue' by these less-frightening aliens, he'd been afraid to sleep in the dark. He knew now that monsters really did lurk about, and he needed to see his surroundings clearly the moment he opened his eyes. It was embarrassing, although no one probably knew what he did. Also, no one seemed to care. When he was in his bedroom, everyone left him alone. The privacy was appreciated — but also unnerving. He couldn't quite trust that anything was being done for his benefit. It wouldn't surprise him if the one called Val had eyes on him through his security system.

Not that it mattered. He'd learned to accept what he couldn't change and survive in any way possible. Suicide had only briefly touched his mind in those terrible early days. He'd been true enough to his faith to not go through with it. He'd believed — and still did — in the promise of eternal heavenly peace if he followed God's rules. Taking his own life had not been an option then, and there was no reason to contemplate it now. Only the most chopsy of people would resent the privileged life he was currently leading. He was always warm and well-fed and had lovely clothing that he was allowed to wear instead of the often-enforced nudity back in the castle. No one had hit him since he'd left the castle, not even Merlin, although his son had come close at one point, and his body was his own. No one forced themselves inside him or used him for pleasure in other ways. For the first time in over a hundred years, his body didn't ache or bleed. There was no reason to want to end his time on Earth, other than this persistent and nagging anxiety that threatened to swamp him every minute of every day.

He pushed down that feeling, which was particularly insistent due to his nightmare, and focused on the mundane. After relieving himself in the glorious effectiveness of modern plumbing, he headed for the shower. He was careful to avert his gaze as he passed the long mirror above the sink counter. Looking at himself was something he avoided as much as possible. He might not be a victim of violence anymore, but his body still bore the markings of it. There was hardly a section that didn't contain a scar from knives, pokers or whips that had been used to bring him under his master's control. Even when he'd capitulated, the lessons had continued, especially if he'd dared to make even the tiniest of mistakes. He was hideous in his own eyes, and because sleeping nude had become engrained in him, his battered skin was all too evident.

The coolness of the stone tile floor made his toes curl, but he refused to use the convenience of the heating system. There was something unseemly to him about pampering himself that much. Really, the room was warm enough, and soon he'd be under a spray of water that he could make as hot as he wished. And he didn't need four shower heads. One would do nicely. He tested the temperature before getting in, putting the heat level to just shy of scalding and letting the water sluice over him. The intense heat was cleansing, washing away more than surface dirt. It was fine to spend as long as he wanted, apparently. So said Lucien, and he'd come to depend on the man as something of a kindred spirit and a kindly mentor who helped him navigate through this often-confusing new life. Like Alun, Lucien knew what it was like to be under the control of vicious men. He understood Alun's fears, even without his having to express them. Alun trusted in the man's advice. So, he didn't hurry to wash, and no matter how long he took, experience taught him that the water never ran cool.

This ability to wash was another blessing long denied him. He often showered more than once a day because it felt so good to be clean. And yet, he never truly did. Some part of him always felt dirty, defiled, no matter how hard or often he scrubbed at his skin and hair. Back in Wales, he'd been forced to ignore it, making due with tepid sponge baths and cold rinses from rain water. Now, it seemed that the more he washed, the dirtier he felt. He knew it was nonsense but he couldn't shake it. And the longer he stood under that spray, the more his mind insisted on focusing on unpleasant matters. Keeping busy was his best defense.

With that thought in mind, he hurried to finish, no longer enjoying the experience. This was how it always ended. The soft towels at his disposal made quick work of drying him. His closet and drawers were filled with more clothing than he could possibly use. He grabbed items at random — a sweater, jeans and socks. Underwear was available, but really, that was something that made no sense to him. Small clothes were for rich people, unless it was about keeping warm, which it wasn't for him. It was enough to have the barrier provided by what he did tug on. Low boots in soft leather completed his dressing. His final act to get ready for the day was to brush and pull back his hair in a slick tail. He didn't mind it being wet because, again, the whole house was warm. He didn't have the patience for using that air-blowing contraption Lucien had given him.

Before he left his room, he gathered the wet towels and dirty clothing from the hamper. He went straight down to the laundry room and threw in a couple of loads in the machines that existed for the purpose, adding others' that were waiting in the baskets. Washing wasn't his job in this house. Frankly, nothing officially was, which bothered him. Doing nothing was not in his nature, and the lack of duties disturbed him more than any amount of hard labor did. He wanted to be useful, and the appliances made everything almost a joy to do.

Once that was done, he proceeded to the kitchen. Here again was an area that wasn't his assigned domain, but there were a lot of mouths to feed, even with some having been captured. The fresh reminder of how his son had been taken from him made him stagger. He gripped the counter until his heartbeat steadied and his vision cleared. It was too easy to spiral into fear and despair and much better to shove his feelings aside and channel his energy into starting breakfast. He knew that those who ruled the kitchen, alien and human alike, wouldn't fault him for it. In fact, it continued to surprise him how often he was praised and thanked for his efforts. With what little confidence he possessed, he prepped for breakfast, allowing himself the time for a cup of tea and a couple of pieces of toast. Hunger was a thing of the past, but he didn't have much of an appetite on the best of days.

Omelets were a staple of the household, so he chopped vegetables and sautéed them while warming multi-cartons of eggs on the counter. He started on sausages next, with an eye to cooking them nearly through so that it would be easy to finish them when breakfast started in earnest. Then he made the decision to bake buns, knowing that anything not eaten here would be sent to the place where homeless children were fed.

He had to put aside his disappointment about not being able to go there anymore. He'd found such fulfillment in the work, but Alex, the leader who was so different than Dracul, yet no less forceful, had forbidden it. It was dangerous for any of them to leave the house now, although the building itself had been breached easily enough. Really, at this point, nowhere was safe—not that he mentioned that indelicate fact to anyone. It still didn't make sense to him, either, that anyone would worry about him. Dracul was unlikely to target him, and if he did, why would it matter? The concern for him was both touching and confusing, such common feelings these days.

So he did what he'd always done—just got on with things.

He was taking the first batch of buns out of the oven when the doorbell pealed. He'd no sooner moved his head in that direction than two aliens, the ones known as Val and Willem, vaulted down to the first floor from the top of the stairs with guns in their hands. Their dramatic appearance caused him to wobble his tray and he scrambled to catch the buns before they fell on the floor. He landed on his knees with a jarring thud that made him wince, but he'd saved all but one of his buns. Then already jackhammering, his heart skipped a beat when he heard the voice of the visitor.

"Hey, guys, what a warm welcome. Are those guns stuck in my face for me, 'cause I, you know, come in peace and all that."

The tone of the human cop, Sergeant Jefferson—Craig—was easy-going, yet Alun heard the steel underneath it. This was a man who didn't scare easily and was someone to fear in his own right. It didn't surprise Alun that the aliens didn't appear to succumb to the sergeant's dominant nature, but his own reaction to the man was unexpected. He should have given him a wide berth, as he did with all men, human and alien alike. Yet he found himself perversely drawn to the cop. After his initial reaction to hearing the man's arrival, Alun's nerves calmed with the sound of the banter continuing between the human and his alien hosts.

"It's too-fucking-early o'clock, Jefferson. We weren't expecting visitors." This from Val, the scary security chief who was nevertheless always respectful to Alun.

"Yeah, but here's the thing, my man, Dracul's goons aren't going to ring the bell, so I had that logic going for me."

"Forgive us if we're a bit jumpy," Willem replied.

"I hear you… Hey, Alun." Alun froze and looked up to see Craig hurry over to him. He had to fight the impulse to cringe away. "Let me help you." The man grinned as he crouched beside him and reached for the tray.

Alun was momentarily mesmerized — and not by fear. This man was unlike anyone he was used to dealing with. It wasn't only his looks, either, although his dark skin was unusual in Alun's personal experience, even before his enslavement. No, it was the way he telegraphed both trustworthiness and concern with a single expression. True empathy showed through his dark brown eyes and, at the same time, made Alun feel secure. It conveyed an 'I've got you' sentiment that let Alun know he didn't have to worry about anything. Craig was in charge, although not to dominate. And the easy smile he gave encompassed his whole face, a genuine warmth that infused Alun with a sense of calm and protectiveness.

It also left him tongue-tied. He opened his mouth but nothing came out. He didn't know what to say or how to react. He simply allowed the man to relieve him of his burden, freeing him to juggle the buns that had fallen. Only one had touched the floor and rolled across it.

Val scooped it up and shoved it in his mouth. "Hmm, delicious."

"It's not even iced, like," he heard himself say before he could stop his tongue from wagging. He shrunk back instinctively in anticipation of a blow that he understood wasn't coming, but that he feared nevertheless.

Craig took him gently by the arm and helped him to his feet. Funny how that gesture hadn't startled him in the least. "No worries. I don't think our giant friend here cares about those kinds of details, although apparently he follows the five-second rule. You know…" he added when Alun could only blink back at him in confusion. "If it doesn't stay on the floor for more than a few seconds, it's safe to eat."

"Yes, of course." Alun didn't know where to look or what more to say. It wasn't for him to dictate what Val or anyone else in this household ate. It had been silly pride that his buns weren't finished to his liking that had caused him to speak without thinking. That had gotten him into more trouble than he cared to think about. He was nothing and his feelings of no consequence in this world and forgetting that was a dangerous thing.

"I should finish the rest, though." He didn't move to do so, however, his mind a muddle from Craig's proximity and touch. It was hard to think with him there. Alun both wanted those fingers to stay curled around his arm and longed to shake off the touch. Being in the presence of this human confused him.

Craig smiled and let go of Alun to put the tray on the counter. "Is there anything I can do to help?"

Alun almost laughed out loud at the idea that such a virile, commanding man should act like a kitchen slut. No, that wasn't right. No one here called anyone that slur for cooking and cleaning. It was hard to stifle the way he'd been forced to think and talk, even of his own derogation. But Emil cooked, and he was a fierce warrior. Somehow, though, the idea of Craig putting on an apron and helping him ice buns seemed inappropriate. Alun would much rather serve him — and not because he felt he had to. He *wanted* to, which was just one more confusing thing about the man.

Turning away, he said, "No, thank you. There's nothing much to it." The timer for the second batch went off in another oven. The kitchen had an astounding four to use. He hurried to put the buns in his hands onto the first tray in order to fetch the newly-finished ones. He put their tray next to the ones he'd previously baked, careful not to look at Craig. The man was too much of a distraction.

"Would you like some coffee?" The question came to him in a flash and he was pleased that he'd thought to start a pot for the early risers.

"Sounds wonderful. I can get it. Thanks."

"No, let me." His boldness made his cheeks heat. "You're a guest, like."

Craig moved to lean against the kitchen's island. "If it's no trouble…"

"None at all." He was quick to assure the man and went to fill a mug. "How do you take it?" Although he'd never been permitted to have any at the castle, he'd learned that coffee was a personal drink with lots of choices about how it should be altered, not so different from tea.

"Black is fine. No sugar, either. I'm a simple guy," Craig added with another grin.

Uncomfortable with so much pleasantry thrown in his direction, Alun busied himself with picking up the carafe. "Well, that's easy." He was also perversely disappointed that he couldn't do more to make the man happy. "Here you are."

As he passed the mug over, the backs of his fingers brushed those of Craig's. The brief touch caused a little spark of awareness and he was surprised by the warmth. He'd grown used to being touched by cold beings.

"Thanks." Once again, Craig gave him a broad smile that reached his eyes. It seemed to be the man's default expression. He was almost like Annika in that respect, naturally joyful. Except this was an adult, not a child, and even with the misery he must see every day, he'd still not lost that appealing quality. It made for a nice change from the grimness that now pervaded the home, a small oasis that lifted Alun's spirits — not that Alun dared do more than glance in his direction.

"I could use a hit of caffeine," Val said from across the dining counter on the other side of the kitchen.

Alun startled at the sudden request. "Yes, of course." He started to turn away from Craig, but the man caught him gently by the arm and kept him in place.

"Get your own damn coffee, Mr. T. Alun's not your slave." Craig winked and took a sip of his own drink.

Unsure of what to say or how to react, Alun fell back on his usual passiveness, allowing Craig to hold him, even as he fretted over Val being forced to get his own coffee. The grip around his arm loosened and morphed into a kind of stroking, a reassurance without words. Alun stopped worrying about Val and began to wonder how he would find the strength to move away from this unexpected attention. He searched for some hint of menace or even demand, and finding none, he decided to leave it to Craig to decide what would happen next.

Doing so wasn't new to him. He'd never been in control of his life, going from a dutiful son who had left his beloved school room to head for the mines to an enslaved whore for an alien monster. This, however, was the first time in which he felt no resentment. He trusted this man to have his best interest in mind, although the why of it alluded him. After all that he'd been through, this kind of assertive behavior should scare him to death.

The situation resolved itself in the form of Damien, who literally jumped into it by taking the last few steps of the staircase with a leap. He landed with a thud that was nothing like the almost-silent entry of his alien lover moments before. And he bobbled a moment before straightening with a look on his face that telegraphed his obvious glee.

"Man, I love my new superpowers."

Willem walked over and gave him the kind of passionate kiss that always called up some unnamed longing in Alun. "Easy, baby. You aren't invincible. I don't want you breaking a leg during your transformation."

"You worry too much." Damien rolled his eyes in a form of disrespect that made Alun cringe. He still expected such an act to end in a severe blow.

Craig gave Alun's arm a gentle squeeze before releasing it. "Don't worry. It's just banter between lovers."

Surprised that the man had read him so well, Alun gave him a grateful smile before stepping away. The proximity was becoming uncomfortable now, especially as others were joining them.

"Hey, Alun, thanks for the prep." Damien sauntered into the kitchen area with the confidence of someone who knew he belonged there. "And you made buns. Awesome."

The gratitude made him even more uneasy. "They still need icing."

Damien nodded. "Sounds good... And while you're doing that, I'll fix you an omelet."

Alun widened his eyes with alarm. "Oh, no, I had some toast already. There are warriors who need feeding first. And Mackie's coming," he added as the pregnant changling lumbered down the stairs with his hand on his lower back. Alun winced inside with sympathy. He knew how hard it was to carry a baby inside a body that had not been readily designed for it. Unlike the alien who'd impregnated Alun, however, Val strode to help the human who was pregnant with his son.

Damien shook his head, commanding Alun's attention once more. "It takes no time at all to make one with all this prep done. No one will wait for long. So, what do you like in yours?"

Alun was at a loss, considering what he ate had never been a choice and he hadn't gotten used to the idea of making such decisions. He instinctively looked to Craig, who was watching over the rim of his mug. He felt stupid needing help with such a simple question.

"How about a little of everything?" Craig suggested. Alun found himself nodding before turning his attention to his buns, which was where it belonged.

"Everything it is," Damien replied.

The simple problem having been resolved sent a wave of relief through him. He concentrated on finishing his buns and valiantly tried to ignore the focus of the man standing behind him.

"I'll get out of your way," Craig said.

The sound of the man's footsteps leaving both relieved and disappointed Alun. The conflicting emotions were too hard to unpack, so he fell back on old habits and turned numb to it all.

I am such a jackass. Craig chastised himself, even as he took a position on the other side of the dining counter. He hadn't moved far away from the focus of his interest, yet hopefully he'd stopped making the guy uncomfortable.

After sleeping like the dead on his kitchen floor, of all places, he'd moved to his bed only to lay there the rest of the night with his gaze fixed on the ceiling, trying to make sense of his new, weird reality. Was he really involved with ancient aliens who were the origin for the vampire legend? And were they truly locked into a thousand-year battle over controlling Earth? This was some serious sci-fi shit. It would be easy to dismiss it all if not for the mountain of bodies that had been carted out of Club Lux, along with the freaky shit that he'd witnessed that couldn't be the work of a human.

Those memories kept haunting him — one man using the strength of many, along with a cartoonish speed, to carry a wounded comrade up the stairs, fangs gleaming white before sinking into the blood vessels of another's wrist to suck blood for an instant transfusion. Then there was the deal-sealer — a man he'd once loved and totally trusted telling him that this was all real. Yeah, Trey had broken his heart, and rightly so, given his own infidelity, but the man was rock-solid in the head department. If he said these were alien vampires, one could take that information to the bank.

Nothing, however, that he'd seen or heard had the same impact as the one man he currently watched with a rudeness that his mama would chastise him for. *Alun*. That name, that face, had dominated his thoughts, shoving the rest aside with regularity every time he'd tried to focus on something else — something relevant, such as how he could protect his species from an escalating alien war. Every effort he'd made to lay out plans for the near future had been upended by the intrusion of Alun's lovely face. The memories of their first encounter at *Our Safe Place* in particular were strong and warm. They weren't tainted by the horror of the massacre.

It had been a time in which Craig had only had to worry about how he might approach someone coming off an abusive relationship, as well as adjusting to how, for the first time, he was attracted to someone who was more of a twink than a carbon copy of himself. That new reality was more of a mind-bender. He understood trauma, although only from a professional standpoint, more than his own shifting view of with whom he might spend the rest of his life. Alun's experiences hadn't seemed like an insurmountable problem. The man needed time, space and patience. He had a long road ahead of him to regain his self-esteem to forge a future. Alun had a lot of baggage.

Alun had a *womb*.

That one fact from Trey's hasty information dump stood out among all of the crazy shit rattling around in Craig's head. It was now being reinforced by the arrival of an obviously pregnant young man who was also *not* transgender, which meant his state had been artificially created through the ingestion of blood from the scariest of the scary hulks occupying this house. Well, maybe it was more accurate to say it had occurred through a natural process, if one counted an alien event as *natural*. The jury was still out on that. There was no denying, however, the solicitude and plain old love that this otherworldly creature was showing his human husband.

"Val, how many times do I have to tell you that I am perfectly capable of walking?" The boy, Mackie, spoke with a long-suffering tone that was belied by the way he curled into his man's embrace.

This one image was enough to convince Craig that he was on the right side. As he watched with unabashed interest — because it was way better than staring at Alun like a creep — Val carried Mackie over to the large sectional sofa across the room and gently placed him there.

The alien ran his hand down the back of his husband's head. "I'll get your breakfast."

"Here." Alun raced out of the kitchen area with a plate filled with an omelet, a couple of sausage links and an iced bun. He held it out to Mackie. "Have this."

Mackie beamed at him. "Thanks."

Before he could take it, though, Val intercepted him. "That's Alun's."

Mackie's face fell. "Oh, then you should keep it. Damien will make one for me."

Alun practically shoved it to the boy. "No worries. I've already had some toast and can wait for more. You can't. Do you want a glass of milk or calcium-fortified orange juice?"

Mackie looked at Val in an obvious plea for the guy to make the call. There was some kind of BDSM thing going on, highlighted by the leather collar worn by the boy. That was a little disturbing, except he knew that plenty of humans were in the lifestyle and happily so. It didn't necessarily bode ill for the alien's behavior.

With an audible sigh, Val took the plate and passed it to his husband. "Thanks, Alun. I'll get the drink, and you'll have both milk and juice," he added with a look at his husband, who was already stuffing his face.

Alun stood wringing his hands. "It's no trouble. I'm happy to—"

"Alun!" Damien called from the kitchen. "Here's another omelet for you." The cook put the plate on the counter next to Craig and gave him a slightly warning look before retreating back to the stove.

There was almost a defeated expression on Alun's face as he padded to the counter and slipped into a chair. "Thank you."

He's not used to the kindness. He doesn't know what to do with it. That realization wasn't exactly a bombshell. Craig understood the complex emotions that plagued survivors of abuse. It was hard for them to accept another's generosity, to believe that they were worthy of it. They didn't trust easily and were always on the look-out for a change for the worse. And on top of every other emotional baggage the man carried on a daily basis, he had to be out of his mind with worry about his son.

Although Craig had picked up on the fact that Merlin had been a difficult kid, he hadn't missed the quiet ferocity with which Alun had defended him among the angry crowd of aliens the other night. He bet that as nice as everyone was being, they didn't necessarily realize that aspect of Alun's feelings. They probably weren't thinking that they had to reassure him, but someone did.

Taking a chance, he slid closer to Alun and plunked his ass down on an adjacent chair. He was careful not to get too close. Man, he'd been a dumbass the way he'd taken the liberty of touching Alun and even holding him in place so that he didn't cater to Val with an ingrained need to please. It had been gratifying that Alun hadn't jerked away or shown any other signs of fear. It was also good to see that Val had learned his lesson and was getting drinks for his husband instead of expecting Alun to do it.

He watched Alun pick at his food for a few seconds before saying, "It's hard to have an appetite, isn't it?"

Alun froze for a few seconds before glancing his way. The guy never quite looked him in the eye, which was understandable and frustrating. "I'm not used to eating much." He took a small bite of omelet. "It's delicious, though. I should be more grateful."

"Bullshit," he said as gently as he could. Alun was startled enough to look fully at him for a few seconds. "These people made the decision to bring you into their home. The least that they owe you is good and plentiful food. You don't owe them anything."

Now Alun looked at him as if he had lobsters crawling out of his ears. "You say the strangest things. Sorry," he added hastily. "That was rude."

"It's okay. You can be as rude as you like. You don't owe me anything, either. I'm only trying to help you understand your worth. And," he added with a shake of his head, "I can see in your eyes that you don't believe that you have any."

Alun almost bristled, which was a damn good sign. "That's not true, mun. I have a lot of useful skills that help the family."

"I'm not talking about your role as domestic help, but let's put that aside for the moment. What I meant about your lack of interest in eating was that it's because you're worried about your son."

With a drop of his fork, Alun curled into himself before clutching at his chest with one hand. Beneath the thin-knitted sweater he wore, there was a distinct outline of a chain and what might be a cross that he now had his fingers around. That surprised Craig. He had assumed the aliens didn't worship the way many humans did and wouldn't have tolerated their slaves doing so. He certainly didn't expect to see signs of Christianity. This unexpected news gave him an 'in' where Alun was concerned.

Reaching inside his own long-sleeved T, he pulled out the cross his parents had given him when he'd graduated from the police academy. He made a point of holding it up for Alun to see. "I find that this gives me hope and courage when I most need it. I'm not sure if anyone is actually listening when I pray, but it's a source of comfort, nonetheless. It reminds me of Sundays with my family, going to church and eating a big dinner with everyone around the table. It really isn't something I should hide away."

So saying, Craig deliberately let it hang against his chest where it could be seen. After a few seconds, Alun did the same with his. It was lovely, bigger than Craig's, shiny gold and a crucifix, not just a cross. Alun kept his hand around it for even longer before slowly releasing it and picking up his fork again. He took a larger bite of his omelet than he had before.

"I'm *that* worried about him," he said eventually in a low voice. "Merlin."

"I know and understand. He's your son. Of course, you are." He dared to pat the man's arm but was careful not to indulge himself by keeping it there. "They'll get him back."

Alun merely nodded and kept eating, slowly, steadily. By the time the others had come down in greater numbers, the man's plate was clean and Damien had placed one in front of Craig. It was double the size of Alun's and everything on it smelled delicious.

"Thanks, man." He made a point of trying the bun first and he didn't have to fake his delight. "Fantastic. Would you mind giving me the recipe?" he asked between bites. "I'll see if I can sweet-talk my mama into making them for me."

As he slid off his chair with his empty plate and utensils in hand, Alun smiled — not a big one, but genuine, to Craig's way of thinking. "You don't bake, then? Of course not, you're a warrior."

It was silly, but something about Alun referring to him in that medieval way made his chest puff up. "It's not that. I would like to cook but my efforts have proved disastrous. It's in everyone's best interest if I stay out of the kitchen."

Alun's smile increased. "I'll be happy to make them for you any time." With that, he hurried to help Damien.

Craig grinned like a maniac, pleased with that small gesture of — dare he think — affection? An arm slung around his shoulders unexpectedly enough to make him jump.

Willem bared his teeth in a mockery of the smile that was now wiped off Craig's face. "If you hurt him, we'll rip out your throat."

Craig only had to cough once to find his voice. Really, this was another good sign. These aliens were protective of Alun. He appreciated the threat, actually. "I hear you, man. You've got no worries on that account."

With a nod and a pat, Willem stepped back. "Good. Eat up quickly. We've been doing some satellite recon of Dracul's hidey-holes and have a meeting planned for right after breakfast. We could use another set of eyes and some brain power to plan our next move. We assume you're here to help, not ogle."

Serious now, Craig went into cop mode. "Damn right I am."

PUBLISHING

Sign up for our newsletter and find out about all our romance book releases, eBook sales and promotions, sneak peeks and FREE romance books!

About the Author

Samantha Cayto is a Boston-area native who practices as a business lawyer by day while writing erotic romance at night — the steamier the better. She likes to push the envelope when it comes to writing about passion and is delighted other women agree that guy-on-guy sex is the hottest ever.

She lives a typical suburban life with her husband, three kids and four dogs. Her children don't understand why they can't read what she writes, but her husband is always willing to lend her a hand — and anything else — when she needs to choreograph a scene.

Samantha loves to hear from readers. You can find her contact information, website details and author profile page at https://www.pride-publishing.com

9 781839 438950